"I wanted to thank you for tonight."

"I didn't do anything," Callie said.

"Yes, you did." Tyler swallowed. "I've been so wrapped up in family and work that I haven't taken the time to go out and enjoy myself with other adults. So thank you for going along. I'm not sure I would have gone alone."

"Really? You seemed anxious to go when Riva asked us."

"That was for your sake. You needed a break." He shrugged. "Turns out, so did I."

The clouds uncovered the moon, illuminating her face. He leaned closer and touched his mouth to hers. He'd been wanting to do that all night. As soon as their mouths met, he knew it was a mistake.

This wasn't the one chaste kiss they'd shared in high school.

This was the real thing.

Dear Reader,

When I originally conceived the plot of *Prince Charming Wears a Badge*, I had no idea it was a twist on *Cinderella*. But then I saw the live-action version of the movie *Cinderella*, where they go into much more detail about Cinderella's life. When I saw how she was treated by her stepmother and stepsisters, I saw the similarity to my story.

The main difference, or the twist, is that my Cinderella, Callie James, doesn't wait around for her prince to find her. She studied hard and got a full scholarship to college and never returned home. At least until she's forced to. And that's where she finds Tyler Garrett, a true prince of a man.

I hope you enjoy this twist on a favorite fairy tale. I'd love to hear from you at lisa@lisadyson.com. Check out my website, www.lisadyson.com, for upcoming releases.

Wishing you a happy ending,

Lisa Dyson

LISA DYSON

Prince Charming
Wears a Badge

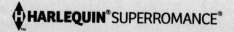

Recycling programs
for this product may
not exist in your area.

ISBN-13: 978-0-373-61006-8

Prince Charming Wears a Badge

Copyright © 2016 by Lisa Dyson

Printed in U.S.A.

Lisa Dyson has been creating stories ever since getting an A on a fifth-grade writing assignment. She lives near Washington, DC, with her husband and their rescue dog with a blue tongue, aptly named Blue. She has three grown sons, a daughter-in-law and four adorable grandchildren. When not writing, reading or spending time with family, Lisa enjoys traveling, volunteering and rooting for her favorite sports teams.

Books by Lisa Dyson

HARLEQUIN SUPERROMANCE

Resorting to the Truth
Catching Her Rival
A Perfect Homecoming

Visit the Author Profile page at Harlequin.com.

To my prince of a husband, Michael

Acknowledgments

A special thank-you to my friend
attorney Benjamin W. Glass, III
for answering my many questions
about the legal system.
Any mistakes are entirely my own.

CHAPTER ONE

A FEW DAYS ago Callie James was planning a romantic surprise for her boyfriend.

Now she found herself in front of a judge who held Callie's future in her hands.

She swallowed the lump in her throat that held back the bile churning wildly in her digestive tract. Her folded hands on the defense table were damp as she waited for the judge to speak.

Callie never got into trouble. Sure, she'd received a speeding ticket once and had the occasional library book fine, but that's as far as it went. She'd never come close to the possibility of jail time.

The judge turned her attention from the papers in front of her to the scattered observers in the courtroom. She cleared her throat and looked over horn-rimmed reading glasses to focus on the prosecution side of the room. "The charge is malicious destruction of property?"

"Yes, Your Honor." Her now ex-boyfriend, Andrew, who happened to be a Maryland Assistant State's Attorney, rose from his seat at the prosecution table and straightened his conservative navy-and-white diagonally striped tie, which he wore with his equally conservative navy suit.

"You're prosecuting the case on your own behalf?" The female judge's wizened eyes narrowed in disapproval.

"No, Your Honor," he said quickly and looked down to his right.

A much younger but similarly dressed man seated next to him stood up. "ASA Ross, Your Honor."

Was this guy even out of law school yet? He had the haircut of a six-year-old and the lanky build of a fourteen-year-old who was wearing his father's suit.

When the judge smiled at ASA Ross, Callie figured this was it. They were all conspirators in her downfall. They were going to lock her up and throw away the key.

"Harvey Goodman for the defense, Your Honor." Callie's lawyer was her financial firm's house counsel and the only person she could think of to call. Harvey was nearing retirement age and she just hoped he wasn't out of his league. His expertise was in mergers and acquisitions—he probably hadn't litigated since law school. Which was likely about the same time he'd bought his suit, whose buttons strained over his middle.

"Thank you, Mr. Goodman. I understand your client rejected the state's plea agreement?"

"Yes, Your Honor," Andrew interjected, and Harvey nodded.

"Mr. Slater. If you're not prosecuting the case," the judge admonished, "then please allow Mr. Ross to speak."

"Yes, Your Honor. I apologize." Andrew played the admonished attorney well.

ASA Ross spoke. "The plea was rejected."

The judge wrinkled her nose as she looked over the papers on her large, wood-paneled desk that placed her a few feet higher than everyone else in the courtroom. "Mr. Slater, you're claiming Ms. James came into your apartment, lost her temper for no apparent reason, and then threw your Dresden vase—value forty-five hundred dollars—on the floor and left?"

"That's correct." Andrew's tone was sharp but deferential.

"No apparent reason?" The whispered words were out of Callie's mouth before she could stop them, earning her a stern look and a shush from Harvey.

"You'll have your chance, Ms. James," the judge told her then turned to Andrew. "How would you classify your relationship with Ms. James?"

Andrew glanced quickly at Callie before answering. "A romantic one."

Callie coughed and immediately lowered her head when the judge glared at her.

"Keep quiet," her lawyer whispered out of the corner of his mouth.

"How long have the two of you been involved?" the judge asked Andrew.

Too long, Callie realized, but hindsight was always twenty-twenty.

"A few months" was Andrew's answer.

Except that the incident had taken place on their six-month anniversary. The reason Callie had been taking Andrew a romantic dinner when he'd had to work late. Or so he'd said that's what he was doing.

"Do you have anything else to add?" the judge asked.

"No, Your Honor." Andrew took his seat.

The judge turned to Harvey and Callie. "Ms. James, you've rejected the state's plea agreement?"

Callie rose, displeased when her voice was shaky. "That's correct, Your Honor."

Sounding incredulous, the judge stared straight at Callie. "May I ask why? You do know that if you don't accept the plea that consists of paying restitution, then you can be subject to not only reimbursement but also a fine of twenty-five hundred dollars and up to three years in prison if found guilty?"

Callie inhaled, straightening her spine. "I understand, Your Honor." Her lawyer had explained in depth. "I didn't lose my temper, and I can't admit to causing damage when I'm not sure I did it. If I did break the vase, then it was accidental and happened because Mr. Slater—" She stared at Andrew, narrowed her gaze, and said calmly, "Because Mr. Slater is a lying ba—"

"Objection!" Andrew was on his feet so fast he nearly toppled over the table in front of him.

The judge banged her gavel at the sudden commotion in the gallery. "Order!" Bang, bang, bang. "Order!"

When everyone quieted, the judge first reprimanded Andrew in a no-nonsense manner. "Your objection is moot, Mr. Slater. This is an arraignment, not a trial. And I'll remind you for the last time that you're not the one prosecuting this case." Her gaze went to ASA Ross.

"Of course, Your Honor." Andrew had the decency to lower his head in deference before taking his seat.

Then the judge addressed Callie. "Ms. James, please keep your personal opinions to yourself and stick to the facts."

Callie nodded. "I'm sorry."

The judge straightened her back and folded her hands on the desk in front of her. "Why don't you tell me your version of what happened and why you won't accept the plea agreement?"

As Callie began to explain how she'd been going to surprise Andrew with dinner because he said he'd be working late, the anger rushed through her as if she were reliving it. She unclenched her fists, relaxed her shoulders and blew out a breath, techniques she'd always used successfully to diffuse the first signs of anger.

"So you brought him dinner. Then what?" The judge's smirk said she didn't want to hear about some lover's spat.

"It was our six-month anniversary." Callie glanced at Andrew. Her confidence got a boost when he colored with embarrassment. "I had a key to his apartment and I didn't bother knocking since he'd told me he was still at work. I took the food directly to the kitchen and heard a noise in the bedroom." Callie swallowed. There was that pesky bile again. She shifted her weight from one foot to the other. "Thinking Andrew had gotten home earlier than expected, I went to surprise him." She drew in a breath. "He was in bed with a...woman." Callie had other names for Andrew's former colleague but refused to lower herself to their level.

A choking sound from the back of the room had Callie and several others turning.

Heat suffused Callie's face and spread through

her body as she relived Andrew's betrayal. There was the woman, standing at the back of the court-room as if she belonged. So sure of herself that she'd come to observe Callie's further humiliation. How long had their affair been going on? Was it serious or merely a one-night fling?

Callie didn't care. Once a cheater, always a cheater. She'd never take Andrew back.

The judge gave her a little prod. "What happened next?"

Truthfully, Callie wasn't a hundred percent sure. Everything had blurred as she'd run out of the apartment. The blood rushing in her ears had been so loud that if she *had* knocked over Andrew's precious vase, she hadn't heard or felt it.

"I ran out of the apartment and went home." Callie shrugged her shoulders. "I have no recollection of knocking over his vase, accidentally or on purpose. I do know that I didn't throw it."

The next thing she remembered was waking to the ringing phone, her pillowcase wet from tears, thinking Andrew had wanted to apologize. Instead he'd wanted her to reimburse him for the stupid vase. The thing was ugly, with some kind of battle scene on it, but he'd bought it in Germany several years ago and claimed it was very expensive.

Callie had refused to pay him and a few choice words to describe her feelings about his betrayal had remained unspoken. In return, he'd offered her a few hours to think about her options. The only *option* she'd been interested in was the one where she'd never see him again.

She'd gone to work as usual the next day. When she hadn't heard back from him, she'd assumed he'd come to his senses and realized it was unfair to make her pay for something she didn't break.

The following morning she'd awoken to banging on her apartment door. Two officers were there to escort her to the Montgomery County Detention Center. She'd spent several hours in an interrogation room until her lawyer made arrangements for her arraignment. At least she hadn't been subjected to a jail cell.

She'd sworn to herself right then and there that she would never, ever, get involved with an assistant state's attorney again. Or a lawyer. Or anyone else who could put her in this kind of position.

For that matter, she was swearing off men altogether.

Period.

The judge drummed her fingers on her desk, appearing to want Callie to say more.

"Your Honor, if I did knock over Mr. Slater's vase, then it was by accident." Callie couldn't help adding, "An accident caused directly by Mr. Slater's own inexcusable actions."

The judge's brows rose but she kept her focus

on Callie while raising a hand to quiet Andrew, who was halfway out of his chair.

He pinched his lips shut but not before glaring at Callie as he sat.

She guessed he didn't expect his private "affair" would come out in public. He probably thought he'd scared her and she'd gladly pay for his precious vase now.

"Then you admit you broke the vase?" the judge asked.

"No."

"No?"

"I don't remember bumping into it or breaking it, so I can't say for sure that I broke it. We only have his version of events, and I'm not about to accept the opinion of a known liar."

The judge nodded. "Thank you." She turned to Andrew. "Mr. Slater, did you see Ms. James break the vase?"

"Well—"

The judge nodded, pursing her lips. "That's what I thought. Do you perhaps have a witness who will come forward to verify that Ms. James broke the vase?"

Andrew looked to the back of the room where the witch was now seated, shaking her head vigorously.

Andrew turned back to the judge. "No, I don't."

"So it's a 'he said, she said' case?"

Andrew looked at Callie, disgust on his face. "Unfortunately yes, Your Honor."

"And you still think you can be successful at trial?" The judge wanted to know.

Again Andrew glanced to the back of the courtroom before answering. He straightened. "Yes, I do."

The judge addressed Callie. "I know you don't want to accept the plea agreement from the state, but I have an alternative so as to stop wasting the court's time and the state's money."

Callie waited for the judge to continue, her knees knocking. Maybe she should have just given Andrew the money for his ridiculous vase.

Then again, why should she give him the satisfaction? He'd already gotten what he wanted. Callie glanced back at the woman she'd last seen straddling him.

Callie straightened her shoulders and raised her head high. She had nothing to be sorry for.

"Ms. James, I don't know whether or not you broke Mr. Slater's vase. And if you did, I don't know if it was on purpose or by accident. So my solution to this is Solomonesque." From the confused looks the judge was getting from around the courtroom, Callie wasn't the only one who didn't get her meaning. "King Solomon, people. You know, cut the baby in half and all that?"

Callie still didn't understand.

"Okay, Ms. James, you will pay for half of the vase." She looked at the papers in front of her. "That comes to two thousand, two hundred and fifty dollars." She looked at Andrew. "That means, Mr. Slater, you will be responsible for the other half."

Neither party spoke.

"Is that agreeable to both of you?" the judge asked.

"But—" Callie was about to say no. The whole thing was *not* fair.

The judge held up a hand. "Let me remind you, Ms. James. If you don't accept this agreement, then bail will be set and a trial date chosen. Mr. Slater will likely have time to convince a particular witness to testify and back his version of events, leaving you to defend yourself in front of a jury of your peers, and you seem to have no witnesses to make your case."

Callie couldn't believe it. Andrew was going to win because, no matter what she did, she would have to pay.

She spoke through clenched teeth, fisting her hands so tight that her nails dug into her flesh. "I have no other options?" She was an expert at controlling her temper, had done it out of necessity, but she was a hair's width away from losing it.

The judge watched her carefully. "No, you don't. And I'm going to add something beneficial to your overall well-being. I don't know if you broke Mr. Slater's vase, but, frankly, you appear to be wound way too tight. I'd like you to get some anger management therapy."

Callie's eyes nearly popped from their sockets. *Was the judge kidding?* Callie held back the hysterical laughter choking her. "Why do I need therapy when he's the one who lied and cheated?" She pointed at Andrew, quite pleased with himself. She snapped her mouth shut.

"You're making my point, Ms. James," the judge cautioned. "I'm beginning to think you may have broken the vase on purpose." The judge made a note on her papers. "So I need to know if you accept the plea deal. Pay for half the vase, seek therapy, and I'm going to add one hundred hours of community service to the deal."

"Community service?" Her lawyer finally spoke up. "That's completely unfair, Your Honor."

"Mr. Goodman, your client can gladly turn down the plea and go to trial. I won't repeat what I said before about a possible fine and jail time. I think she understands."

Callie went numb. Why was she being punished and Andrew came out the winner?

"May I have a moment with my client?" Harvey asked.

"A moment," the judge said. "I have other cases pending."

"Yes, Your Honor." Harvey turned to Callie

and lowered his voice. "I'm recommending you take the deal."

"What!" She whispered but several heads turned in her direction. "I can't take the deal. I'm not guilty."

"If you don't, then you could end up in jail. You know he's going to get the other woman to testify against you."

"Will this go on my record if I accept the plea?" She'd made a name for herself in the financial world. This could ruin her career.

"I'll ask for it to be expunged after you complete your therapy and community service," Harvey said.

Community service. *You've got to be kidding.* She pictured herself in a reflective vest as she picked up trash along I-270 on a hot July day.

"I can probably get your community service limited to some pro bono tax returns for struggling businesses," Harvey told her.

That didn't sound so bad. And she could probably handle a few sessions with a shrink. Heaven knew she had enough childhood stuff to fill a few hours.

"Okay," she finally said. "As long as it all gets expunged when I'm done."

Harvey addressed the judge. "There are two conditions we'd like to attend to, Your Honor. The matter of expunging Ms. James's record and some kind of proof of the value of the vase."

Nice touch, Harvey. Paying for half wouldn't be a financial burden for Callie, but the principal of paying for it definitely irked her.

The judge made notes. "Those conditions are acceptable." Then she turned to Andrew. "Mr. Slater, can you provide the court with a proper document?"

"I'd be happy to do that, Your Honor."

Callie was tempted to wipe that smirk off his face but instead breathed in and out, in and out.

The judge turned to the clerk. "Have both parties sign the appropriate documents." She banged her gavel. "The court is in recess for fifteen minutes."

Everyone stood until the judge exited the courtroom through her private door. Loath to speak to Andrew ever again, Callie whispered to Harvey, "Get me out of here."

"Callie!" Andrew came up behind her as she hurried down the courthouse hallway.

She slowed her pace but didn't stop completely. "What?"

Andrew hesitated a few seconds before blurting out, "I want my key back."

Of course he did. She stopped, dug through her hobo bag and struggled to remove his key from her ring. Instead of throwing it at him like she wanted to, she very smoothly held it out to him.

He tossed it a few inches in the air and caught it, his pleasure at her expense almost more than she could bear. "You know I only want the best for you."

She stared at him, curious why he felt the need to say anything to her.

"That's why I suggested the judge add therapy to the plea."

He'd suggested it? Then she was right about them all being in cahoots. She kept her tone neutral. "So you think I need to control my anger?"

He shook his head. "No, I think you need to start expressing your feelings." He looked down the hall to where his bed partner waited and then back at Callie. "You're a wonderful person, Callie, but you're as emotionally reserved as a rock."

SEVERAL WEEKS AND anger management therapy sessions later, Callie's therapist harrumphed and scratched his head. Nearly halfway into today's session and he was clearly frustrated. Callie suspected he was trying to bring out some anger in her, or at least some kind of emotion. In her defense, she'd spent years bottling up those emotions and she wasn't sure she knew how to unleash them. Or wanted to.

Dr. Hammond seemed perfectly nice. He was

a middle-aged man of average height, average weight and above-average intelligence as far as Callie could judge. Just not the person with whom she was comfortable sharing her innermost thoughts.

"Let's get back to your mother," Dr. Hammond said in his monotone voice. "She died when you were very young?"

"Yes." A pink bathrobe and fuzzy pink slippers constituted her faint memory of the woman who'd died when Callie was three. She didn't even remember her face, forced to consult one of the few faded pictures she'd held on to.

"Were you upset when she died?"

"Of course I was upset," she said evenly. "Who wouldn't be? I was young and had no mother." Callie's pulse sped up, so she took control of her breathing. In and out. In and out. "But I couldn't do anything about it and it wasn't her fault that she was killed."

"Are you still angry?"

Callie's brow furrowed. Her mother had been gone twenty-six years. She missed her or, more specifically, she missed having a mother figure. She didn't know what it was like to have a mother to turn to in tough times. Like when she'd caught Andrew cheating.

She spoke calmly. "Car jacking is a horrific act of violence, but I don't dwell on it."

"Are you close to your father?" Dr. Hammond shifted in his seat and crossed one leg over the other.

"No."

"When was the last time you two spoke?"

Callie did the math in her head. "About eleven years ago."

Dr. Hammond's eyebrows rose. "That's a long time." When Callie didn't comment further, he asked, "What was the circumstance that led to your loss of communication?"

Callie nearly smiled at Dr. Hammond's formal turn of phrase rather than simply asking why she'd shut her father out of her life. "I left for college."

"I see."

No, he probably didn't, but Callie couldn't disclose her personal demons to this stranger, no matter how soothingly he spoke.

"Did you and your father have an altercation?"

"No."

"Would you like to rekindle a relationship with him?"

She hadn't even considered it. "That's not an option."

Dr. Hammond cocked his head and asked, "Did he molest you?"

Callie's eyes widened and she straightened in her chair. "No, of course not. He'd never do that." Her father was the sweetest man she'd ever known. Maybe too sweet, blinding him to the deceit surrounding him.

Dr. Hammond watched Callie through narrowed eyes and finally nodded as he made notes in his file. "Let's move on to your stepmother," Dr. Hammond suggested.

Let's not. "What about her?" *Breathe deeply. In and out.*

"How old were you when she came into your life?"

Callie's stomach churned. "She was my mother's friend, her maid of honor when my parents married."

Dr. Hammond made another note. "How would you characterize your relationship?"

Callie couldn't do this. She couldn't discuss her stepmother. "She's my father's wife." She took a halting breath. "Can't we talk about something else?"

Dr. Hammond was silent for several minutes. "Callie, I'm at a loss here. The court sent you to me, but I can't help you if you insist on burying your emotions. You need to open up."

Callie didn't know what to say. She'd spent most of her life keeping her thoughts and emotions to herself. Any anger burning her insides remained unspoken. That's what kept her out of trouble.

Until recently.

Most people would have screamed and yelled at Andrew and the woman on top of him, but Callie didn't operate like that. She'd learned early on to curb her temper, no matter how unfair the circumstances. After that, only once had she ever lost complete control of her temper. It was a slipup as a teenager and she was lucky it hadn't ruined the rest of her life.

"I don't know what you want me to say. Nothing in my past has anything to do with me finding my boyfriend in bed with another woman." She fisted and relaxed her hands several times. "It didn't make me lose my temper and break an expensive vase. Though I almost wish I had so at least I'd be paying for something I actually did."

The more she'd thought about it since court, the more she was positive she couldn't have broken Andrew's vase. The ugly thing always sat on a shelf right outside his kitchen, so she never even would have come near it as she ran out of his apartment. The only way she might have been responsible is if it had fallen when she'd slammed his apartment door as she'd left—but she wouldn't have slammed the door. That would have been a loss of control that was completely out of character for Callie.

"Our time is almost up for today." Dr. Hammond leaned forward. "I was hoping I wouldn't have to do this, but I want you to go spend time with your father and stepmother." When Callie opened her mouth to speak, he raised a hand to stop her. "I want you to voice, face-to-face, whatever your feelings have been about them. Even if in the end you haven't settled things, at least you won't be carrying your hurt inside where it's obviously tearing you apart."

This couldn't be happening. "Can't I just write letters to them, pour out my feelings, and then burn the letters or something?" She'd seen that on shows countless times and it always seemed to make the person feel better.

Not that she needed to feel better. She was just fine. Especially now that she was free of cheating Andrew and single again.

"I'm afraid not," he said. "I've already made arrangements for you to continue your community service in Whittler's Creek."

"But—"

"Our time is up." Dr. Hammond repeated as he stood. "We'll continue therapy by phone while you're away. You can email my receptionist with the best time for you once you know your community service hours."

Callie stood up, her mind a foggy mess. "What about my job?" How would she explain needing time off? How long would it take? A few days? A week? Longer?

Breathe. In and out. Slower. In...out.

Dr. Hammond put a hand on her elbow to show her out. "I'm sure they'll allow you to take a sabbatical once you explain." He handed her another piece of paper. A formal letter on his personal stationery. "Use this if necessary." He handed her another sheet of paper. "And here's where you report for community service at 8:00 a.m. Monday."

She glanced at the information. Office of the Chief of Police, Whittler's Creek, Maryland. Great. What were the chances this small-town law enforcer was someone who didn't know her or about her past?

CHAPTER TWO

LATE SUNDAY AFTERNOON Callie reluctantly drove the hour and a half from her home just inside the Washington, DC, beltway to the town where she'd grown up in western Maryland. She'd spoken to her boss Friday afternoon and arranged to telework while she was away. Her boss hadn't been happy about it, but he'd had no choice. She'd made the company a lot of money the past few years. They couldn't afford to lose her, especially knowing there were several other financial firms that would gladly hire her immediately after this fiasco in Whittler's Creek ended.

When she reached the sign welcoming her to Whittler's Creek, her heart began to beat double-time. How had she gotten herself into this? Was it too late to give Andrew the entire amount for the stupid vase? Probably.

Callie's plan for today was to arrive in town and immediately head to her father's house to get their reunion over with. She loved her dad and missed having him in her life. But she couldn't get past the feeling that he'd let her down all those years ago.

She drove through the "downtown" area of Whittler's Creek that consisted of two blocks with a few small, family-run businesses, as well as a bank and the police station where Callie would report tomorrow morning. She continued on toward the outskirts of town and made a left turn on the winding uphill road that led to her childhood home.

When she reached the long driveway, she pulled over onto the gravel-and-dirt shoulder to gather her courage. She pressed the button to turn off the engine of her dark red sports car—the one she'd splurged on, buying it outright with her last bonus.

She could see the house farther up the hill. It didn't appear much different than when she'd lived there all those years ago.

The house held painful secrets, but from the outside you'd never guess it was anything but run-down.

The white clapboard was dingy and one of the dark green shutters was missing, while several others hung slightly crooked. The landscaping needed work. The grass needed to be mowed and the evergreen bushes near the front door were overgrown. One of the large oak trees in the front yard was dead. The next big storm could knock the tree into the house if it wasn't taken down soon.

Callie hadn't called ahead to let her dad know she'd be coming. It wasn't that she didn't want him to know, it was more that she didn't want to give her stepmother a heads-up. This visit would be difficult enough without giving the woman prep time.

Callie stayed in her car for quite a while, gathering her courage to face her past. There were only a few other houses down this quiet road. Not even one car passed by as she sat there.

Her stomach was in knots. She should have eaten lunch, but she'd figured an empty stomach was better than a full one that could reverse direction if her anxiety got out of control.

Which it was definitely threatening.

She uncapped the water bottle in the center console drink holder and took a long swig. The cool liquid somewhat soothed her dry mouth but offered no relief to her stomach. She replaced the cap and turned her attention back to her father's house.

A car was visible in the detached garage, the door having been left open. She hoped that meant her father was home, but she'd been gone too long to know if it was her father's car or her stepmother's.

It was now or never. She would prefer never, but that wouldn't make her therapist happy. Callie needed to get this over with and move on.

The engine turned over when she pressed the start button. Taking a deep breath, she reached for the gearshift and froze.

She reminded herself that she was an adult now. Not the eighteen-year-old who'd left home for college eleven years ago. She could stand up for herself, could leave whenever she wanted. No one could force her to do something against her will.

She wasn't that scared little girl, so easily intimidated.

She put the car in gear and slowly pulled back onto the two-lane road riddled with potholes that still hadn't been patched from last year's harsh winter.

She carefully turned right into the long driveway leading to her childhood home and stopped abruptly.

Her head throbbed.

Before she could change her mind, she threw the car into reverse and backed out onto the street to face the direction from which she'd come.

A single bead of sweat ran down her temple. Not from the heat but from anxiety.

Without another glance at the house, she gunned the engine and headed back through the downtown area.

She hadn't realized she was holding her breath until she let it out as she passed the sign saying Thanks for Visiting Whittler's Creek, Come Again.

She knew of a small hotel in a neighboring town that she could check in to for the night. After breakfast tomorrow, she'd look for a more semi-permanent housing solution, rather than pay daily hotel rates.

She'd also work on reinforcing her courage.

MONDAY MORNING TYLER GARRETT rubbed his face with both hands, barely able to control the urge to bang his head on his desk as he surveyed his crowded office.

He was Whittler's Creek's Chief of Police, not a financial guru. He had no way of deciphering the mountain of binders and documents that had been packed into boxes and were now taking up much of the walking space in his already cramped office.

He'd received an anonymous email late last week about discrepancies in the town's financial records. With no ability to track down where the email had originated, he had immediately requested a court order before the records could be doctored. After Judge Parsons had signed off on it, Tyler had requested the records be brought to his office from a building down the street. He'd never imagined there would be so much paper involved.

What happened to going digital like the rest of the country?

Then he considered where he was living. A small town in western Maryland. Even though a few residents commuted to DC or Baltimore, the majority had lived here most of their lives and rarely ventured more than an hour or so away. They preferred to keep their lives simple.

His phone rang. "Chief Garrett."

"Good morning, Chief Garrett. This is Dr. Jeffrey Hammond. I'm a psychologist in Bethesda and I have a court-ordered patient who will be coming to Whittler's Creek to do her community service. I sent you an email over the weekend with the details."

Great. Just what he needed. Another criminal coming to town. "I haven't gotten to email yet this morning." He glanced at the banker's boxes surrounding his desk and shook his head.

"I understand." Dr. Hammond went on to give Tyler a few details. "I'm not at liberty to explain too much about Ms. James's current situation, but she grew up there and still has family in town. I trust that you will provide adequate supervision for her court-ordered community service?"

"Absolutely." Ms. James? As in Callie James? If that's who it was, he hadn't seen her in years. Not since he'd witnessed her explosive temper the night he'd walked her home from a party. He'd had a huge crush on her, asking her out several times but getting the same negative response from her

each time. The night of the party he thought he'd
been the luckiest guy in Whittler's Cove until her
true personality revealed itself.

He fired up his dated desktop computer while
Dr. Hammond continued talking.

"Thank you for understanding and for your dis-
cretion." By the time Dr. Hammond disconnected,
Tyler's computer was finally opening the email
program.

He needed to take a look at the town's budget and see about new computers. How was he
expected to do his job if he couldn't even check
email in a timely fashion?

He wiped sweat from the back of his neck. The
air-conditioning was on the fritz again, too, and
the outside temperature on this July morning was
already in the low eighties.

The program finally opened and he found Dr.
Hammond's email. There it was. Callie James.
Grew up in Whittler's Creek and has family is-
sues to deal with.

No kidding. Callie's stepsister used to hang out
with Tyler's sister back in high school, and the
stepsister had been a terrible influence on Isabelle.
Thankfully, the two young women had gone their
separate ways after high school.

Had Callie changed since high school? Obviously not, if she had community service hours to
fulfill. According to his sister and what he'd wit-

nessed, Callie could be as mean and nasty as an angry wasp.

What about physically? Had she let herself go as much as others he'd seen around town? She'd always kept her light blond hair long, allowing it to swing to and fro or weaving it into a thick braid. Was it still long? Did she still twist it around her fingers when she became nervous?

He remembered her cupid's-bow lips, shiny with lip gloss. How he'd always wanted to taste her mouth, wondering if she used fruit-flavored gloss like some of the other girls their age. But he'd kept his distance because his sister had always insisted that Callie had an explosive temper. He hadn't believed it until he'd seen it firsthand.

Was that what had forced her return to Whittler's Creek? Had her temper done her in?

A loud knock on the frame of his office door had him opening his eyes. He hadn't even realized he'd closed them. "Yes?" he said to the youngest of his three patrolmen on the Whittler's Creek Police Force.

"You have a visitor, Chief." Pete Meyers ran a hand over his bald head. He was only a few years older than Tyler's thirty, but between losing his hair and being overweight by a good forty pounds, Pete looked older than his years. "Callie something."

"Callie James." She'd come up to the doorway behind Pete.

Tyler would have recognized her voice without even seeing her.

Physically, she was everything he remembered and more. She wore a navy suit jacket and matching pencil skirt that stopped a few inches above her knees. Her filmy white blouse had several of the top buttons open to reveal multiple strands of large gold chains around her neck. Her neutral-tan pumps added about four inches to her average height.

She still had the ability to heat his blood, but he was an adult now and knew better than to get too close to a smoldering fire.

"Thanks, Pete." He waved Callie in and rose from his chair. Her deep blue eyes with long lashes gave her an innocent quality. "Have a seat." He pointed to one of the two beat-up chairs on the other side of his desk. He sat when she did. "I apologize for the heat. The AC repairman was here three times last week, but the system needs to be replaced." He swallowed, feeling like he was babbling. "I haven't seen you since high school, Callie. How have you been?"

She crossed one bare leg over the other. "Pretty good, until I had to come back here."

He nodded, forcing his eyes from her legs to her face.

"What about you? I didn't realize you were the one I'd be reporting to." She looked around his cramped office. "What are you doing back here? Weren't you going to West Point? Planning to make the Army a career?"

"I left the Army. Plans change." He didn't want to get into the details of his own life. That wasn't why she sat across from him.

"So you're the Chief of Police now?"

"That's right. For about a year now." He checked the email again from Dr. Hammond. "It says here you need to perform community service hours. You couldn't do them where you're living?"

"I was going to, but Dr. Hammond thought I should come back here to see my family."

"How long has it been?"

She twisted a lock of her still-long hair. "Eleven years. I guess he figured it would take more than a day trip for me to resolve things to his satisfaction."

"Eleven years is a long time to not see your family." He couldn't imagine how painful it would be if either of his young daughters someday decided to stay away from him for that long.

She shrugged. "If I'd been given a choice, I would never have come back."

WHEN TYLER DIDN'T COMMENT, Callie turned the focus on him. "What about your dad? Is he still living in town?"

Tyler hesitated and cleared his throat. "He died almost a year and a half ago."

Callie leaned forward. "I'm so sorry. He was a great guy." Tyler's dad had been very active in youth sports when they were growing up. As the owner of Garrett's Hardware Store, he'd had flexible hours, allowing him to be on the practice fields after school. He was also very generous when it came to sponsoring teams. Callie's softball shirt with Garrett's across the back came to mind. "What about the store? Is someone still running it?"

Tyler shook his head. "Dad closed it when he got sick. He sold the inventory and gave up the lease. The furniture store that was next door—Pratt's—expanded into the space."

"That's too bad."

"It was for the best. Dad had an inoperable brain tumor and it was either close the store then or my sister and I would have had to do it after he passed away."

"Neither of you wanted to continue running it?"

"Isabelle definitely had no interest. And, at the time, I wasn't sure what I was going to do."

Isabelle's best friend had been Callie's stepsister, Wendy, who'd had a major crush on Tyler. Had the two of them ever gotten together? Pushing the question to the back of her mind, Callie opened her mouth to ask why he'd left the Army—she had a hunch there was a story to that—but he changed the subject before she could bring it up.

"Now, about your community service…" He consulted his computer while she took in his broad shoulders. He'd gone from slim teenager to well-built adult. "You're only the second person I've had report to me to fulfill their hours. I'll have to see what I can find." He clicked a few keys.

"What did that other person do for their service hours?"

He looked at her with his deep-set, dark brown eyes. As a teenager she'd thought of them as puppy-dog eyes, but on a grown man they were downright sexy. "He loaded and unloaded mulch into a truck and spread it at the elementary school. He did some other landscaping, too." Tyler glanced at her and took in her outfit from head to toe. "I'm not sure landscaping is right for you. Besides, you're not dressed for work like that."

She heated at his perusal. "I have clothes to change into." In truth, she'd worn her office clothes, hoping the Chief of Police would see her as a professional and not someone ready to do hard labor. Not that she wasn't strong, but if she had to do community service, she might as well do something that would benefit the community. It never crossed her mind that Tyler would be the person holding authority over her. She doubted he'd give her any kind of break, though, no matter how she'd dressed.

"That's good." He clicked keys on his computer again and the printer in the corner, partially hidden by banker's boxes, came alive.

Tyler stood to retrieve what he'd printed. He glanced at the page and then handed it to Callie. "You can report to this address tomorrow morning at eight. There's a volunteer group, mostly seniors, who have planned a clean-up of the city streets."

"Are you talking about picking up trash?"

His dark, well-groomed eyebrows rose. "Do you have a problem with that?"

Her hands clenched and unclenched automatically. "Of course not." She rose. "I'll be sure to be on time."

She was outside his office when she heard him add, "You might want to wear gloves and shoes you don't care about. Oh, and long pants. You never know when you'll run into poison ivy or the occasional snake."

She shivered at the thought. "Great," she muttered to herself. She should have guessed that he'd give her a nasty job rather than one she was actually suited to. He hadn't even asked about her skills.

For that matter, he hadn't asked her anything about herself. Was he still holding that outburst against her? The one she hadn't held back that last night before leaving for college? She'd thought letting him walk her home from that party would be nice. She'd planned to leave for college the next day and he'd made it clear all summer that he was interested in her.

But even if she could go back and do everything differently, there was no way to a happy ending. One of two things would have happened regardless. Either her stepsister would find a way to hurt her physically or emotionally because she wanted Tyler for herself, or, sooner or later, Tyler would have discovered how dysfunctional her family really was. What he'd witnessed that night was a mere hint of the reality.

Fine. His disinterest didn't bother her. She had things to do and she'd get them done and get out of town.

She should have thought to bring old shoes with her, not that she really owned any. She tended to clean out her closet every spring and donate to the local women's shelter. They were always looking for gently-worn work clothes, shoes and purses so disadvantaged women could go on job interviews and hopefully make new lives for themselves and their children. Callie was happy to help them out.

She got into her car and turned the air-conditioning up to maximum. She twisted her long hair into a bun and secured it with a few bobby pins from her purse. The heat in Tyler's office had been stifling. The town was obviously in a financial bind if it couldn't replace the AC or even Tyler's ancient computer.

She pulled out of the small visitors' parking lot next to the police station and headed to her appointment to see about a room for rent. It was the only option she'd found on Craigslist within a twenty-mile radius.

Callie could have lived out of a hotel, but she preferred to not waste her hard-earned money. And she'd save a lot if things worked out with Mrs. Thompson.

The house was a few blocks from the police station. When Callie had lived in Whittler's Creek, this home had been occupied by Mrs. Thompson, her husband and their four children. The children must be grown by now since the youngest was only a year older than Callie. Mrs. Thompson had been the one who'd listed the rental.

The large Victorian home with its wrap-around porch sat on an oversize corner lot. It was probably a hundred years old, but from the outside it looked pristine. Especially compared to her father's house that was only about half as old.

The pale blue painted clapboard and white gingerbread trim appeared fresh. The lawn was mowed and there were flowers blooming everywhere Callie looked. Definitely a pleasant place to come home to after picking up trash all day.

When she'd communicated by email with Mrs. Thompson yesterday, Callie had discovered that the woman had turned her home into a boarding-house after her husband died. Callie assumed it was for financial reasons. One of her daughters had been living with her but had recently moved out, leaving an empty room to rent.

Parking beside the curb, Callie straightened her clothes and walked to the front door. Even close up, she could see how well-kept the property was.

Mrs. Thompson answered the door almost immediately after Callie rang the bell. "Come in! Come in!" She stepped out of the way for Callie to enter. If Callie hadn't known Mrs. Thompson was in her late fifties, she would have guessed her as being closer to fifty. The petite woman with auburn hair and not a single gray had a welcoming smile and an energetic attitude to go with it.

She drew Callie in for a hug, catching her off guard. "It's so good to see you after all these years," Mrs. Thompson said.

Callie hadn't known Mrs. Thompson very well, but the woman obviously remembered her. Mrs. Thompson had been the team mom on Callie's softball team and she had also been the room mother in her third-grade classroom.

Mrs. Thompson kept an arm at Callie's waist as she ushered her from the entryway, down a short hallway and into the kitchen with its white cabinets, yellow walls and royal blue accents. "Come, we'll have something to drink and you can tell me what you've been doing." She named both hot and cold drinks.

Callie swallowed, still in shock by the warm reception. "Coffee sounds good." Unlike the police department, the AC in Mrs. Thompson's house was in good working condition.

"So, tell me what you've been up to, Callie," Mrs. Thompson said as she busied herself getting the coffee.

"Well, since grad school, I've been living in Silver Spring. I'm a financial analyst at a large firm in Bethesda."

"How wonderful! I'm sure you're great at what you do."

Again, Callie didn't know how to react to Mrs. Thompson's enthusiasm. She hadn't gotten even close to that reaction from Tyler. He'd appeared guarded. Did he really hold what happened all those years ago against her? Couldn't he at least be friendly?

She'd been nervous as hell when she'd first seen him today. He was a mature version of the handsome teenage boy she'd crushed on in her past life, but her teenage reaction to him hadn't changed. Her mouth had gone dry, her heart beat double-time and words had been hard to find.

"I'm doing something I love," she told Mrs.

Thompson, "so I think that helps to make me good at it." Callie didn't know why else she was so successful at choosing the right investments to make others a lot of money, but it had certainly been financially rewarding for her personally, as well.

Mrs. Thompson set a cup of coffee in front of Callie, who'd taken a seat at the counter. "What do you like in it?"

"A splash of something white," Callie said with a smile. "Skim, whole milk, cream, half-and-half. I'm not choosy. I think needing to add it is psychological because I've told myself I don't like black coffee."

The two women chuckled while Mrs. Thompson retrieved some cream from the fridge. They spoke for a few minutes about things going on in town while they drank their coffee.

"I never asked you why you're back," Mrs. Thompson said. "I'm guessing it's family related."

"Something like that." Callie wasn't ready to divulge too much yet, especially before her family knew she was in town.

"I get it. You need a place to escape instead of staying at your parents'. Sometimes family can be overwhelming." Mrs. Thompson took the last swallow of her coffee.

Callie merely nodded and then changed the subject. "So you've been renting out rooms for several years?"

"Since right after my Jeffrey died. It's been almost five years now."

"I'm sorry for your loss, Mrs. Thompson."

She nodded. "Thank you. And, please, none of this Mrs. Thompson nonsense. I'm Poppy to everyone."

"Poppy." Callie still felt like the young girl who used to live in Whittler's Creek, not an adult on the same level as others in town.

Poppy put their cups in the dishwasher. "I think I told you the rent is one fifty a week and that includes breakfast and dinner. We do family style for whoever is here at six o'clock. If you miss it, there are always leftovers for you to heat up later."

Callie nodded. The rent on her condo was four times that and no meals were included. She'd often thought about buying a condo or house instead of throwing away so much money on rent, but with the unstable real estate market, it was too big a risk. And she'd probably never buy a house. A bigger place to take care of wasn't practical since she had little spare time as it was.

"I'll show you around and you can decide if this is the right place for you," Poppy said as she led the way through the dining room and into the living room. "Feel free to use any of the rooms down here. I like my guests to feel as if this is their home, too."

Callie knew before going upstairs to see her

bedroom that she would accept Poppy's invitation to stay here. She'd never lived anywhere that was this welcoming. Her current home was just a place to return to when not working. She had no one to greet her or to miss her. No pleasant family dinners—not that she'd grown up with them.

"Here's where you would be staying." Poppy gestured to the doorway at the top of the open staircase.

Callie stepped into a large room that held a queen-size bed with brass headboard and footboard, a full-length mirror on a brass stand and a small love seat positioned in a bay window that let in lots of light.

Poppy opened a door to show her a small closet and then crossed the room to open another door. "This is the only room on this floor with a private bathroom."

"This is a wonderful room," she told Poppy. "I'd love to stay here."

Poppy smiled. "I'm so glad to hear that. My daughter, Molly, really loved this room."

Another question popped into Callie's head. "So who else is living here right now?"

Poppy pointed to the next doorway down the hall. "This room is being rented by a young man going through a divorce, but he told me just last night that he'd be moving out at the end of the week. So I'll need to put another ad on Craigslist."

Callie was wondering if she'd like his room even better when Poppy said, "His is the smallest and has no private bathroom."

"What about those two rooms?" Callie pointed down the hall. "Is one of them yours?"

"Oh, no. I've got my own suite in the attic. Those rooms are rented by my nephew and his two young daughters. I hope that doesn't make you change your mind. I forgot to mention that there would be children in the house. Although they're very well behaved."

Callie smiled. "That's not a problem at all." She wasn't used to being around kids, but how difficult could it be for what she hoped would be a short time before she went back to her old life? And then she remembered who Mrs. Thompson's nephew was.

"Oh, you might even know my nephew. I think you're about the same age and he grew up here, too. It's Tyler Garrett. His sweet little girls are Alexis and Madison."

CHAPTER THREE

LATER THAT MORNING Callie was finally settling into her room. *Poppy was Tyler's aunt.* Amazing how much she'd blocked out when she'd moved away.

She'd been surprised to hear that he and his daughters lived with Poppy. She would have expected Tyler had a place of his own. Especially with two children.

Poppy hadn't mentioned Tyler's wife. Had Poppy not mentioned her because she wasn't someone from town whom Callie would remember? Or was Tyler a single dad with custody of his children? He might even be a widower for all she knew.

She'd hung up what she could in the small closet and used the large oak dresser with a beveled mirror for the rest of her things. Then she checked her email on her laptop and didn't want to think about what she was missing back at work.

Close to lunchtime she decided to take a walk to see how much things had changed in town. She'd really like to go for a run to rid herself of her pent-up energy and frustration, but it was too hot and humid for that. Early morning or dusk would be a better time.

She'd changed into shorts, a tank top and her running shoes earlier, so she closed the door to her bedroom as she left and exited the house through the front door. There were no outside locks on the bedrooms, only a lock when you were inside the room. Obviously the crime level was pretty low and locks weren't a necessity. Just one more thing she'd have to get used to again while being back in a small town.

She headed the few blocks toward the downtown area, such as it was. Just as Tyler told her, Pratt's Furniture Store had expanded into the space where Garrett's Hardware used to be. Next to Pratt's was a bakery that hadn't been there before. A gift store was next to it, also new since she'd lived here.

On the other side of the street was the First National Bank, looking exactly as she remembered with its tan-brick façade. She crossed the street when she saw that the little drugstore next to the bank was still there.

This was where she'd hung out after school when she was able. She wondered if they still had the counter and a few booths where they served juicy burgers and shakes so thick you needed a spoon to eat them.

She opened the glass-and-metal door and stepped inside, feeling like a teenager again. Nothing had changed. The counter and booths were still there, the Formica chipping on the tabletops as was the wood laminate on the benches. The stools at the counter, circa 1950s, were metal circles with red-vinyl inserts that had seen better days.

"Callie?" The woman behind the counter was staring at her, eyes wide.

Callie smiled. "June!" She came up to the counter where the woman stood on the other side. "You're still working here!" She sat on the empty stool in front of June. "How are you?"

"I'm good," June told her. "And you look like life is treating you okay, too."

"Thanks. I'm surviving down inside the beltway." These days she could add "barely" to surviving and still not be accurate enough.

June was probably in her early forties by now. She'd been a young mother working at the drugstore when Callie was in high school. Her husband had gone on disability after he was in a tractor accident at their farm a few miles from Whittler's Creek and June had taken the job to make ends meet.

Callie ordered a burger and shake, figuring she'd run off the excess calories later. After June sent the order to the short-order cook, she turned back to Callie and asked, "So what brings you to town? I haven't seen you in what? A decade, at least."

Callie should come up with an answer for the question that would be asked every time she ran into someone she knew.

"I've got some things to take care of in town," she said vaguely, hoping June didn't have a follow-up question.

"Well, it's great to see you." She had another customer to take care of and she stepped away.

Callie spun her stool a hundred and eighty degrees and looked around again while waiting for her food. A feeling of déjà vu came over her, or at least a step back in time.

It wasn't long before June delivered her food. Callie hadn't realized how hungry she was until she smelled the burger in front of her. "Thanks, June." She put a blob of ketchup on her plate for her fries. "So what have you been up to? How are your kids?"

The two caught up while Callie ate, interrupted occasionally by other customers. So far, no one else had come in that Callie recognized.

She was wiping her mouth after her last bite of burger when the bell over the door rang, signaling that someone was entering the store. Callie turned in that direction. It was her stepsister, Wendy Carter. Their gazes collided. Wendy looked away first, as if uncomfortable. Interesting. Not the same cocky teenager Callie remembered.

She couldn't help but notice Wendy's appearance. Her jeans and plaid shirt looked like they'd been washed a hundred times or more. Her hair needed something—a cut, deep conditioning— Callie couldn't say. And her complexion… Callie had never seen anyone with such a sickly appearance. She was pale, with tinges of green and yellow on one cheekbone. As if she'd been bruised a week or so ago.

"Hello, Callie," Wendy said stiffly when she came up to the counter. "I didn't know you were in town."

"I got here yesterday," Callie said just as stiffly.

"What can I get you, hon?" Thankfully, June interrupted their awkward exchange to take Wendy's order.

Callie had nothing more to say to the stepsister who had mentally and sometimes physically tortured her when they were growing up in the same house.

While Wendy placed a take-out order, Callie pulled out the money she'd stuck in her pocket to pay the bill June had left when she'd delivered Callie's food. Even the handwritten green checks that had to be added manually were the same as when she was a kid. She didn't bother asking if they now took credit cards. She'd planned ahead and taken out cash from an ATM before she'd arrived in Whittler's Creek. Callie laid enough money on the counter to cover the bill, as well as a healthy tip.

"Have you been to see my mom and Bart?" Wendy's question caught Callie by surprise.

"Not yet." Not until she gathered her courage.

Wendy didn't comment, merely nodded and then concentrated on a fingernail.

After waving goodbye to June, Callie was almost out the door when Wendy said just loud enough for Callie to hear, "You don't belong here."

Callie turned to Wendy, wondering if she'd heard correctly. "Excuse me?"

Wendy sneered. "You heard me. Go home. No one wants you here."

Callie remembered to breathe, in and out, in and out.

When her stepsister turned away, Callie assumed Wendy had nothing more to say.

So she continued out the door to the sidewalk and relaxed her hands when she realized her nails were digging into her palms.

IT HAD BEEN a long afternoon of frustration.

Tyler's job had been straightforward until that email about financial fraud showed up in his in-box. He'd spent the afternoon trying to find someone to audit the town's finances, but no one could do it for at least another month.

Thirty days was way too long to wait. It would give whoever was responsible the time to find out that an investigation was under way.

He'd appropriated a storage locker for all the records and they'd finally been moved, so at least they weren't cluttering up his office anymore.

He closed his computer and straightened his desk before letting the receptionist know he was leaving for the day. "I'll have my cell if anyone needs me."

"Yeah, yeah," Donna mumbled. "You say that every day. When was the last time anything happened in this town?"

Tyler had to think a minute. "When Mr. Rawlins got drunk and was waving a shotgun around."

Donna's eyebrows rose. "You know that was last month, right?"

"Seems like last week," he quipped. "And how quickly you've forgotten the standoff at the bank that secured this job for me in the first place." She did have a point, though. His job was mainly administrative.

Not that he expected to stay in this position until retirement, but he couldn't complain when the job and this town gave his daughters the stability they needed.

A little while later, he arrived at Aunt Poppy's,

his family's temporary home, to hear giggles and commotion coming from the kitchen. He headed there to greet his daughters and see what they were up to.

Aunt Poppy watched the girls while he worked, and staying with her just made sense while their house was under construction. This week they were attending a day camp to give his aunt a break.

"Hey, what's going on in here?" The words were barely out of his mouth when Alexis and Madison came running into his arms. He picked them both up and squeezed, making them giggle even more.

"Hi, Daddy." Alexis, the older of the two, kissed his cheek loudly. Madison, two years younger at four, did the same to his other cheek.

He was about to ask about their day when he noticed Callie across the room. She was hard to miss in those formfitting shorts and tank top.

He put his libido in check and got down to reality. What was she doing here? For that matter, what was she doing in the same room with his daughters?

"Where's Aunt Poppy?" he asked instead when he didn't see her anywhere nearby.

"She ran an errand," Callie explained. "I said I'd be here with the girls until she got back. I'm renting a room from her while I'm in town."

She was staying here? He was silent, wondering how to tell her to stay away from Alexis and Madison without causing an incident.

"You don't mind, do you?" Callie's puzzled look told him she didn't know why it would be a bad idea for her to be around his children. "I don't have much experience around kids, but yours have been great. And Poppy only expected to be gone twenty or thirty minutes. She needed something for dinner that she forgot to buy earlier. I offered to go, but she said it would be faster for her to go since I wasn't familiar with the store."

"Um, no. It's fine." He put the girls down, purposely not looking at Callie when he answered. He'd speak to his aunt privately about his concerns.

"Ms. Callie was telling us about when she used to go to the same camp as us." Alexis was bouncing as she spoke.

"Is that right?"

"Uh-huh. And she even took a bus like we do."

He glanced at Callie and then back at his daughters. "You know I went there, too."

"You already told us that, Daddy." Madison was very serious. "But you don't remember singing the same songs as us. Ms. Callie has been singing them with us. She knows all the words."

"Well, let's not wear her out. Who wants to go on a short bike ride before dinner?"

Both girls raised their hands and began dancing around the kitchen. "Can Ms. Callie come, too, Daddy?" Madison had stopped moving to ask the question.

He glanced at Callie then back at Madison. "Well—"

"I don't have a bike to ride," Callie told Madison. "So you'll have to go without me."

Tyler didn't know if she was giving him an out or if she really didn't want to go, but he was grateful for her answer.

"Go put on sneakers and I'll meet you at the garage after I change clothes."

When the girls were out of earshot, Callie said, "I'm sorry they put you on the spot. Don't feel obligated to include me just because I'm staying here now."

He decided to be honest with her. "I won't. In fact, it would be best if you avoided being around my daughters."

She awoke the next day with a feeling of dread. Picking up trash along the side of a road was not her idea of a productive day. Remembering Tyler's advice, she donned jeans and a T-shirt. Then she put on the pair of shoes she'd picked up last night at the big-box store that had opened outside of town since she'd been gone. For ten bucks, she could afford to ruin them. She pulled her hair into a ponytail and secured a baseball cap—another new purchase—around it. She applied a slathering of sunblock to her exposed skin and put the bottle into her small backpack, along with the water bottle and energy bars already there. Then she headed downstairs to grab breakfast and the prepackaged Greek salad she'd bought for lunch.

Driving to the community center, she thought back to her reaction the previous evening when Tyler had announced that he'd prefer she avoid being around his daughters. Her hands tightened on the steering wheel. His comment had confused her, but she'd been too shocked to question him about it. Instead she'd gone for a long run to blow off steam.

Callie arrived early at the designated meeting place. A few people were at the community center already and she introduced herself, leaving out the real reason she was there. Tyler had told her that everyone else was there voluntarily, so no one should think twice about her participating.

"We're so glad to have you join us," a tall gentleman, probably somewhere around seventy, told her. "I'm Gary, and this is my wife, Liz." He gestured to a petite woman about the same age with neatly styled, short blond hair.

Callie smiled and shook hands with both of them. "I'm Callie James. Nice to meet you."

"Are you new in town?" Liz asked.

"Actually, I grew up here. I'm back for a visit." That was pretty close to the truth.

"James?" Gary scratched his head. "Are you related to Bart?"

Callie shouldn't have added her last name during the introduction. "He's my father." She'd be more careful from here on out because she didn't want her dad hearing that she was in town before she could contact him herself. It was bad enough that Wendy knew she was in Whittler's Creek.

"Great guy," Gary said before they were interrupted by others coming into the building to join the group.

When Poppy arrived, her eyes widened at seeing Callie. "I didn't know you were participating in this. We could have driven together."

"Oh, well." Callie was surprised to see Poppy, too, and didn't know how else to respond. She wondered if Tyler had told her the real reason Callie was there. If he *had* confided in her, then Poppy was very good at pretending ignorance.

At least Poppy would be able to vouch for Callie being where she was supposed to be today. Otherwise, Tyler was relying on her honesty about fulfilling her service hours. Based on last night's comment to Callie about not wanting her around his girls, why would he take her on her word?

Callie was quiet as conversations continued around her. Poppy suddenly grabbed her arm and said, "I want to introduce the two of you." She guided Callie over to a handsome man, close to Poppy's age, with a healthy tan and thick salt-and-pepper hair. "This is Gino Borelli. He's moving in next weekend." Poppy and Gino made eye contact and Callie could have sworn there was a spark between them. "And this is Callie James," Poppy told Gino. "She moved in yesterday."

"Hello there, neighbor," Gino said as he and Callie shook hands.

"Are you new in town?" Callie asked before he could ask her anything.

He shrugged. "Not new. I lived here a long time ago. Now my business has brought me back and I can once again be in the company of this lovely lady." He gestured to Poppy. His words would have sounded silly if not for his faint Italian accent.

Poppy must have thought so, too, because she was blushing like an adolescent.

"Let's get going," someone finally said, and the gathering moved out of the building and onto the sidewalk. Back at the community center, they'd been given reflective vests to wear. There was nowhere to hide when you were wearing bright orange.

In all the discussion going on, Callie didn't hear where they were going to do this cleanup. So she just followed along with the group of about a dozen people.

They walked quite a ways before stopping. "This is our street," a woman announced. Callie couldn't remember her name, but did recall the woman seemed overly excited to be doing this task. "Let's divide into two groups and each take one side of the road. I have extra garbage bags when you need them." Along with the reflective vests, they'd been given two orange trash bags each. "When a bag is full, tie it carefully and leave it on the shoulder. A county trash truck will pick them up later."

That was a relief. At least they didn't have to haul other people's garbage back to where they'd started.

As the group divided into two, Callie found herself with Poppy and Gino, as well as three others. Callie donned her rubber gloves and noticed she wasn't the only one who'd brought them. Then they fanned out on their side of the street and began the arduous task of picking up garbage.

Callie was amazed at the stuff she found. She had a difficult time deciding what was worse— the used condoms that she'd covered with dead leaves before picking them up, or the used diapers that had been neatly balled up and tossed on the side of the road.

On second thought, that clear plastic container with a half-eaten sandwich covered with maggots was definitely the worst thing she'd had to deal with.

She could only imagine what Tyler had in store for her tomorrow since, after today, she would still have ninety-two of her one hundred service hours to complete.

WHEN SHE RETURNED to Poppy's, the first thing Callie did was strip down and shower until she felt clean again. Between the heat and the disgusting trash, she wasn't sure she'd ever be able to wash it all off.

Before leaving the community center, Callie had told Poppy that she wouldn't be around for dinner. She was sure Poppy wondered what was going on with her, but she only said there would be leftovers in the fridge if Callie changed her mind.

In truth, when Callie smelled dinner cooking after she'd showered, she realized she was starving. Maybe she could bring her dinner up to her room. That would satisfy her hunger and Tyler wouldn't be upset about her being around his daughters.

There was a knock on her door.

"Come in." She'd been reclining on the love seat by the window when Tyler opened her door and entered. She immediately sat up, her feet touching the floor.

"Hi." He stood right inside her doorway, his

hand on the doorknob. He wore his work uniform that somehow still looked fresh. It was black pants and a short-sleeved white shirt with epaulets, a gold badge on his breast pocket and an embroidered patch on one sleeve. His tan made him look even better in that short-sleeved, white dress shirt. Although not a look you'd find in *GQ*.

"Hi." She clenched and unclenched her fists, not wanting to reveal how she felt about him not wanting her around his girls. Although, maybe he'd changed his mind and that was why he was here.

"I wanted to let you know that, for the next two days, your service hours will be at the community center. Poppy said everyone enjoyed having you today and they are spending the next two days doing a deep clean on the building."

Great.

When she just looked at him, not saying a word, he continued. "Then on Friday, they open the center to serve dinner to those in need. So you'll be cooking or doing whatever they need you to do."

She still didn't speak.

"Any questions?"

She shook her head.

"Is there something wrong?"

Should she ask him the question burning in her gut? She spoke before thinking it through. "Why don't want me around your girls? What are you afraid of?"

He stepped farther into her room and turned away to shut the door for privacy. When he turned back to face her, his expression was serious.

"My girls have been through a lot before we came back to Whittler's Creek. I don't know the details of your arrest, but I know it had to do with malicious destruction of property."

"That's the charge, but I didn't do it. I just have no way to prove my innocence."

"That might be true," he said, "but I can't forget that you had quite a reputation for being a hothead when you were growing up here."

Callie straightened. "A hothead?" What was he talking about? Her hands clenched so tight that her short nails dug into her palms. As a young child, she'd vented her frustration, but she'd soon learned that behavior only made matters worse. "Who told you that?"

"It doesn't matter. Besides, I saw your temper for myself."

"Are you talking about the night before I left for college?" Was he kidding?

"Yes. The night I walked you home after that party and you yelled at your stepmother."

He was basing his opinion of her on that one night?

She spoke as calmly and deliberately as she was able. "First of all, that was eleven years ago. Second, I *finally* yelled back at my stepmother because I'd had enough over the years and I knew I was leaving the next morning."

"What about the chair you threw?"

She narrowed her eyes. "What chair?"

"I stood outside your house to make sure you were okay when I heard all the commotion. That's how I heard the argument between you and your stepmother. At one point, I heard a crash."

"Why would you think I threw a chair?"

"After the crash, I heard your stepmother yell that you would have to pay for the chair you broke."

"But you didn't see me break it, did you?" She reminded herself to breathe, in and out, in and out.

"No, but you can't deny what I heard."

"That's true. Those were my stepmother's exact words." Callie swallowed before admitting more to Tyler than she had to even her therapist. Like how her stepmother had blamed Callie for the broken chair because she'd claimed Callie had made her angry enough to throw it.

Luckily for Callie, she'd learned as a young child how to duck from flying objects when her stepmother became enraged.

CHAPTER FOUR

"FROM YOUR RESPONSE, there's obviously more to the story," Tyler said to Callie. "Why don't you tell me what actually took place?"

"You believe your version of events that night, so hearing mine won't change your mind." Callie spoke without emotion.

"I don't understand."

"That makes two of us." She rose from the love seat. "I'd really rather not talk about this. You can believe what you want. Just know that I'd never do anything to upset or hurt your daughters."

He nodded, deciding to drop the subject for now. Someday soon he'd love to circle back to it, wondering how she would reconcile what his sister, Isabelle, had told him about Callie's hot temper. Or maybe he needed to speak to his sister about it next time they talked. Had she exaggerated Callie's disposition? If so, why?

He checked his watch. "I need to make sure the girls get their dinner. Please don't skip coming to dinner because of what I said yesterday."

He left her room then, confused by their conversation. He still wasn't ready to have her be around his girls when he wasn't there, but their brief interaction had brought up more questions about her.

He went down the hallway to speak to his daughters, but they weren't in their room. He entered his own room and quickly changed from his work clothes into shorts and a T-shirt. Then he headed downstairs in search of his daughters.

"Hey, girls, wash up for dinner." He arrived in the kitchen to see both Alexis and Madison sitting patiently at the table.

"We already did, Daddy," Madison told him, raising her hands, palms outward, to show him.

"Yeah," Alexis added. "We've been helping Aunt Poppy with dinner and we always need to wash our hands before we do anything in the kitchen."

"Good rule." Tyler grinned. "So you two cooked dinner?"

The girls giggled. "No, Aunt Poppy cooked," Madison said. "We just set the table and got ice for the glasses."

"The water pitcher was too heavy for us to pour it." Alexis was very serious as she explained.

"I'm glad you're helping Aunt Poppy." He glanced at his aunt taking a tray of roasted asparagus from the oven. "Just don't get in her way."

"Oh, they're not," Poppy told him over her shoulder. "They're good helpers."

"Glad to hear it." He turned to the girls again. "Tonight is our appointment with Dr. Patty."

"Yay! I love going there!" Madison was bouncing in her seat. "She has fun toys."

"Okay, then don't fool around during dinner so we're not late for our appointment."

"Appointment?"

He spun around to see Callie had entered the kitchen.

"The girls and I have a weekly appointment on Tuesday evenings." Just like she didn't want to talk about the past, he wasn't ready to confide the reason his girls needed to see a therapist once a week.

"We like Dr. Patty," Alexis told Callie. "And if we don't want to talk about our mommy, then we don't have to."

Callie opened her mouth as if about to say something.

"Did you change your mind about joining us for dinner?" Aunt Poppy chose the exact right moment to change the subject.

"Yes. If that's okay," Callie told her while looking at Tyler.

He nodded and said to his daughters, "Let's add a place for Ms. Callie." The girls jumped out of their seats to get her silverware and a napkin, while he got a plate and a glass down from the cabinet. The girls then put ice in her glass and he poured the water from the pitcher.

"Thank you," Callie said. "I didn't mean for you all to make such a fuss." She seemed overwhelmed by the rush to make a place for her at the table.

"We're glad you're joining us," Aunt Poppy told her as she brought the dish of asparagus to the table to join the meatloaf and mashed potatoes.

"Everything smells and looks delicious," Callie said. "I really worked up an appetite today."

"Me, too," Aunt Poppy agreed as she took her place at the table. "I don't usually make such a heavy meal this time of year, with the heat and all."

"I'm glad you did," Tyler told her. "Your meatloaf is the best I've ever eaten."

As the conversation switched from what the girls did at day camp to the threat of thunderstorms overnight, Tyler checked the time. "We need to get going, girls. Take your plates to the sink so we can get into the car."

He'd been lucky to find Dr. Patty Schmidt and even luckier that she allowed them to have a seven o'clock time slot on a Tuesday evening so he didn't have to leave work to bring the girls.

In the nearly a year that they'd been seeing the therapist, he'd noticed a positive change in both his daughters. When they'd first returned to Whittler's Creek to take care of his dad when he got sick, they were very quiet and withdrawn. Nothing he said or did could bring them out of it. Now, thanks to working with Dr. Patty, they were blossoming into chatty little girls who seemed happy and confident.

He could only hope that what they'd been through while he'd been deployed to Afghanistan would someday be a very distant memory.

THINKING THE DAY spent picking up trash was the worst, Callie changed her mind at the end of the next day after cleaning the community center. She'd been put in charge of the kitchen and had spent the entire day cleaning off the grease and grime built up on surfaces she could barely reach—the small ledge over the commercial stove, the top of the double-wide refrigerator. If it had a surface, then it needed to be cleaned. At least she knew how to make it sparkle.

Maybe she should thank her stepmother for that. Callie was always assigned kitchen cleanup and was constantly told that she hadn't done it correctly, no matter how long she'd worked at it.

By the time Callie returned to her temporary home at Poppy's, she was tired and filthy. She stood under the hot shower in her bathroom for too long before finally drying off and putting on fresh clothes. She really wanted to slip into bed, but she'd gotten an email from her therapist that afternoon. He wanted to set up an appointment to video chat at seven o'clock that evening.

When she checked her bedside clock, she saw it was close to six-thirty already. She might have missed dinner because of her long shower.

She hurried downstairs, determined to get something in her complaining stomach and saw that everyone was still at the table.

"Sorry I'm late." She shoved her still-wet hair back from her face. She should have put it into a ponytail, but it would take longer to dry that way. "I really needed a shower."

"We're having chicken casserole," Alexis told her. "It has carrots and peas and potatoes in it."

"Sounds delicious," Callie said.

"It is." Madison put a bite of chicken on her fork and stuck it in her mouth to demonstrate.

Callie smiled and said to Poppy, "I have a seven o'clock call, so I'll apologize now for eating and running."

Poppy pointed to Callie's place at the table, already set. "You do what you need to. The girls knocked on your door, but when you didn't answer, we went ahead and started."

"That's good. I must have been in the shower when they knocked." She noticed Tyler was missing from the table. "Where's Tyler tonight?"

"He's got some police training he does Wednesday nights, even though this town doesn't see much criminal activity. Tyler likes his officers to be ready, so he instituted regular training sessions."

Callie nodded and took her seat. She scooped out some of the casserole onto her plate and took a slice of the warm bread Alexis passed to her.

Callie took her first bite and whatever spices Poppy had added to the food danced on her palate. "You were right, girls, this is delicious."

Both girls spoke at once and kept up the conversation while Callie gulped down her dinner. She looked at the bright blue clock on the wall near the table and wiped her mouth. She had about three minutes before her therapist called. "Sorry." She jumped up from her seat and took her plate to the sink to rinse it and put it in the dishwasher. "I need to run."

"That's okay," Poppy said. "We understand. Go do what you need to."

The last thing she wanted to do was spend an hour with her anger management therapist, but she had no choice.

Her therapist called right on the dot.

"Hello, Dr. Hammond," she said when his face appeared on her laptop screen.

"How's it going, Callie?"

She filled him in on what she'd done since arriving in town.

"Have you seen your family yet?"

This was where she could have told him about chickening out in front of her father's house, but she didn't. Instead she decided to give him a tidbit that would hopefully satisfy him. "I ran into my stepsister on Monday."

"Your stepsister?"

He looked down and Callie heard the rustling of papers.

"You've never mentioned a stepsister."

"You never asked."

Pause. "I'm asking now." His tone was stern and slightly irritated.

Callie swallowed. "I have a stepsister and I ran into her on Monday."

"How old is this stepsister and what's her name?"

"Wendy is a year younger than me, so she's twenty-eight now."

"And the two of you lived in the same house from the time your dad remarried?"

"Yes."

The doctor was silent for an overly long time. "Why haven't you mentioned her before?"

Callie shrugged. "I didn't want to talk about her."

"Do the two of you get along?"

"No." Callie's answer was immediate and came out harsher than she'd intended.

"Tell me about it."

She didn't want to talk about Wendy. "I don't know what you want me to tell you." That was a lie. She knew exactly what he wanted her to say.

"Why didn't you two get along?"

"I don't know. She hated me the minute she walked in the front door of my house."

Dr. Hammond wrote something down. "Did she bully you?"

Callie hesitated. "Yes. You could call what she did bullying." With all the cyber bullying going on these days, Callie could only imagine how much worse Wendy's treatment of her might have been if they'd had social media growing up. Texts and emails were bad enough in those days.

"What kind of things did she do?"

"Can't we talk about something else?" Callie really didn't want to relive her childhood with him.

"I think we're finally making progress," he said. "Tell me what Wendy did to you."

Callie inhaled slowly. Her hands were at her sides, off camera, while she sat on her bedroom love seat for their session. He couldn't see her hands fist and relax.

"What didn't she do? She called me names, she played mean tricks on me, she spread lies about me. She even spit on me." She'd done even worse things, but Callie didn't want to delve into them.

"That must have been very upsetting," the doctor said in his calm voice.

"No kidding." She couldn't help her sarcastic tone.

"Did you do anything to retaliate?" he asked.

"I didn't dare. If I'd tried, she would have worked twice as hard to hurt me back."

"What about telling your father and stepmother? Didn't they step in to discipline her?"

That was a joke. "No, they didn't do anything to stop her."

Dr. Hammond's eyebrows shot up. "Really? You told them what was going on and they didn't handle it?"

Callie shook her head. She swallowed the lump in her throat before speaking. "I told my stepmother about what Wendy did once and she told me to stop being a baby and if I told my father I'd be punished." Her stepmother's form of punishment. Something else Callie didn't want to recall.

"So your father didn't know about your stepsister's treatment of you?"

"I went to him once, and he said he'd take care of it, but Wendy continued to harass me." Her dad *had* talked to Wendy but she'd gone immediately to her mother, who'd then punished Callie for telling her dad. Her stomach tightened. That was the first and last time Callie had gone to her father for help.

"You didn't go back again to tell him it hadn't stopped?"

"Isn't our time almost up?" she asked instead.

His gaze went to where he kept a clock across from his desk. "We have five minutes left."

She needed to change the subject away from her family.

"You didn't answer my question," he persisted.

"What did you ask?" She knew very well what he'd asked, but her mind had gone blank when it came to changing the subject.

"Why didn't you tell your father that your stepsister was still bothering you?"

Bothering her? That was definitely whitewashing the situation, but she didn't correct Dr. Hammond. At least not today with five minutes—or less—left in their session.

She sucked in a breath. "Because I got punished for telling on Wendy." Her hands fisted at her sides.

Dr. Hammond made a notation and looked up as he asked, "What kind of punishment?"

Before she readied herself to answer, his phone rang. He held up one finger. "I'm sorry. I usually have my phone turned off. This must be an emergency." He picked up his cell phone to look at it. "Yes, I'll have to call this person back right away." He pressed something on the phone and the ringing ended. "Let's stop here for now and we'll pick it up next week at the same time. Does that work for you?"

She nodded, hoping her words came out clear as she said, "Yes, that's fine."

By the time she closed her laptop, she felt wrung out emotionally and didn't know if she could continue to do this week after week.

And all she'd told Dr. Hammond so far was that she'd seen her stepsister, who'd bullied Callie their entire childhood. She'd barely scratched the surface.

The sun had long set and a partial moon was barely visible in the cloudy sky when Tyler parked on the street in front of Aunt Poppy's. Training had gone well that evening and he was pleased to see the improvement in his officers since he'd taken over as Chief of Police.

He walked up to the porch, lit only by matching globes on either side of the front door. His foot was on the bottom step when he realized someone was in the shadows, seated on the far side of the porch glider.

"Callie?"

"Hi." Her voice was so soft he could barely hear her.

"Is everything all right?"

She didn't say anything at first. "I'm fine." Her legs were tucked under her body and her arms were crossed over her chest.

He wanted to disagree, considering her body language and quiet tone of voice, but he didn't. "I'm going to get myself a beer. Would you like one?" He didn't know why he was pursuing a conversation with her. He should just leave her alone.

He couldn't see her reaction, except for a slight turn of her head in his direction.

"Sure," she finally answered, not moving from her curled-up position.

"Let me check on the girls and I'll be back with a couple of cold ones in a few."

His eyes had adjusted to the dimness enough to see her nod, so he went into the house.

The girls were already in bed and asleep, their night-light allowing him to make his way between their twin beds. He gently kissed them good-night on their foreheads and covered up Alexis, who tended to kick and squirm all night. He quietly exited their bedroom, closing their door as he left.

In his own room, he changed from his uniform into shorts and a T-shirt. Then he slipped his bare feet into a pair of canvas shoes to go down to the basement fridge where he kept the beer. He jogged back up the stairs with two beers and went out the front door to the porch. "I should have asked if you wanted a glass." He held out a bottle to Callie. He'd already popped the top with the opener he kept on top of the basement fridge. "I can get one for you."

"This is fine." She uncurled her legs and reached for the bottle. "Thank you." Her fingers brushed his momentarily. She took a long swallow and he wondered why he'd even noticed when their hands touched.

Instead of sitting next to her on the glider, he pulled a rocker closer and sat before taking a long swallow of ice-cold beer. "Mmm, that's exactly what I needed."

When Callie remained silent, he grasped for something to say in the uncomfortable silence. "Bad day?"

She set her beer on the small, white-wicker end table next to the glider and folded her hands on her lap. "Let's just say that days in Whittler's Creek are nothing like what I'm used to."

"How's the cleaning going at the community center?"

"We made a huge dent today, but there's still a lot to do tomorrow."

"Must be exhausting work. You have an office job, right?"

"I do." She picked up her beer and took a sip. "It's not so much the physical toll. I work out several mornings a week." She set the beer back on the table. "It's the filth. I swear this must be the first time in a dozen years that some of that stuff has been touched with a cleaning rag."

"You're probably right. Do you think you'll be done after tomorrow?"

She hesitated, as if considering his question. "If we get the same amount of people to help out as we did today, I think we have a good chance of finishing."

"Great." But he'd said it jokingly. "That means I'll have to find something new for you to do after Friday's soup kitchen."

"I'd prefer more work like at the soup kitchen, but I'm sure you'll come up with something disgusting like picking up trash and cleaning out grease traps." She sounded resigned to the fact.

He chuckled. "I'll see what I can do."

She tucked her bare feet under her. "How was training? I think that's what Poppy said you were doing tonight."

He nodded. "It went well. I inherited my three officers and decided they could use regular training. So we work on something different every week. Tonight we did target practice at the gun range over in Lewisburg."

"Seems more like playing than working." She sounded as if she could use something like that.

"That's how I've tried to structure the training so everyone wants to participate. How was your evening?" he asked. "I hope my girls haven't been too annoying."

"They've been fine. I didn't really see them much after dinner."

"Were they playing outside or did Aunt Poppy take them out somewhere?"

"I don't know. I was in my room." She paused. "I now have a standing appointment with my therapist on Wednesday evenings."

He was surprised at her admission, although he already knew from her therapist that she had court-ordered sessions. He didn't know why and didn't feel he should ask. Instead he said, "My daughters have been seeing their therapist for over a year now and they've gotten a lot out of it. I hope you get a similar result."

Callie didn't say anything while she took a long drink of her beer and then set it back down. "I'm not sure what kind of results I'll get since seeing the psychologist wasn't my idea."

"You're not happy about having to talk to him?"

Her head shot in his direction. "How did you know my therapist was a man and not a woman?"

His beer was halfway to his mouth when his arm froze. "Because Dr. Hammond is the one who contacted me about your community service hours."

"Oh. Sorry. I forgot that he would have been the one to speak to you."

He took a long swallow of beer. "He seems like a nice guy. Although I only spoke to him that one time."

"He's okay I guess. He just wants me to talk about stuff that I'd rather not relive."

He got the distinct feeling there was a lot more to Callie's past than he knew. "I can't say enough good things about the girls' therapist. Believe it or not, when we first came back to Whittler's Creek, Madison barely spoke." His youngest daughter was making up for it now with her constant chatter.

"I'm glad it worked out for them, but I was doing just fine without bringing up the past."

"And that had nothing to do with why you're doing community service and forced to talk to a psychologist?" The words were out of his mouth before he thought them through. "Sorry. I don't mean to be argumentative."

She took a long swallow of her beer, her head back and her neck elongated. "You're right." She uncurled her legs and stood. "If I hadn't confided in a certain jackass, who then used my past against me, then I wouldn't have been forced to do any of this." She walked by him to the front door.

He reached out to grab her arm to stop her. The look she gave him made him release her immediately.

She continued to the front door, paused with

one hand on the screen door and stared at him. "Thanks for the beer." She lifted the beer bottle in a toast. "Good night."

With that, she disappeared into the house, leaving him to go over their conversation and where he'd gone wrong. Not a difficult thing to figure out. Note to self: avoid talking about what she did that caused her to come back to Whittler's Creek against her will.

Suddenly the front screen door came open and Callie appeared out of breath. "Quick. Your daughter needs you. She's screaming her head off. Sounds like she's having a nightmare."

Tyler jumped up and took off up the stairs to the girls' bedroom. Just when he was comfortable enough to brag about how well adjusted the girls were, one of them was having a nightmare.

He recognized Madison's screams before he opened the bedroom door. He rushed to her bed and gathered her in his arms until she quieted. "Hush," he whispered into her hair. "It's okay. Daddy's here. There's nothing to be afraid of. You're okay now."

Madison's heart pounded rapidly against his chest and her breathing was quick and shallow, even after she finally stopped screaming.

When she seemed calm again, he laid her back on her pillow. Her eyes never opened and she probably wouldn't remember the episode when she woke in the morning. Thankfully, she rarely did.

If only she could forget the reason for those nightmares in the first place.

CALLIE HAD FOLLOWED Tyler up the stairs, ducking into her own room while he headed straight to his distraught daughter down the hall.

To make sure everything was okay, Callie stood right inside her doorway to listen. Her entire body was shaking. Hearing one of the little girls crying out in fear had affected her more than she ever would have expected.

Did the girls often have nightmares? What had they been through? Tyler hadn't shared any details. But obviously something traumatic had occurred if they'd been seeing a therapist regularly.

Tyler's soothing whispers could be heard as the child quieted to a whimper and then there was silence. Callie found herself comforted by his tone, as well. Her breathing slowed as she began to feel normal again.

After a few more minutes she heard him leave his daughters' room. She quickly closed her bedroom door as quietly as possible. She didn't want him to know she'd been listening.

She got ready for bed, hoping to have a dreamless sleep. Like every night of her life, she left the light in the bathroom on so she wouldn't be in complete darkness while she slept.

CHAPTER FIVE

By LUNCHTIME ON Friday Callie was relieved to be cooking food to serve for dinner that night at the community center's monthly soup kitchen.

Though she'd never be known for her cooking, after two days of heavy cleaning she was glad to be doing something that had nothing to do with dirt and grime.

Today she was following Poppy's directions in the kitchen. She'd peeled more potatoes than she'd ever seen in her life. Thankfully the community center kitchen was equipped with a food processor, so she used it to slice the potatoes instead of having to cut them all by hand. She'd never make it through the first round in one of those TV food challenges because her knife skills were far from the best.

When the potatoes were sliced and put into large aluminum pans, she covered them with cold water. Poppy had told her earlier that they would be making au gratin potatoes, a dish Callie had eaten many times but never cooked.

Alone in the community center kitchen, she

dried her hands and went looking for Poppy to get her next instructions. She stepped into the large dining room that was set up for dinner and found most of the volunteers seated at a table near the door. They were taking a lunch break. Poppy looked up from her conversation with Gino and waved Callie over.

"Get your lunch and join us," Poppy suggested.

"We've got plenty of room here," Gino added as he rose. He gently nudged the person next to him to make room at the table and then slid a chair into position for Callie.

"Thank you." Her words were barely a whisper. She was once again overwhelmed by how welcoming these people had been to her. They'd all been so friendly, asking about her as if they were really interested. She wished she'd known them when she'd lived here. Maybe then she'd have felt like she had someone safe to confide in about her home life.

"Callie James? Is that you?" A woman about Callie's age with a bright pink stripe in her jet-black hair had stopped eating.

"Yes, that's me." Another second went by before Callie realized who the woman was. "Riva?"

Callie's childhood friend smiled wide. "That's *me*!" She got up and came around the table to Callie's seat. Callie stood and the two women hugged. "How are you, girl? I haven't seen or heard from you since high school graduation. You're not even on Facebook or Twitter or nothin', 'cuz I've searched for you." Riva spoke as if Callie had committed a mortal sin.

"I'm doing well," Callie told her, not adding that she wasn't on social media because she didn't want her family contacting her. She looked at the table and realized everyone was watching them. She and Riva had been pretty good friends in high school but they were practically strangers now. "How are you?"

"I'm okay." Riva gestured to where she'd been sitting with her lunch. "I better finish eating. But let's get together later and catch up." She obviously didn't want to spill her guts in front of an audience, either.

"Sounds good. Maybe after we serve dinner?"

"Works for me," Riva said as she stepped away.

Callie sat back down and opened her salad. She needed to find something else to eat besides the prepackaged food from the local grocery store. She'd tried each of their salads and was getting sick of them already. At her office, she kept a supply of frozen, healthy microwavable meals, but here in Whittler's Creek she didn't always have a microwave available.

The afternoon sped by and, before she knew it, some extra volunteers had arrived to help serve.

Callie assumed they were coming there after their day jobs ended.

"Are there always this many volunteers?" Callie asked Poppy shortly before they began serving.

"We usually get a pretty good turnout. Since the recession several years ago, everyone in town seems ready to pitch in to help those who haven't yet recovered."

From the amount of food they'd prepared, Callie guessed there would be many diners tonight. Personally, she hadn't been as affected by the recession as others. Being here in Whittler's Creek put it all into perspective, though.

"Put those potatoes on that burner over there." Poppy pointed to a place on the long serving table set up with the food. "You did a good job on them."

Callie warmed with pleasure at the compliment, no matter how slight. It might actually be the first when it came to her cooking. "Thank you." She was pretty proud of her accomplishment. Au gratin potatoes might not sound like much to most people, but it was huge for Callie who'd never been taught to cook.

From across the room, Callie saw Tyler walk in. He was wearing his uniform. Her first thought was that he was here on police business until he began greeting people and shaking hands. He finally made it over to the food table and they made eye contact.

"How's it going?" he asked.

"Pretty well." She gestured to the table overflowing with food in metal catering dishes over flaming kerosene canisters. "Looks like we're expecting a lot of people tonight."

Tyler nodded. "I seem to remember we get anywhere from a hundred and fifty to two hundred."

Callie's eyes widened. "Really? I'm surprised there are so many in need of a hot meal in this area."

"They come from all over. We don't ask for any proof of need. Some people just show up because of that."

"So why are you here? To make sure I'm working?" She tried to make it sound like she was kidding, but she knew there was an edge to her voice.

"No, I figure Aunt Poppy will tell me if you've gone AWOL. She's here frequently to help out." He smiled and it softened his words and made her heart flutter erratically. "I usually try to come by and lend a hand when I can. It's not easy with the girls."

"Where are they? Did someone else pick them up from the bus?" Callie realized Poppy had been at the community center all day.

Tyler nodded. "They're having dinner at a friend's house tonight. The friend's mother brought the three girls home from the bus. I just talked to her on my way here. They were playing in the sprinkler and planning to watch a princess movie after dinner."

She nodded. "That's good. I'm glad they've made friends in town."

"Five minutes, everyone!" Poppy made the announcement and then looked over the table to make sure everything was in order. She'd given out assignments and Callie was to serve her potatoes.

"I better wash up." Tyler disappeared into the restroom and Callie went into the kitchen to put on clean gloves. By the time she came out, Tyler was standing at the station next to hers, ready to serve green beans, with an apron covering his uniform and latex gloves that matched hers.

She wondered if Poppy had purposely put them beside each other and then decided probably not.

Poppy had more sense than to play matchmaker where Callie and Tyler were concerned. Or so she hoped.

Tyler was pretty sure Aunt Poppy had put him next to Callie on purpose. Since he'd been back in town, she'd made no secret of the fact that she thought his daughters needed a mother and he needed a wife.

He disagreed, at least with the wife part. He'd

done that once and it had turned out poorly to say the least. Disastrous was a closer description.

He glanced at Callie next to him. She was certainly attractive. With her hair in some kind of knot on the back of her head and a minimum of makeup, she still touched something inside him that had been dormant for years. Even the apron she had on over her jeans and fitted, light blue T-shirt didn't detract from her beauty. Neither did the cheap sneakers and latex gloves she wore.

She had a way of making him feel the same way he had when they were teenagers. He'd glimpse her in the school hallway and his hormones would go into overdrive, just like now.

"Hey, Chief, how's it going?" Tyler's thoughts were interrupted by the man on the other side of him serving ham.

He turned in his direction. "Not too bad, Jim. How's the furniture business going?" Jim was the oldest son of the Pratt family, probably in his late forties, who'd taken over his dad's furniture business and had expanded it into Tyler's dad's old hardware space on Main Street.

The two men exchanged pleasantries for a minute or two before diners began entering the building. Business was steady as people moved down the line for nearly an hour before it slowed.

"Looks like stragglers now that the initial rush is over," Jim commented to Tyler.

Tyler nodded and scooped up green beans to serve to the next person in line. "Green beans?" The words had barely come out of his mouth when he realized Wendy Carter, Callie's stepsister, was holding a plate of food and waiting for him to put beans on it. "Oh, sorry." While he emptied the spoonful of beans onto her plate, he said, "Is that you, Wendy?"

She nodded.

He hadn't seen her since he'd been back in town. She'd certainly changed since high school, and not for the better. Her hair was clumpy, as if it hadn't been washed or even brushed in days. She was slightly hunched and didn't meet his gaze, as if embarrassed to be seen getting a free meal.

He didn't know what else to say and she remained mute until she reached Callie and her potatoes. Tyler watched the exchange between the two women. At first Callie didn't notice Wendy and Wendy hadn't looked up to see that it was Callie serving her.

"Wendy?" Callie mimicked his surprise at seeing Wendy.

Wendy raised her head and as soon as she saw Callie, the expression on her face turned to anger and something else. Hatred was the only word he could come up with.

"What the hell are you doing here?" Wendy's vitriolic question was barely loud enough for him to hear. She didn't let Callie speak before going on in an angry whisper. "You always thought you were so much better than us. I guess there's no denying that now."

"Wendy—" He shut his mouth when Callie put a hand on his upper arm. She met his gaze with eyes pleading for him to let her handle it. He barely nodded and she turned to face Wendy.

"Would you like potatoes?" Callie held a spoonful of potatoes out to Wendy as if nothing had happened. Wendy accepted the potatoes and moved down the line.

When she was out of hearing range, Tyler asked Callie, "Why is she so angry at you?"

Callie shrugged. "Who knows? She's been angry at me since she and her mother moved in when I was three and she was two."

"Really?" He had a hard time computing that information. Wendy had always been nice to him, especially when they were teenagers. In fact, he'd always thought Wendy might have had a crush on him, but he hadn't been interested. At the time, Callie was the only one who'd interested him.

And now he was finding that interest in her renewed.

THE KITCHEN AND dining areas were nearly cleaned up a few hours later when Riva came up behind Callie. "Some of us are going to Abbott's when we're done here. You want to join us? You're welcome, too, Tyler." He'd been drying the large catering dishes that Callie had washed.

"I don't know—" Callie was still pretty shaken up after her run-in with Wendy and didn't feel like going to a pub.

"Come on, we haven't seen each other in years," Riva reminded her. "Just come for one drink so I can hear what you've been up to. It's Friday night, for heaven's sake."

"We'll be there," Tyler answered for her.

"Great. See you there!"

As soon as Riva stepped away, Callie turned on Tyler and spoke more calmly than she felt. "What was all that about? Saying I'd be there? You have no right—"

He held up a hand, palm out. "Hold on. You obviously need to unwind. All work and no play will put you in the hospital with a nervous breakdown."

She tilted her head and scowled at him. "Not likely."

"Then what if I say that for every hour you spend having fun, I'll count it toward your community service?"

Her eyes widened. "You can do that?"

"I can do whatever I want. I was given authority over you and your service hours. I just need to sign off to say you completed them."

Callie quickly looked around to see if there was anything else to be washed. She pulled the plug to drain the water from the sink, rinsed and dried her hands, and untied her apron. "Then, let's go."

The clock in the nearly empty dining room said almost nine, which meant she'd worked a twelve-hour day. No wonder she was tired.

But she was also anxious to catch up with Riva, so she headed out the door ahead of Tyler.

"We can drop your car off at the house and take my truck if you want. No need for two cars."

Abbott's was a few miles from Poppy's and his suggestion made sense. So why was she hesitating? "Sure. Thanks." Probably because she'd noticed that being close to him brought back all the old feelings she'd had for him when they were teenagers. The feelings she'd been forced to keep hidden or face the wrath of her stepsister who'd thought Tyler belonged to her. But Wendy no longer had any power over Callie and any feelings she might have for Tyler were grown-up feelings that had grown-up consequences.

She had nothing to worry about as long as she kept her thoughts to herself. Which shouldn't be too difficult since she was pretty sure he considered her a nuisance that he was saddled with for the next few weeks.

When they reached the house, they each went to their own bedroom. Callie would have liked a shower, but didn't want him to wait for her. She merely washed her face and put on fresh makeup. At least she hadn't been doing manual labor today, just cooking and cleaning up afterward. She released her hair from the bun she'd worn all day and fluffed it enough to make her reasonably happy with it. She donned fresh skinny jeans with a white tank top and canvas wedge sandals before heading to the front door.

Tyler was waiting for her, looking extremely appealing in his dark jeans and deep navy T-shirt that hugged his torso as well as his biceps.

"You look great," he said to her before she could say it to him.

"Thanks. You, too." His hair was damp, as if he'd taken a shower. The scent of his manly soap was intoxicating as she got closer to him. Riding in his truck was going to be pure torture. "I hope you haven't been waiting long."

He held the screen door open for her. "Absolutely not." He looked at a pretend watch on his wrist and then winked at her. "At least not more than an hour or two."

Her mouth opened and her eyes narrowed. "As long as I didn't make you wait too long."

He chuckled at her comeback and then put a hand to her lower back to usher her out the front door. "You know, you're not so bad when you relax." He was so close behind her that his warm, fresh breath tickled her neck.

She ignored the goose bumps he raised. He had a good sense of humor and that went a long way with her. Until just now, she'd only witnessed it with his daughters and others. She was beginning to think being around him tonight wouldn't be so bad. Especially when he opened her truck door and assisted her in.

Sitting that close to him on the drive to the bar made her acutely aware of him. The combination of his natural scent and the soap he'd used were enough to make the short trip a cruel form of torture.

"There you are!" From the table Riva and a few others had taken over at Abbott's Pub, her old friend saw them as soon as they entered. She waved as she came to greet them at the door. "We've got a couple of pitchers going," she told them over her shoulder as she led them to the table. "One's a wheat and the other's an IPA. Way too hoppy for me." She said the last almost under her breath.

When they reached the table, Callie recognized a few people she hadn't seen since high school. Riva introduced everyone, although it was difficult to hear because the bar was so noisy. While everyone shifted seats to make room for Tyler and Callie, Tyler poured them each a glass of beer.

"Wheat?" he asked close to her ear, holding the glass out to her.

She took the cold glass, noting he'd poured it perfectly without too much foam. "Thanks." She took a sip, wondering how he knew her preference of beer. "How did you know I wanted this one?"

His lips curved slightly upward. "I poured one of each. If you wanted the IPA, then I would have been happy with the wheat beer."

"Oh." She had nothing else to say. He could be quite the gentleman when he wanted to be.

She took a minute to finally look around. Like the drugstore, Abbott's had also remained the same. The dark brown Colonial-style tables and chairs were marred with scratches, the paneled walls had numerous illuminated beer logos covering them, and the long, aged bar was lined with patrons quenching their thirst. Since it was Friday night, the small corner stage had a three-piece band playing classic rock.

Callie had left town at eighteen, too young to be served a drink here, but she and her friends had come many times for the food. They made the best onion rings, perfect with a burger after a high school football or basketball game.

Before she knew it, Riva pulled her close to speak to her privately. "So what's up with you two?" she said in a stage whisper so as to be heard over the live music and conversations going on around them. "I saw you walk in together. Did you finally get the guy you lusted after back in high school?"

"Shh!" Callie looked over her shoulder to see if Tyler had overheard. "No, we're not together. We just drove in his truck because we're both living in the same house."

"The same house!" Riva's voice was definitely louder than a whisper that time.

Callie reached out to squeeze Riva's forearm. "Be quiet!" She felt like she was back in high school again. "We're both renting rooms from his aunt."

"You're not staying with your family?"

Callie shook her head. Riva knew some, but not all, of the details about her former home life and now was not the time to fill her in. Riva only knew how mean Wendy was to her when she'd seen it firsthand at school or out in public.

"I prefer having my own place," Callie told her. "And this way I'm not inconveniencing anyone." She needed to move the subject away from such a depressing topic. "Tell me what you've been doing. I didn't realize you were living here in Whittler's Creek."

Riva nodded. "I moved back about a year ago. Chuck and I divorced."

"I'm sorry to hear that."

"My mother broke her ankle and I came back

to help her. Once she recovered enough, I realized I had nothing to go back to in upstate New York where I kept running into Chuck and his girlfriend of the month."

Callie didn't know what to say. Her life before coming back to Whittler's Creek had been comparatively good, with little chance of running into her ex. As long as she stayed out of the courthouse.

She took a long drink of her beer and realized her glass was nearly empty. She needed to slow down, even if she wasn't the one driving. At least she'd gotten dinner when they ate leftovers at the community center after everyone in need had eaten their fill.

As if reading her mind, Tyler came up behind her with a pitcher. He poured the rest of its contents into her glass, making it come up to halfway. "Thank you," she said. "You're better than a server."

He grinned then said to Riva, "I'll get us another pitcher and be right back with it."

Riva held up her glass that was three-quarters full. "I'm good for now."

He gave her a thumbs-up and left them alone again as he headed to the bar.

Riva leaned in. "He's *so* hot!" She sounded breathless. "If you're not interested, then at least let me take a shot."

Callie was caught off balance. Luckily, she didn't need to reply because Riva was pulled away by someone else in the group.

"Need more?" Tyler appeared with a full pitcher, interrupting her thoughts about him and Riva.

She shook her head, covering her glass with her hand. She wondered why she had even hesitated about giving Riva the go-ahead when it came to Tyler. "I'm okay. I drank the first glass pretty quickly."

He shrugged. "I'm driving." He showed her the glass of soda in his other hand.

"I know. I'm just a lightweight." And she didn't like to be out of control. She reached for her purse. "I need to give you some money. How much was the pitcher you bought?"

"Seven bucks, but don't worry about it."

She'd forgotten how much less expensive things were in this part of the state. "I can pay my own way."

He stared her down. "I'm sure you can." His look dared her to say more. "If you insist on making everything fifty-fifty, then you can buy more beer for Poppy's. The fridge is in the basement." He named a local brewery that he liked. "But feel free to buy whatever you'll drink, too."

"That seems like a fair deal." She sipped her beer because she suddenly felt tongue-tied. He had a way of looking at her. As if he could see right through her skin to her core. As if he recognized her inability to talk about her past and her close-to-insane need to be in control.

And now she was pretty sure he could see how attracted to him she was.

CHAPTER SIX

"DINNER WAS DELICIOUS," Gino told Poppy when they sat in her living room long after Alexis and Madison were settled into bed. "Your lasagna was even better than I remembered."

"Thank you." She took the glass of wine he'd poured her and sat on the opposite end of the couch from him. Her face heated at the compliment. She knew she was a decent cook, but somehow hearing it from Gino made her feel both proud and a little embarrassed.

Unlike Tyler and Callie who'd stayed behind and eaten leftovers at the community center, Poppy had planned ahead and made lasagna. She and Gino had been eating a late dinner when Tyler and Callie had come home to change before going out.

"Those girls are very well behaved," he said, setting his wineglass on a coaster on the coffee table. "I can't imagine how difficult it's been on them and Tyler. Being a single parent isn't easy. My daughter did that for a while when her husband was deployed, and with three kids under five, it took a lot out of her."

Poppy nodded. "Tyler's a good father. Everything he's done has been for them."

"So tell me, what made you decide to run a boardinghouse after Jeffrey died?"

Gino and her husband had been good friends. When Jeffrey died five years ago, Gino had been nearly as grief-stricken as Poppy.

She shrugged. "I guess I needed people around me. I was in my midfifties at the time and I thought if the house was full again, like when the children were growing up, then I'd survive on my own." Her breathing accelerated and her hands shook. She placed her wineglass next to Gino's on the coffee table. "You never told me why you're back in town."

Gino picked up his glass, took a long swallow, and set it down again as if delaying his answer. "It's a business deal I've got going on. If it works out, then I'll settle down here for good."

"That would be nice," Poppy told him. "We haven't seen you much over the years."

He looked directly into her eyes. "You have to know that it killed me coming back and seeing you and Jeffrey so happy."

A huge lump formed in Poppy's throat. She'd dated Gino before Jeffrey. They'd even talked about marriage and their future together. "You made choices," she reminded him. "You chose to leave me behind."

"And I'll never forgive myself for that." He'd moved to Canada for a business opportunity instead of staying with her. Poppy couldn't leave her mother at the time because she'd had terminal cancer.

"You should. It's all in the past. You and Maura were happily married for a long time. And you have three wonderful children." She didn't bring up that Maura had taken her own life a year before Jeffrey died. She'd battled depression since the birth of their first child.

"I'd like another chance, Poppy." His statement caught her by surprise. "Tell me it's not too late for us."

"I don't know—"

He quickly rose from his seat and sat next to her on the couch. He took her face in both hands and stared into her eyes. Then he placed his lips on hers.

For the first time in decades, she felt truly wanted.

TYLER WAS GLAD he'd agreed to go to Abbott's. He'd spent very little time with anyone outside of work besides Poppy and his daughters since he'd returned to Whittler's Creek. Tonight he was enjoying catching up with old friends and getting to know the others at the table a little better.

A few minutes ago Riva had pulled Callie away from him. The group's conversations had divided into women at one end of the long table and men at the opposite end. He couldn't help himself when he was tempted to watch Callie. Every once in a while she would look his way and catch him. He'd give her a smile or a wink or a little wave. Her embarrassed expression at getting caught looking at him made her all the more sexy.

After a heated discussion about the looming baseball trade deadline, Tyler realized the women were getting up from their seats. He caught Callie's eye and they nodded to each other to indicate they were both ready to take off.

"It was great seeing you guys," Tyler told the group.

Pete, an old high school buddy, said, "You should join us more often. In fact, we're all meeting at the park on Sunday for a cookout. It'd be great if you came, too. We're each bringing our own food and drinks." He gestured in Callie's direction. "Feel free to bring someone with you." He waggled his eyebrows. "She's always welcome."

Tyler decided to ignore Pete's obvious interest in Callie and asked, "Will there be kids there?"

"Sure. Several of all ages." Pete pointed around the table, listing the adults who had kids. "That's right. You have a couple of kids, too, don't you?"

Pete not only had no children, but no wife or girl-friend, either.

Tyler nodded. "Two daughters, six and four."

"Bring 'em along. The kids all have a great time together. We like to organize games with them."

Tyler said his final good-night to everyone and he and Callie left together. He waited until they were in his truck to broach the subject of Sunday's get-together.

"A cookout?" Callie repeated.

"Yes. You know. Hamburgers, hot dogs, pasta salad a dozen ways, watermelon, as well as ants and flies."

The last made her chuckle, which was his intent. He was finding that she loosened up greatly if he kept her off guard with humor.

"Except for the bugs, it all sounds great," she said. "But what about my community service hours?"

"What about them?"

"Don't you have something for me to do on Sunday? I want to get through them quickly so I can return to my life."

Her statement jolted him back to reality. Of course she'd be anxious to leave. "I figured you'd need the weekend to recover. There's really no-where to assign you when people are mostly off from work and businesses are either on reduced hours or closed."

"Oh."

They were almost back to Poppy's and he didn't want to leave things awkward between them. "Remember, I told you I'd give you credit for the time you spend having fun and relaxing."

"I thought you only said that to get me to come out tonight."

"That was my original plan, but I'm willing to extend it to Sunday's picnic."

She paused for longer than he liked. "In that case, I accept." They spent the next few minutes talking about what food they could make that they both liked and that Alexis and Madison wouldn't balk at.

Tyler parked his truck in front of Aunt Poppy's and turned off the engine. Callie immediately unbuckled her seat belt and had her hand on the door handle. "Wait." He reached across the split bench seat and placed a hand on her upper arm.

She turned her head in his direction. "What is it?"

"I wanted to thank you for tonight." He dropped his hand from her arm.

"I didn't do anything."

"Yes, you did." He swallowed. "I've been so wrapped up in family and work that I haven't taken the time to go out and enjoy myself with other adults. So thank you for going along. I'm not sure I would have gone alone."

"Really? You seemed anxious to go when Riva asked us."

"That was for your sake. You needed a break." He shrugged. "Turns out, so did I."

The clouds uncovered the moon and her face was illuminated. He leaned closer and touched his mouth to hers. He'd been wanting to do that all night. As soon as their mouths met, he knew it was a mistake. This wasn't the one chaste kiss they'd shared in high school. This was the real thing. The sparks that flew would grow to a full-blown inferno between them, if allowed to.

He was sure she was about to end the kiss until she placed her palm on the side of his head, covering his ear. Her thumb caressed his cheek. He tilted his head and deepened the kiss. Her mouth was hot and tantalizing, and she was kissing him back with fervor.

Wanting to pull her closer to him, he reached for her right thigh but his seat belt stopped him. He reached between them to release it while not breaking contact with Callie, but she pulled away. "What are you doing?" she asked, peering at the seat.

He undid the seat belt with a click and let it rewind out of his way. "I was trying to unbuckle so I could get closer to you. I guess I'm out of practice making out in a vehicle." He laughed at himself and she smiled.

"Maybe that's a sign," she suggested.

Not what he wanted to hear. "A sign?"

"More like a reminder. That this is just temporary. As soon as I finish what I came here to do, I'll be leaving Whittler's Creek."

"You mean your service hours?"

She didn't answer right away. "My service hours are just part of the reason I had to come here."

He waited for her to continue. He remembered their conversation about her talking to her family. Her paperwork had also said she had issues to deal with concerning them.

"I still need to visit my family."

"You haven't seen them since you've been back?"

"No."

"Have you spoken to them? On the phone? By email?"

She shook her head, only visible because of the moonlight.

"Besides your sister, do they even know you're in town?"

"*Stepsister*," she corrected sternly. "I don't know. It depends on whether Wendy told her mother or my father that she saw me."

"So is that your plan for tomorrow—go see them?"

She shrugged. "I hadn't really thought about it, but I guess tomorrow is as good as any other time if you have nothing for me to do. I have to do it before I speak to my therapist again, so if we're picnicking Sunday, then tomorrow is the only day I'll be free."

"Will you give them a heads-up that you're coming?" He could only imagine the shock of seeing Callie after all these years.

"I hadn't thought about that, either. I guess I could call." She paused. "I went to go see them when I first came to town. I even pulled into the driveway."

"What happened? Were they not home?"

"I don't know." Her voice lowered to a whisper. "I chickened out."

"That's hard to believe." She always came off as strong enough to deal with anyone or anything.

She shook her head. "I couldn't go through with it."

"Do you think you'll be able to do it tomorrow?"

"What choice do I have? I can't leave town until I've done everything my therapist thinks I need to do."

A FEW MINUTES later Callie was alone in her bedroom. She hadn't wanted to discuss her family situation with Tyler any longer, so she'd said goodnight and walked into the house.

More than anything, she'd wanted him to kiss her again. The truth was that she wanted Tyler.

There was no denying it. And this wasn't her teen-age fantasy anymore. This was a red-blooded woman wanting an extremely hot man.

A man she couldn't have. Correction. She *could* have him—he'd made that clear in his kiss—but that didn't make it a smart idea.

She had to face the fact that she would be leaving Whittler's Creek as soon as she possibly could. And Tyler was settled into the town, along with his daughters. The daughters he didn't want her to be alone with.

She went into her bathroom to wash her face and brush her teeth. She'd been about to change into her nightshirt when there was a quiet knock on her door.

Her heart sped up, anticipating Tyler at her door. Who else could it be? She automatically fluffed her hair and went to answer the knock.

"Hi," he greeted her.

"Hi."

He pulled something from behind his back. "You left this in my car." He was holding her cell phone.

She took it, their fingers sparking as they grazed. Heat traveled through her at an alarming rate. "Thank you. It must have slipped out of my purse." The words were barely a whisper as she focused on his mouth.

The mouth she so wanted to taste again.

"You're welcome," he whispered back and then their mouths met in a bone-searing kiss.

They weren't in his truck anymore. They were standing and he'd pulled her body tight to his. She ran her hands over his back, loving the play of his muscles, and he grabbed her backside and lifted her off the ground. Her legs came around his waist and she slid her arms around his neck when he stepped into her room and closed her bedroom door with his foot. He tasted hot and sexy, and he was easily the best kisser she'd ever come in contact with.

Just as she was imagining what he looked like naked, he slowly lowered her until her feet touched the floor. He leaned his forehead against hers. "I should go."

That wasn't what she'd expected or even wanted to hear. She didn't say anything.

He took a step back. She wanted to grab him and press herself into his hard and hot body.

But she didn't.

Instead she stood there like an idiot, not saying a word. Not telling him he didn't have to go, that he could stay.

"This is where you tell me I don't have to go," he said as if reading her mind. He smiled. When she still didn't say anything, he added, "My girls…"

She nodded, unable to speak. His daughters were the perfect excuse for him to leave.

"So you're visiting your family tomorrow?" Good way for him to get her out of the mood.

"I guess so. What are you up to?"

"I need to check on my house."

"Your house?"

He nodded. "I bought the old McCutcheon house and I'm having work done on it before the girls and I move in. That's why we're living here."

That answered the question she'd had when she'd first discovered he was staying at Poppy's. The McCutcheons had lived on the hill overlooking the town. Every Christmas they would light up their house with thousands of little white lights and you could see it from anywhere in town.

"I've always loved that house," she told him.

"Me, too." He opened her bedroom door and moved to the doorway, his hand on the doorknob to close it behind him. He leaned in as if to kiss her again, but she came to her senses quickly. She put her hand flat on his chest and stopped him. In answer to his questioning look, she said, "If you kiss me again, I'm going to drag you in here and have my way with you."

His eyes widened and then he grinned devilishly. "That sounds like a challenge."

She laughed quietly. "I mean it."

He grew serious. "So do I." Their eyes locked

until Tyler spoke again. "Have dinner with me tomorrow night."

She blinked. "Are you asking me out on a date?"

He shrugged. "If you want to call it that, then, sure. I'd like to spend time with you, somewhere that we're not tempted to jump into bed right away. A public restaurant is a good place to start."

"I agree, as long as you give me a tour of your house." She would probably appreciate a night out after spending time with family tomorrow.

"Absolutely." His eyebrows rose. "That was easier than I thought."

"You're not calling me easy, are you?" she teased.

"Not at all. Not even after your comment about having your way with me." They both laughed, keeping as quiet as possible so they didn't wake anyone in the house.

"I hear Aunt Poppy walking around up there," Tyler said, pointing to the ceiling. She'd had a private suite built for herself in the attic after her husband died. "I hope we didn't wake her."

"Sounds like she's coming down the stairs," Callie said. They both stepped into Callie's room. Tyler closed the door, leaving a small gap for them to watch the attic door, waiting for Poppy to come through it.

But it wasn't Poppy who stepped into the hallway. It was Gino, who'd moved into the room next to Callie's a few days ago. He was wearing a white T-shirt and boxers as he skulked down the hall and into his own bedroom, closing the door behind him.

Callie and Tyler looked at each other, their eyes wide with shock and amusement. "Poppy and Gino?" Callie whispered.

"Sure looks like it."

AFTER A FITFUL night's sleep because sizzling dreams of Tyler kept waking her, Callie finally got out of bed. It was nearly nine o'clock, much later than she'd expected to get up as she showered and dressed for her visit to see her dad.

She wore white capris with a pink-and-white-striped tank top. Because it was supposed to be in the nineties, she French-braided her wet hair to stay cool. When it was time to get ready to go out with Tyler, her hair would be dry and she could undo it. She always got compliments when she wore her long hair full and kinky from a braid.

She went down to the kitchen to see about coffee and something to eat when she ran into Poppy cutting up vegetables Callie assumed were for dinner.

"Good morning," the older woman greeted her.

Remembering Gino sneaking downstairs from Poppy's room, Callie suddenly found herself tongue-tied. "Good…good morning." She helped herself to a coffee mug and began pouring herself a cup from the fresh pot.

"Did you sleep well?"

"I guess so." Probably not nearly as well as Poppy had after Gino had left her. Callie admonished herself. The two of them had as much right to be together as anyone else.

"Something bothering you?" Poppy's question sounded sincere.

Instead of telling Poppy the truth about her dreams of Tyler, she told a partial fib. "I'm going to visit my dad today and I guess I'm a little nervous. It's been a long time since we've spoken."

"It must be stressful for you. I'll be around later if you want to talk when you get back."

"That's kind of you," Callie said, putting a slice of bread in the toaster.

"I mean it. I'm a good listener and every once in a while I come up with a good piece of advice."

Poppy's words made Callie smile. "I'm sure you do and I really appreciate the offer. I'm going to hope for the best and I'll let you know how it turns out."

Poppy nodded and went back to cutting vegetables.

Callie got out the peanut butter to spread on her toast, as well as a knife and plate. By the time she was finished with breakfast, it was late morning.

She cleaned up her dishes and took her cell phone into the living room to call her dad.

Her heart beat wildly as the phone rang. What if her stepmother answered? What would Callie say? Would her stepmother tell her not to come? She was about to hang up when she heard her dad's voice.

"Hello?"

"Hi, Dad. It's Callie."

There was silence on the other end.

"Dad?"

"Is...is that really you, Callie?"

Tears came to her eyes. She hadn't realized how much she'd missed this man. "Yes, it's really me."

"How are you? Where are you?"

Callie chuckled nervously. "I'm fine. I'm here in town. In Whittler's Creek." She paused. "I was wondering if I could come by to see you."

"Of course!" He nearly shouted into the phone. "When can you get here?"

They made a plan for Callie to come right over and then disconnected. She looked at her silent phone, a little shocked at how easy it had been to talk to her dad. He sounded really glad to hear from her.

Feeling better about going, she went upstairs for her purse and, before she knew it, she was driving the same road she'd driven when she'd first arrived in Whittler's Creek almost a week ago.

This time she didn't hesitate. She pulled right into the driveway as far as she could go. The same car she'd seen the other day was in the open garage.

She wasn't even out of her vehicle when her dad came out the front door to greet her. He enveloped her in a warm hug and she was taken back to a time she didn't want to think about.

With an arm around her shoulders, he said, "Come on in. I fixed us some lunch."

"I don't want to be a bother," she told him, sure she couldn't eat a single bite with the way her stomach was in knots.

"No bother at all. I was just fixing lunch. Making an extra sandwich is no trouble." He held the front screen door open for her and she stepped inside.

Sitting primly in a chair on the far side of the living room was the woman Callie least wanted to see. She seemed small and frail, her now-gray hair stringy and unkempt. With an afghan over her legs, she had her hands folded on top of it. She didn't say anything to Callie, merely stared at her as if not recognizing the stepdaughter she'd raised.

"Ellen?" Her father spoke calmly to her stepmother. "You remember Callie, don't you?"

Ellen didn't respond. Where was the stern taskmaster who'd made Callie's life a living hell?

"Is she okay?" Callie asked softly.

"She's had multiple strokes," her dad said just as quietly.

"Oh." Saying she was sorry to hear that would be an outright lie, so she said nothing more.

"Let's go into the kitchen. I'll bring Ellen a tray with her lunch and then we can sit down and get reacquainted."

That sounded like an excellent plan. "I'd like that."

Not only did her dad need to fix Ellen's lunch, but he needed to help her eat it, too. By the time she finished and he came to join Callie in the kitchen, nearly half an hour had gone by.

"How long has she been like this?" Callie asked.

Her dad paused with a plate in each hand. "About a year and a half." He nodded vigorously. "Her first stroke was two days before Christmas."

"Do you have any help coming in for her?" she asked when they began eating. He had aged considerably since she'd left home. He'd been a tall man in his prime, a recognizable figure from afar, but now he slumped over, as if life had beaten him down. His previously dark hair had grayed and thinned, his skin was pale.

"Oh, no. I can manage on my own. Besides, insurance won't cover that."

She should check on it for him. "Maybe I can help pay for someone to come in."

"That's not necessary." He took a bite of his sandwich. "Tell me what you've been doing."

Taking that to mean her normal life and not since she'd arrived in Whittler's Creek, Callie filled him in. "I'm a financial analyst and I'm living near DC."

"Are you married?" He glanced at her left hand. "Seeing someone?"

She shook her head. "No, not right now." He didn't need to know about Andrew, and Tyler had only kissed her a few times.

They chatted for another forty-five minutes before her dad asked how long she would be in town.

"Probably a few more weeks," she said as he walked her to the front door. She mentally did the math for when she would complete her service hours.

"Do you think you could come by again?"

Again, her eyes filled up. "Of course." And she meant it. She hugged him tight, anxious to make up for the years they'd missed out on.

With her stepmother incapacitated, she discovered she no longer feared coming back.

CHAPTER SEVEN

ON THE DRIVE back to Poppy's, Callie assessed the visit with her dad. He'd never asked where she was staying. Because he'd wanted to avoid the subject? If they'd spoken about it, would he have felt the need to invite her to stay with him and Ellen?

Not that she'd have accepted. She'd barely recognized Ellen as the same person who'd raised her. Her stepmother had been subdued, but that didn't mean Callie would ever be comfortable in that house. Whether Ellen was there or not. Callie had too many awful memories to spend even one night there.

She relaxed her hands that were gripping the steering wheel.

She and her dad had carefully skirted several other subjects, too. Like, why he hadn't contacted her in all this time. She'd sent him letters, gifts at Christmas and for his birthday, as well as an invitation to her college graduation. He'd never responded to any of them. Yet if he was angry with her for not returning before now, he never let on.

Callie parked on the street in front of Poppy's, right behind Gino's SUV. Tyler's truck was gone.

She wondered where they were having dinner and what to wear. Tyler hadn't said whether this was a casual or dressy evening, although touring his house that was under renovation in heels might not be wise. She was really anxious to see the inside of the house that she'd always considered a perfect home. She also looked forward to a relaxing evening after her visit with her dad.

She went directly to her room, avoiding the commotion in the kitchen. It sounded like Tyler's girls were "helping" Poppy. From the delicious smell when she entered the house, Callie guessed they were baking something.

A few minutes later there was a knock on her bedroom door.

"Hi," she said when she opened it to Tyler. She was surprised at how happy she was to see him. Probably because her day was going so well, not counting the concerns she'd had after leaving her dad's.

He smiled and returned her greeting. "I just got back from work. There was a traffic accident over in Bridgeport and they needed some extra assistance."

"Was it bad?"

He shrugged. "No one hurt. An oil tanker

spilled its contents and the road had to be closed. I've been directing traffic around it."

She nodded. "So you're exhausted, and the last thing you want to do is go to dinner with me?"

"No, no!" He laughed. "That's not it at all. I came by because we hadn't made specific plans for tonight." He narrowed his eyes at her. "You aren't trying to back out, are you?"

She tilted her head and smiled. "Would I do that?"

"Absolutely," he said bluntly then smiled. "Too late. We have a reservation at Chez Louis for seven o'clock. We can go see my house before then. Work for you?"

"Sounds good. I love French food." Chez Louis was one of the nicest restaurants in the area. One she'd never been able to go to when she'd lived in Whittler's Creek. "Will I be able to wear heels around your house or should I bring other shoes?"

He pursed his lips. "I didn't think of that. I'd bring other shoes. Inside isn't bad, but the landscaping has been torn up and it might be muddy after last night's thunderstorm."

She nodded. "So what time should we leave?"

"How about five-thirty? That should give us enough time to see the house and get to the restaurant on time."

"Daddy!" One of his daughters was calling him as she came up the stairs. "Look what we made!" Madison held a plate of cookies out to him. "Try one."

He did as she asked and took a large bite. "Mmm," he said with overdone enthusiasm. "This is delicious. My favorite."

"You say that every time," his daughter reminded him.

"But this is my absolute favorite."

She lowered the register of her voice. "You always say that, too."

He laughed and patted her head. "I guess you found me out. I love all cookies."

Callie was enjoying their exchange, wishing she'd had a closer relationship with her father. Between traveling as a long-haul trucker and Ellen's interference, Callie'd rarely had one-on-one time with him while growing up.

"Would you like one, Ms. Callie?" Madison held the plate out.

"I'd love one. Thank you." Callie took one and bit into it. "This really is delicious." Tyler hadn't embellished his review at all.

Madison grinned.

"Aunt Poppy could open a restaurant with her recipes," Tyler said. "Although I don't mind that we don't have to share."

Madison asked if either of them wanted a second cookie. Callie declined, but Tyler took two more before his daughter went back downstairs.

After swallowing a mouthful, he said, "So I'll see you about five-thirty?"

She nodded. "I'll be ready."

He turned to head down the hall to his room while she admired his trim body and wondered what the evening would bring.

TYLER SPENT THE rest of the afternoon with his daughters, playing the prince to their princesses followed by soccer at the local elementary school.

When they got back, the girls went to find Aunt Poppy while Tyler grabbed a shower. He could count the number of dates he'd been on since his divorce on one hand. So he was more than a little apprehensive about the evening with Callie.

It was only dinner. He'd eaten thousands of meals in his lifetime. He had manners. He knew how to have a pleasant conversation. So why was he worried?

As soon as he saw Callie come down the stairs to where he stood by the front door, he knew exactly *why*.

She wore a formfitting dress in a dark red. She would probably call it some other name, but he lived in a world of eight-pack crayons. The dress was sleeveless and stopped inches above her knees, leaving her long legs bare. She wore tan high-heeled sandals and carried a pair of running shoes in one hand and a small purse in the other.

...st above where her dress had scooted to
...several more inches of bare legs.

...e jerked his attention back to the road.

...I'm sure the work you've done on it has only
...de it better," she said.

"I hope so. I had an architect friend help. Some-
...ne renovated the house in the eighties, but they
didn't remain true to the original. My friend was
adamant about not losing the character of the
house and restoring it to its original time period."

"I've never been inside it," Callie told him.
"What kind of things did they do?"

He made a left turn onto the street where his
house sat at the top of the hill. "They put those
off-white Formica and oak-trimmed cabinets in
the kitchen and all the bathrooms."

"Oh, no," she said. "They scream 'eighties' all
by themselves."

"There was also a lot of stenciling of geese,
hearts, things like that. The worst was that they
replaced the bathtubs, which were probably claw-
footed, with one-piece vinyl shower enclosures."

"Sounds like it's a huge project."

"Much bigger than I'd anticipated." He reached
the driveway and stopped. "This is as close as I
can get to the house. I'm risking a flat tire if I pull
into the driveway."

While Callie switched shoes, Tyler came around
to help her out of the truck. She placed a hand on

Her hair was loose, flowin...
and moving with the stirring ...
ried down the stairs.

"You look great," he said when s...
bottom step.

She smiled and looked even sexier, ...
possible. "Thank you." She eyed him ...
down, taking in his gray slacks, light blu...
shirt with the collar open, and a black jacket.
look pretty great yourself."

He was out of practice getting compliments s...
he changed the subject. "Ready to go?" At her nod
he opened the door and she went out ahead of him.
The rear view of her wasn't too shabby, either.

He helped her into his truck and came around
to the driver's side. He put his hand on the door
handle and sucked in a breath. Nothing to be worried about. Nothing to be worried about.

Except that when he opened his door, her light,
sweet scent had already filled the cab of his truck.

He was a dead man.

"Are you okay?" she asked.

Her question knocked some sense back into
him. "What? Yes, I'm fine." The engine turned
over and he pulled away from the curb. "My house
still needs a lot of work, so I hope you aren't disappointed. I know you said you always loved that
house."

"That's true," she said, her hands folded in her

his shoulder and his hands spanned her waist as he lifted her to the ground without thinking. Their eyes met and he quickly dropped his hands.

He needed to get over this or he'd never be able to enjoy the evening.

So he did what any red-blooded man would do when faced with a woman so sexy he ached with wanting her.

He pulled her in for a kiss that was supposed to end his wanting but instead made him want her even more. She didn't push him away. Her mouth softened and she leaned her body into his.

"Now we don't have to wonder," he said on the fly when he finally released her.

"Wonder what?" Her slightly out-of-breath tone wasn't helping his libido.

"Whether we'll kiss good-night or not. We've already gotten it out of the way."

She smirked. "I wasn't wondering about it."

"You weren't?"

She shook her head slightly. "Nope."

"Oh. I guess it was just me then."

Before he could say anything more, she kissed him. Kissed him good. Made their prior kiss amateurish.

"What was that for?" he asked. His body was in overdrive.

She grinned. "I was just curious."

He liked this game. "Curious about what?"

"Curious whether you would get any more flustered than you already were if *I* kissed *you*."

His eyes widened. "Me, flustered?" She was absolutely right.

Instead of responding she turned a hundred and eighty degrees to take off down the driveway to his house.

CALLIE COULD PRACTICALLY feel Tyler's eyes on her as she navigated her way to the house. The thought made her smile. Even before coming to Whittler's Creek, it had been quite a while since she'd been appreciated for her looks. Andrew had been stingy with the compliments, preferring to focus on himself instead.

She heard Tyler come up behind her as she neared the covered portico. "The house is beautiful. At least, the bones of it."

He stood next to her. "I'm glad you can see that with all the work that still needs to be done." The 1920's brick Colonial Revival needed a facelift, but it appeared structurally sound. "Some paint and a new roof will help," he said. "Thankfully the roof held up long enough that it hasn't leaked and caused damage."

They were both looking up at the peeling dormers in the roof.

He stepped to the front door, key in hand, and

unlocked it. "And, don't worry, the house has been fumigated."

Her eyes widened. "Fumigated?"

He chuckled. "Oh, yeah. It had been empty for years except for some unwanted creatures. Bats in the attic, termites in the walls, mice in the basement."

Callie shivered as she stepped through the front entrance. "And you're sure they're gone?"

"As sure as I can be." He took her hand. "Come on. I'll show you the kitchen. I've been doing that and the bathrooms first. Then I'll get to the bedrooms and finally downstairs."

"You're doing all this by yourself?"

"I've done a lot of it, but I've contracted out some of the more difficult things. I can demo and dry-wall, and I can even do some of the plumbing, but things like electrical I leave to an expert."

She was pleasantly surprised at his ability, especially when they reached the kitchen. "This is wonderful!" She walked around on the black-and-white tiled floor to see the multitude of white cabinets, shelves and glass-fronted cabinets. "I love the countertops." She ran a hand over the black quartz embedded with pieces of clear glass in it.

"The butler's pantry is over here." He led her into a narrow room with similar cabinets and countertops running its length. There was even a second sink.

Next they went into the dining room that had peeling paint and a built-in corner cupboard. On the opposite end was a large bay window that drew her attention.

"Oh! You can see into town from here!" The view was breathtaking. The mountains were visible on the horizon because it was such a clear day.

"Yeah, the view is one of the best features of this house. I'm going to add a deck off the back of the master so I can enjoy my morning coffee out there since it faces the same way." He pulled on her arm. "Come on, I'll show you the upstairs."

She'd barely had time to glance at the large staircase when they came in because they'd immediately gone to the kitchen. But now she got to admire its magnificence. "This will be gorgeous when it's all done."

His expression said he was pleased she could see the potential there.

"How much longer do you think it'll take to finish or at least until you can move in?"

They began walking up the stairs to the second floor. "Much longer than I'd expected when I started this thing." He chuckled. "Maybe I should assign you to do your community service hours here."

She froze, her pulse beating furiously against her temples.

Tyler continued as if he hadn't noticed her reaction. "And with many more days like this, I'll never get it done."

"Days like this?" Her voice trembled slightly.

"Being called in to help out with the traffic accident," he explained.

"That happens often?"

"More than I'd like." He showed her the bedrooms and hall bath and then they ended the tour in the master bedroom.

"Are you okay?" he asked as they entered the largest of the bedrooms.

She nodded. "I'm fine." But that was a lie.

She concentrated on the empty room that had a tray ceiling, making the high-ceilinged room even more grand. She could see where a king-size bed would go, a sitting area by the front windows and also where Tyler planned to put a deck.

She was about to ask about the attic when his cell phone rang. He held up a finger and pulled the phone from his pocket. "Sorry." He pushed a button to connect the call. "Garrett."

While he listened to his caller, the nagging thought Callie had been pushing down came to the forefront of her mind. Tyler was a police officer. The police chief, in fact. He had power over her.

Just like Andrew had.

He'd been teasing about having her work on his house, but could she trust that Tyler wouldn't eventually abuse his power over her like Andrew had?

By the time they were seated in the restaurant, Tyler was even more confused about Callie's change in mood. They ordered drinks and he broached the subject again.

"Something happened at the house that upset you, but I don't know what. Did I say or do something?"

She looked down at her hands folded in her lap and didn't say a word.

"Look, I can't apologize if I don't know what I did." His frustration was mounting.

"It's not anything you did." She spoke so quietly that he had to lean in to hear her.

"Then what is it?" His ability to stay calm was waning.

She met his eyes. "It was what you said about me working at your house."

He let out a breath. "That's what upset you? I was joking. You have to know that."

She nodded. "Yes, I know it was a joke." She visibly swallowed. "But if you wanted to, you could order me to do exactly that."

"But I don't want to." He was still confused. "I would never take advantage of you like that."

They were interrupted when their drinks arrived. "Are you ready to order?" their server asked in a slight French accent.

"We need a few minutes," Tyler told him. "We haven't looked at the menus yet."

"As you wish. Take your time." The fortyish man nodded and left them.

Tyler had chosen this restaurant because he knew they could have a long, relaxing dinner. Unlike the chain restaurants that couldn't get you fed and out the door fast enough.

Now he wondered if long was really what he wanted.

When they were alone again, Tyler looked to her for an answer. "Why would you think I'd take advantage of you like that?"

She took a long drink of her ice water before replying. "Realistically, I know you're probably a good guy."

"Probably? Gee, thanks."

She remained serious. "You need to understand what happened that forced me to put my life on hold and brought me back to Whittler's Creek. If not for a man having power over me, I would still be living my life the way I chose."

"If you think I like telling you what to do, I don't. I'm hard-pressed to come up with things for your community service."

She nodded. "I know. It just made me remember that you're not just Tyler. You're Police Chief Tyler Garrett, the boss of me while I'm in town."

"The boss of you." He couldn't help it, he waggled his eyebrows. Then he sobered. "Sorry. I shouldn't be finding humor in your discomfort."

"You're right. You shouldn't." But her lips twitched slightly.

"I apologize." He pointed to his menu. "Let's decide what we want to eat and then you can tell me all about what happened to make you land here." He opened his menu. "I highly recommend the crab-stuffed mushrooms. Want to start with that as an appetizer?"

She nodded. "That would be nice."

He realized he'd taken charge. "Unless there's something else that you'd like. I don't want to be pushy."

She smiled at him. Not just a twitch of her lips but a real smile. "You're not being pushy. You're the expert—I've never eaten here before."

He smiled back at her and then looked down at his menu. "I've never been disappointed with the food here. I don't think you can go wrong with anything on the menu."

As soon as their server stepped away from their table after they placed their orders, Tyler reached across the white-linen-covered table to take Callie's hand. "Ready to tell me how you came to be back in Whittler's Creek? I wasn't given details by your therapist, only how many hours you needed to fulfill."

She sighed. "I'd been seeing this guy for about six months."

"Of course you had. There's always a guy making the rest of us look bad." He grinned, trying to lighten the mood.

She ignored his comment and continued. "So, for our six-month anniversary, I brought dinner over to his apartment. He was working late, or so he'd told me, but I had a key to let myself in."

"I can see what's coming."

"You guessed it. He was in bed with a woman. I ran out and went straight home."

"How did his cheating get you in trouble?" He lifted his bourbon on the rocks to his lips.

"He kept calling me and when I finally picked up, he claimed that I'd knocked over a vase and broke it. He wanted me to pay for it, but I said I didn't think I'd done it."

"A vase?"

She nodded. "An expensive but ugly vase. He claimed its value was forty-five hundred dollars."

Tyler nearly choked when he inhaled his bourbon. "Wow! It must have been some vase." He set his drink down. "So you refused to pay for it. So, what? Did he take you to small claims court?"

Callie pursed her lips. "Even worse. He had me arrested."

"Arrested?" Tyler pinched his lips shut when he realized how loud he'd spoken. "They actually arrested you?"

"Yep. Kept me in an interrogation room until

my arraignment. At least they didn't put me in a cell."

"So how did he manage this? Does he know someone in law enforcement or something?"

"He didn't need to know anyone. He's an assistant state's attorney." She continued to tell him about the arraignment and the plea bargain that she'd had no choice but to take.

It all became clear. "So that's why you're so concerned about me exerting my power over you." Saying that made him think of a completely different meaning. Picturing himself over her naked body…

He cleared his throat. "Not that I have any power over you in the first place."

"But you're the one deciding where I do my community service hours."

He shrugged. "Only because I was told to. So you tell me what you'd like to do."

Her eyes widened. "Really?"

"Sure, why not? I'm already running out of ideas."

"Well, when community service was mentioned in court, my lawyer thought I could do some financial work for low-income people." Her mouth twisted. "That was before my therapist forced me to come here to reconcile my past."

Another subject he'd like to delve into, but first things first. She could be the answer to his dilemma. "Don't be so quick to reject the idea," he said. "Tell me exactly what your qualifications are. You're in finance?"

She nodded. "I've got degrees in accounting and finance from the University of Maryland. I've made quite a lot of money for people while working for Dunning and Dunning."

He recognized the investment company and couldn't imagine why he hadn't asked her earlier about what she did for a living. "I have the perfect job for you."

Her eyebrows rose. "Really? You can use my skills in Whittler's Creek? That would be great."

He enjoyed watching her happiness over what he considered a personal win. He explained about the email regarding missing funds and how he needed someone to go over the records to figure out how and when money was taken. "I'm hoping that will shed light on who was responsible."

Their appetizer arrived. The server set it down between them and then placed a small, empty plate in front of each of them.

Tyler stopped the server before he could leave. "I'd like to order some wine." He looked at Callie. "Will you drink some if I order a bottle of white? Unless you prefer red." He was having sautéed scallops and she had ordered the mahi-mahi special.

She smiled when he gave her a choice. "White wine would be nice."

"A bottle of the Italian Pinot Grigio." He pointed to the one he wanted on the wine list. The server nodded and left.

Callie drank the last swallow of her gin and tonic, leaving her with a glass of ice. "Tell me more about the financial problem. You said you received an email?" At his nod, she asked, "Are you able to find out who sent it?"

"I probably could, but I'm more concerned about stopping the drain on the town's finances than uncovering a whistleblower."

"I can see your point. From what I've seen, Whittler's Creek needs every penny it can hold on to."

"That's for sure."

The server came bearing their bottle of wine and, while he opened it, Tyler watched Callie. Since they'd talked about what was bothering her, she'd relaxed tremendously.

He just needed to be on his guard when interacting with her.

Suddenly, as if in slow motion, a patron walking past their table tripped, knocking into their server who was pouring Callie's wine. The wine bottle jerked from over her glass and into her lap.

The whole incident took seconds, not enough time for anyone to react quickly enough before Callie was drenched.

CHAPTER EIGHT

WITH TYLER AND Callie gone for the evening, Poppy was enjoying dinner with Alexis, Madison and Gino. She loved how Gino got along with her great-nieces. They enjoyed his corny jokes, even when they didn't quite understand them. But he laughed, so they did, too.

Poppy's face heated as she recalled last night with Gino. She'd thought her sex life had died when her husband had, but Gino had proved her wrong. She was fifty-nine, but he made her feel nineteen. They'd always had an amazing physical relationship when they were together all those years ago. Who would have guessed their flame hadn't burned out by now?

"Let's help Aunt Poppy by cleaning up the kitchen," Gino said to the girls. He winked at Poppy before guiding the girls to the dishwasher with their plates. Then he said to Poppy, "You sit down and relax." He kissed her quickly and the girls giggled.

"Are you Aunt Poppy's boyfriend?" young Alexis wanted to know.

Gino looked to Poppy, whose face heated immediately, and then answered, "Yes I am." The girls laughed again, silly laughter that allowed Poppy to regain her composure.

Instead of leaving the kitchen, she poured herself another half glass of wine and sat at the table.

"You're really fun, Mr. Gino." Madison put the silverware in the dishwasher basket. "I hope you stay forever."

Poppy smiled, wishing the same thing, but knew better. Gino would finish his business deal, whatever that was, and be on his way to his next adventurous deal.

She'd considered the facts before they'd made love last night, but she'd rejected all the reasons she shouldn't have an affair with him. What if this was her last chance at a physical relationship with a man? Sure, these days fifty-nine was still young—and she felt much younger than the number—but that didn't mean she'd have an opportunity in this small town to find a man like Gino. A man who was attractive, attentive, kind, considerate…she could go on and on.

Poppy focused on what Gino was saying instead of her daydreams.

"So I'll be living here permanently," he said as if in conclusion.

"Here?" Poppy said. "As in this house?"

Gino chuckled, a deep sound that curled her

toes. "Only if you want me to." He closed the dishwasher and turned on the faucet to fill a frying pan to soak. "I was just telling the girls about my plans to buy the old Lincoln Hotel."

Poppy's eyes widened. "You are?" No one had used the Lincoln as a hotel for at least half a century. Several nonprofit organizations had rented the lobby as a meeting place over the years, but Poppy could only imagine what kind of condition the hotel rooms were in. "Won't that take a lot of work to make it habitable?"

"I've got everything set in motion. I should be able to open it as an upscale bed-and-breakfast by next spring."

Poppy then heard the words *complete renovation* and *Michelin star chef*, but she was still trying to process bed-and-breakfast.

Gino stopped talking. He must have finished his explanation. "Why don't you girls pick out a book and we'll read it in a few minutes." He walked over to Poppy and put a hand on her shoulder. "Are you okay?"

She tried to clear her head. "Of course." Her tone was sharper than she'd meant it to be, but she couldn't help it.

"You're obviously lying," he said, pulling out the chair next to hers. He turned it around and straddled it.

"Why would I lie?" Maybe because he'd just punched her in the gut.

"I thought you'd be excited about my plans. I just closed on the property today. When the girls asked me about staying in town, I thought it was the perfect time to let you in on my plans."

"You didn't think this would bother me?"

His eyebrows furrowed. "No, I never considered that at all. Why would it? I figured you'd want me to stick around."

Did he really not see it? "Because turning the Lincoln into a B and B would put it in direct competition with me."

His confusion remained. "But you're running a boardinghouse, not a B and B."

"That's only while Tyler and the girls are here. As soon as they get settled in their new house, I'm ready to make the transition. You knew that. I mentioned it when you asked me about my new website that I was working on last night."

"I guess I was preoccupied with thoughts of taking you to bed."

He had nerve trying to make a joke when this was serious business to her.

She rose from her chair quickly and it scraped the tile floor. "So that's what you think of me? I'm just a distraction until you pull the rug out from under me?" Her voice grew louder the more she spoke. She was breathing quickly, her hurt and anger accelerating.

He stood and tried to take her hand but she pulled it back. "Why are you so upset? I thought you'd be thrilled that I'm staying here. Near you. On purpose."

He stared at her, obviously waiting for her to reply, but she didn't know what to say.

Gino continued. "I thought, especially after last night, that you were as invested in this new phase of our lives as I am." He paused. "I guess I was wrong." He pushed his chair under the table. "I'm going to read that book to the girls. You obviously need time to digest this information."

He disappeared from the kitchen, leaving her to stew.

All the time in the world wouldn't be enough for her to "digest" his plan—a plan that would ruin her business.

"I'm so sorry, *MADEMOISELLE*!" The server who'd just spilled wine on Callie couldn't have been more apologetic as he mopped up the table and basically everywhere except her lap. Another server and the maître d' had come over to give him a hand.

Tyler had risen to help, but the most he could do was hand her his linen napkin.

"Thanks," she said, trying to soak up as much

of the wine on her dress as possible. She remained calm. No need to get upset, she told herself. It was an accident. No one's fault. She breathed deeply, exhaling slowly.

A few minutes later they were back to as normal as possible with the front of her dress still damp. They'd been given fresh napkins as well as the promise of paying for Callie's dry cleaning and a free meal. "I'll bring you another appetizer," their server promised. "One that's hot. Again, I'm so very sorry."

"Thank you," Callie and Tyler both said at once.

Their server picked up the one that had cooled and hurried away.

When they were alone, Tyler said, "You stayed pretty composed through all of that. I'm not sure I would have remained as calm."

She smiled and shrugged. "It was an accident. Getting upset doesn't make the situation any better."

He nodded. "That's true. A good way to look at it. I still don't think I would have been as nice as you were."

She took a sip of her wine. "I doubt that's true." She held up her wineglass. "And the good news is that this is excellent free wine."

He grinned and took a drink from his glass. "You're right." He held his glass out. "Cheers!"

She tapped her glass to his. "To a dry evening!"

"At least from here on out!" They laughed and their fresh appetizer arrived.

"These *are* delicious," Callie said when she took a bite of her crab-stuffed mushroom. She patted her mouth with her napkin and placed it back on her lap. "So let's get back to this financial bind you're in. Where would you like me to work on these records and where are they now?"

He swallowed his bite of mushroom. "They're in a storage locker at the moment. I'll arrange to have them moved, but I'm not sure where. I'll have to think about where there might be a work space for you."

"Sounds good." She was anxious to get back to doing what she did best. Straightening out and enhancing wealth. And if Whittler's Creek had a financial problem, she was prepared to find it.

"So you said your therapist suggested you come back to Whittler's Creek?" he asked.

"Suggested?" She gave him a wry smile. "More like gave me no choice."

"And you obviously didn't want to."

"That's putting it mildly. I told you I haven't been back since high school." She could tell he wanted to know more but she'd spent too much time today thinking about her Whittler's Creek relatives. She changed the subject. "So, tell me why you stayed here after your dad passed away. And what made you decide to leave the military?"

His expression sobered and he focused on his mushroom. "I guess I owe you an explanation since you've shared things with me." He met her eyes. "I resigned my commission because my ex-wife went to jail."

Callie's eyes widened. "Jail? What did she do?" She quickly raised a hand to stop him from speaking. "I'm sorry. If you don't want to tell me, I understand." She was certainly keeping her own secrets.

He shook his head slightly. "That's okay. You're right, I don't like to talk about it. She's in jail because of child neglect, among other things."

Callie's heart pounded. She waited for him to go on.

"While I was deployed, a neighbor called the police when she realized the girls were home alone. At the time, they were only two and four."

Callie gasped. "That's terrible. Those sweet little girls. Any number of things could have happened to them."

"True. Although she locked them in their bedroom so at least they couldn't wander out into the street."

"But there could have been a fire or—" She didn't want to imagine what else could have befallen them.

"You can see why I don't talk about it," he said quietly. "It's both depressing and infuriating. Especially when I add that this happened multiple times. According to Alexis, their mother would often keep them locked in their room even when she was home." He paused, looking as if he was trying to keep his emotions in check. "Alexis said she was always hungry, but she learned that crying about it only got her sent to her room without food."

Callie picked up her water glass with an unsteady hand. She drank as if parched. "What about when you were around? Did you suspect anything? Did the girls try to tell you about it?" Her vision blurred as she spoke, trying not to relive her own childhood. She blinked several times.

Tyler took a drink of his wine. "In hindsight, I should have realized when the girls were ravenous whenever I returned home. Alexis did tell me once that her mom was locking her and her sister in their room, but I thought she meant at night. My ex had said she put a lock on the outside of their door because they'd started wandering around in the middle of the night. She was afraid they'd wander outside while she was sleeping." He ran his hands through his hair. "I had no idea that Alexis meant anything different."

Callie was losing her appetite. "So your ex is in jail. For how much longer?"

He shrugged. "Her original sentence was three years. I divorced her right after she was arrested and admitted what she'd done. I had to get the girls away from her. I got full custody, and she doesn't even have visitation. In fact, she can't have any contact with them until they turn eighteen."

"Good."

His eyebrows rose. "You're not going to give me some flak about mothers' rights?"

Callie shook her head vehemently. "Nope. She got what she deserved. And she obviously doesn't deserve those sweet little girls."

"My feelings exactly."

"So that's why they go to therapy." She said it as a fact, not as a question. "It's helping them? They seem to be well-adjusted little girls, but I don't have any experience with children."

He nodded. "When we first came back to help my dad when he got sick, the girls barely spoke." He smiled slightly. "Now there are times I can't shut them up."

Callie smiled, too. His sense of humor lightened her mood. "They do have a lot to say. Maybe making up for all their quiet time."

"Could be." He finished chewing his mushroom and said, "The good news is that their therapist thinks they're ready to stop therapy."

Callie stared at him. "Really? That's great."

He nodded. "I know. She feels they've put it in the past and, at their young ages, they'll hopefully fill their memory banks with happier times now."

"So that's it. No more therapy?"

"Only if I see a problem. If their personalities change at all, or they seem troubled, I need to contact the therapist. She said it's possible that this will all resurface when they're teenagers or even when they become parents themselves."

Callie's hand shook as she picked up her wineglass. "Do you mean they might be just like their mother when they have children?"

"It's less likely since they've had therapy, but I honestly don't know. I'm not sure anyone can predict that."

What kind of mother would Callie make, considering her background? That was something she'd never even contemplated.

TYLER OBSERVED CALLIE become subdued after he answered her question about the girls' potential behavior. He truly didn't know the answer and wouldn't trust anyone who might try to forecast the future.

He decided to change the subject. "So what's your plan when it comes to seeing your family again? Or are you done after today's visit?"

Their main courses arrived. Callie waited until they were alone again before answering. "I think I might try visiting again. Today went well, and my dad and I have a lot of catching up to do." She surprised herself with her answer.

He nodded. "What about your stepmother?"

Callie froze, staring at him. "What about her?"

"Aren't you going to see her, too? She raised you, right? You only talk about seeing your dad."

Callie chewed her bottom lip, moving her fork through the sauce on her plate. "She's had several strokes and seemed almost catatonic when I was there today. I had no interaction with her, and I have no desire to, now or ever." She paused. "Can we talk about something else?"

"Sure. Of course." He was taken aback, not realizing she didn't get along with her stepmother even now. He'd only witnessed that one argument between them when he and Callie were teenagers. "How about those Orioles? Or are you a Nats fan since you live outside DC?"

She gave him a slight smile. "They're baseball teams, right?"

He laughed and put his hands on his head and shook it. "Oh, no! How can you not be a sports fan?"

She laughed with him. "Actually, I *am* a fan. My company has season tickets for the Nats, and I went to several games earlier in the summer." She leaned in closer. "Although my favorite sport is hockey."

"I'm surprised, but I probably shouldn't be. The Caps are a fun team to root for." He cut into a scallop and took a bite.

They spent the rest of the meal talking about the local pro teams and their chances of having good seasons.

Later, when they pulled to the curb in front of Aunt Poppy's, Callie turned to him. "Thank you. I had a really nice time."

"Me, too." He cut the engine and came around the truck to help her out. He reached for her hand. She stepped out and nearly lost her footing. With both hands, he grasped her waist and lowered her to the ground. He knew instantly, when her body grazed his, that he wasn't going to resist kissing her.

With lips soft and warm, she kissed him back. Her arms slid around his waist and her breasts pressed against his chest. He put a hand to her cheek, tilted his head and deepened the kiss.

He wanted to lift her into his arms and take her to his bed, but he knew better. At least, his mind did. His body had another plan developing.

He ended the kiss and leaned his forehead on hers. He opened his mouth to speak, but the words came out of Callie's mouth first.

"This is a bad idea." She took a step back.

"I know," he said with a grin. "It's just hard to remember why."

She smiled. "How about the fact that I'm going to be leaving soon?"

He sobered. "Not a good idea to get involved in a long-distance romance."

She cocked her head. "Romance?"

He shrugged. "Affair?" He ran his fingers lightly over her bare shoulder and he felt her shiver.

"What about an affair with a time limit?" she suggested, entwining her fingers with his.

He was surprised. "A time limit?"

"Until I have to leave. No commitment, no worries, no hurt feelings."

He didn't have to think long and hard. "That works for me." He paused, capturing her gaze as he brought her hand to his mouth and kissed it. "You're sure about this?"

She nodded. "Absolutely. We're obviously attracted to each other, so why deny it?"

"Okay, then." He put an arm around her waist and they began walking to Poppy's front door. "Your room? My girls sometimes come into my room in the middle of the night."

"Perfect. Wouldn't want to scar them for life because of me."

He gave her a squeeze and then opened the front door, allowing her to go ahead of him.

There was a light on in the front hall, but everywhere else on that floor seemed to be dark. He heard a noise coming from the living room. "What was that?"

Callie pointed in the same direction. "It sounds like someone crying."

He stepped into the living room and, as his eyes adjusted to the darkness, he saw Aunt Poppy curled up in a chair by the window.

"Aunt Poppy? Are you okay?" He stepped closer.

"I'm fine." But she didn't sound fine.

"I'll leave you two alone," Callie whispered to him and left them before he could reply.

After listening to Aunt Poppy tell him about Gino's plans for the Lincoln Hotel, Tyler understood why she was so upset. "And he never mentioned this at all until now?"

She shook her head fervently. "Not a word." She wiped her nose with her balled-up tissue.

Tyler didn't reveal that he knew Aunt Poppy and Gino were sleeping together. She'd be embarrassed, and she was upset enough already. And he had no clue how to help her.

CALLIE DIDN'T KNOW what to think when she woke up in her bed alone the next morning. Slivers of daylight shone through the window treatments.

Tyler never showed up. Callie had stayed up late reading, hoping he'd knock on her door, but no such luck. The book lay next to her on the bed where she'd left it when she couldn't keep her eyes open anymore.

She stretched and got out of bed. Then she

showered and dressed, not knowing what to expect when she ran into Tyler. She had to assume that whatever Poppy's problem was, it had taken quite a long conversation before Tyler could leave.

She smelled food cooking when she opened her bedroom door. She heard voices in the kitchen, so that's where she headed.

Tyler was packing a casserole dish into a container. He looked up and gave her a smile when she stood in the doorway. "Good morning."

She smiled back, although a little tentatively. "Good morning."

He zipped the container and came over to Callie. "Come in here," he whispered, taking her by the arm and directing her into the living room. "I'm so sorry about last night," he said quietly. "Believe me, I'm really, really sorry."

"Is Poppy okay?"

He nodded. "I think so. I'll tell you about that later. She was only part of the problem. Both girls were up during the night."

Callie's eyes widened. "Are they okay?"

"They're fine now. Alexis had a bad dream, and she started screaming, which woke Madison and she began crying, too."

"I can't believe I didn't hear a thing."

His eyebrows rose. "I'm surprised, too. They were pretty loud."

"But you're sure they're okay now?"

"I am. Just nightmares. They were at a park yesterday, and one of the other kids found a small snake—"

"Ew!" Callie shivered.

Tyler chuckled. "It was a little snake." He put his hands out to show her it was about a foot long. "But that's what Alexis was dreaming about."

"I'd have had nightmares, too."

"It was little. Tiny. Like a big worm."

Callie shivered again. "I don't like worms, either."

Tyler shook his head, grinning. "Anyway, they're fine." He rubbed his neck. "So I should have asked you sooner, but I completely forgot about it. There's a picnic today at church, and I wondered if you'd like to join us. That's why Aunt Poppy is making food. You don't have to bring anything, and it's casual. There'll be a short outdoor service and then we'll cook hamburgers and hot dogs. There are games for both kids and adults." He paused and gave her a sexy grin. "Have I sold you on it yet?"

She hadn't grown up going to church. The only time she'd been in one was the occasional wedding or funeral as an adult. "Maybe I could show up after the service. I don't want to embarrass you by doing something wrong."

"Hey, don't worry about it. It'll be *very* casual. Impossible to do something wrong. A few upbeat songs accompanied by a keyboard, a short sermon, and then we eat." He put up a hand. "But if you'd rather not go, I understand. I'm sure the girls will, too."

Callie laughed. "So now you're trying to guilt me into going?"

He shrugged. "Hey, whatever works."

"Oh, wait. What about the picnic with Pete and his friends? Didn't you tell him we'd go?" She'd completely forgotten about it.

"Don't worry. I'll tell him something came up." He leaned closer to whisper, "I think Aunt Poppy could use the moral support." He didn't explain her distress and Callie would never ask.

"Okay, you win," she said on a dramatic sigh. "I'll go. What can I do to help get ready?"

He smiled, a pleased expression, and she grinned back. Spending the day with him, no matter who else was around, was a great idea.

They went to the kitchen to see what Poppy needed, but she had most things ready to go. Callie couldn't help noticing Gino was nowhere to be found, and Poppy's eyes were obviously red and puffy. Callie's heart ached for whatever Poppy was going through.

By the time they made it to the large grassy area next to the church, the girls were practically bouncing out of their car seats. Callie hadn't seen them this excited, and she'd seen them pretty excited at different times over the past week.

Poppy had insisted on taking her own car since five in Tyler's truck would be tight, especially with car seats. Callie had offered several times to drive herself so Poppy could go with Tyler and the girls, but she wouldn't hear of it.

Tyler handed things down to the girls and Callie from his truck bed. There were lawn chairs, a blanket and the food. Between the four of them, they were able to carry everything and Poppy was left with only her purse.

Callie helped Poppy open the food she'd made— a pasta salad and chocolate cupcakes in ice-cream-cone cups—when Poppy said, "Oh, I forgot my hat in my car."

"I'll go get it," Callie offered. "You finish here and I'll be right back."

"Thank you, dear. I appreciate it." Poppy pulled her keys from her purse, which she wore across her body.

Callie hurried to where Poppy had parked next to Tyler's truck. She was unlocking the driver-side door when she heard a voice behind her.

"So you finally hooked him."

Callie spun around to see her stepsister.

Wendy squinted as she faced the sun and she had an ugly expression on her face.

"What are you talking about?" Callie asked.

"Tyler. You've always wanted him. So you heard he was back in town and, here you are, sniffing around after him."

Callie reminded herself to stay calm. She breathed in and out. In and out. "Wendy, I don't know why you think anything I do—or Tyler does—is any of your business, but please go away and leave me alone." Her hands fisted and relaxed as she turned her back on Wendy to get Poppy's hat.

She had it in her hand when she was suddenly pulled out of the car and landed hard on her backside on the macadam parking lot.

CHAPTER NINE

TYLER FINISHED SETTING up their lawn chairs under the tents erected on the church's large side lawn. The weather was beautiful. The sun was popping in and out of the clouds, accompanied by a light breeze, and the humidity was slightly lower than most August days.

"Hi, Daddy." Alexis suddenly appeared in front of him, with Madison not far behind.

"Hi, sweetheart."

"Is it okay if we sit with Brittany and her family?" Alexis's hopeful expression was nearly comical. "Her mother said it's okay."

Tyler looked over to where Brittany's mother was waving her okay from the other side of the chairs. He waved back and then looked down at the girls, who were bouncing in anticipation of his answer. "Okay. Just make sure you behave over there." He looked pointedly at his youngest daughter. "No talking during the service, Madison. If you absolutely *have* to say something, then whisper. I'm talking about things like 'there's a bug on you.' Not 'I have a hair doodad just like yours.'"

"Doodad?" Both girls giggled as they repeated the word.

He gave them a stern look.

"Okay, Daddy, we will," Alexis said.

"We promise," Madison added, her expression dead serious.

He grinned and urged them to hurry.

While his daughters moved their folding pink chairs with their favorite princesses on them to sit with their friend, he looked around for Callie, but didn't see her anywhere. "Have you seen Callie?" he asked Aunt Poppy when she came over to sit. People were still milling around, getting their chairs situated or placing blankets on the grass.

Poppy shook her head and glanced in all directions. "Not since she said she'd go back to my car to get my hat. Maybe she ran into someone she knew."

"Maybe," he said. That was one of the reasons he'd asked her to join them. She might have a more positive feeling about Whittler's Creek if she reconnected with the residents. That had been his experience after his dad had passed away. He'd had no desire to stay on in town—the memories of his dad had been almost more than he could bear. Until he was bombarded with people coming to the house with food and condolences, giving him a warm and welcome feeling. He also found the girls doing well in the pleasant atmosphere, and that's when he decided to stick around.

"I'll walk around and see if I can find her." He checked the time on his cell phone and then put it on vibrate. "We should be starting soon."

Poppy nodded and began a conversation with a woman nearby.

The first thing Tyler did was go to the parking lot since that was where Callie had been headed. Aunt Poppy had parked in the farthest row of the lot. As he got closer to her car, he heard a woman's voice. She sounded angry. *Very* angry.

He couldn't see the person speaking because parked cars were in the way. He assumed a child was being disciplined.

"Who do you think you are?" The woman's tone was harsh.

A quieter voice answered but he couldn't hear the reply clearly.

"I said, don't get up." The woman spoke louder, as if through clenched teeth.

This was not a parent-and-child situation, or at least he hoped it wasn't. Tyler hurried toward the raging voice. He was shocked to see Callie sitting on the ground. "What's going on here?" he asked.

The angry person turned around and Tyler immediately recognized Callie's stepsister, Wendy. She appeared as unkempt as she'd been Friday night. In fact, she might be wearing the same worn-out clothes.

"You don't need to get in the middle of this, Tyler," Wendy said in a more neutral tone. "This is between the two of us."

He stepped in front of Wendy and held out a hand to Callie to help her up. "How did you end up down there?"

Callie brushed herself off and didn't answer, merely glanced in Wendy's direction.

"Did you push her?" Tyler asked Wendy.

"Of course not." Even her laugh sounded mean. "She must have stumbled. I was just coming over to help her up."

Tyler looked at Callie to gauge her reaction. "Is that true?"

"If that's what Wendy says happened," Callie said calmly, "then it must be true."

Tyler knew there was more going on and he was frustrated when Callie so readily agreed with Wendy's version of events.

Before he could ask more questions, Wendy took off. Not toward the group gathered under the tents but in the direction of the street. He didn't know where she lived, but he made a mental note to find out and to keep an eye on her.

"Are you okay?" he asked Callie. She closed Poppy's car door and brushed off the hat that had also landed on the ground.

"I'm fine." She walked past him, her back straight and her head held high. "Let's join Poppy and the girls."

He had to walk quickly to keep up with her fast pace. "What happened back there?"

"I don't want to talk about it."

"I heard some of the things she said. She sounded really angry."

Callie shook her head. "It's fine. Just forget about it."

"Why?" He reached for her arm and made her stop at the edge of the parking lot. "Why should I forget about it?"

Callie hesitated, looked down at the ground then back up at him. "Because Wendy was being no different than she's always been. She's always hated me and she's happy to remind me every chance she gets."

He thought back to everything he knew about the two girls growing up. "But you just calmly took everything she was dishing out."

"Old habits," she said. "Fighting back only got me into trouble."

"How?"

"I was the one who got punished."

He digested her words. "*You* were punished when Wendy was mean to you?"

Callie's eyes welled up and she blinked several times. "I really can't talk about this right now."

She began walking in earnest and took a seat next to Aunt Poppy just as the young female pastor made some announcements.

When everyone rose to begin the service, Tyler had a difficult time concentrating. He couldn't help wondering how bad Callie's life in Whittler's Creek had really been.

Maybe he needed to call his sister, Isabelle, and hear her side of the story since Isabelle and Wendy had been good friends back when Callie lived in town.

ONCE AGAIN CALLIE felt humiliated thanks to her stepsister. As the service continued, and people sang an upbeat song with the accompaniment of a keyboard and guitar, she was no longer concerned about her lack of knowledge when it came to church services. Wendy's treatment of her was now Callie's main focus.

Before the service ended Callie had decided to take off for Poppy's without eating. She didn't think she could enjoy the afternoon after the run-in with her stepsister. She'd have to walk the mile or so home since she hadn't driven to the church. But she could use the exercise to ease her mental anguish.

She turned to Tyler to tell him her plan when someone tapped her on the shoulder. She turned around, still a little skittish, and was pleasantly surprised to see her friend, Riva.

"I didn't know you'd be here today," Riva said. "I'm so glad to see you." She leaned closer. "Wait until you taste the food. I swear some of the people around here are *the* best cooks."

Callie was about to say she wasn't staying when she found herself surrounded by other people she hadn't seen since she'd left town.

"How long will you be in town?"

"Let's get together for dinner."

Everyone seemed to be talking to her at once. She had no idea that so many of the people she went to high school with were members of this church. She was introduced to their husbands and wives and children, and she had a plate of food and a seat at a picnic table without giving it another thought.

"I'd love to catch up sometime," one of the women said, "but right now I need to eat and run." Her preschooler was making it difficult for her to do anything but chase after him.

Callie smiled. "I understand." She pulled a business card from her purse. "My number's on here. Give me a call and we'll get together."

Several people pulled out their cell phones to take down her number. She'd never been a "popular" kid in school, but from the welcome she was receiving, an outsider might assume she had a million friends in town.

"That was quite a welcome," Tyler said about two hours later as they helped with the cleanup.

Callie couldn't help but smile. "It was, wasn't it? I was pretty surprised at how many people remembered me."

"It's a small town. Everyone knows everyone. At least, that's what I discovered when I moved back."

She thought about his comment while tying a full garbage bag and replacing it in the can with a new one. "I guess as a kid I didn't see the town as being friendly. We didn't go to church or socialize with anyone, so my experience was probably completely different than yours."

"True." He took the full garbage bag from her and they walked to the Dumpster. She carried one bag and he had two. "My dad was a member of the American Legion and was also my Boy Scout leader, so we knew a lot of people from those events, as well as from running the hardware store. And my mom was a leader when Isabelle was in Girl Scouts and we were all active in the church."

The mention of Tyler's sister made Callie remember the parking lot incident. "So what's Isabelle doing these days? Is she still living in town? I haven't seen her since I've been back." Callie was trying to be polite but she only cared because she didn't want to run into her.

They threw the garbage bags into the large bin, the lid slamming shut with a loud thud.

"No, she's west of Baltimore. She was engaged and they broke up, so now she's dating some guy she met on one of those online dating services. I haven't met him yet, but she seems pretty happy."

"That's nice."

His head turned in her direction. "That wasn't very sincere."

Callie shrugged. She didn't want to tell him that his sister had been one of the people who'd taken Wendy's side against her. "I'm glad Isabelle is happy."

"Still not selling it. I take it you're not a fan of Isabelle's? I know she and your sister—stepsister—hung out as kids."

"Let's leave the past where it belongs."

They were nearly back to the picnic area when he said, "Someday you'll tell me what really happened back then."

Callie doubted it. She wasn't even forthcoming with her therapist. Which reminded her that she should think about what her therapist would want to hear about her visit with her dad.

Anxious to change the subject, she asked, "Where are the girls?" Callie looked around but didn't see them.

"They went home with their friend, Brittany. She's an only child, six like Alexis, and her mother loves having both of my girls over to play. Brittany and Alexis will be in the same first-grade class next month."

"That's nice for them. Do they live near Poppy's?"

He shook his head. "No, but they live on the same street as our new house."

Poppy waved to them as they got close to the parking lot and said, "I'm taking off. I have my dishes, but you'll need to get the chairs."

Tyler nodded and went in the direction of the chairs, leaving Callie astonished at the good time she'd had this morning. She still couldn't get over how many people remembered her and had gone out of their way to be friendly. She had a lunch date and dinner plans with two different people, while several others promised to call to set up something. She'd even been invited to sub for Bunco Friday night, which she said she'd think about.

They loaded the chairs into Tyler's truck and the two of them drove back to Poppy's.

"Have you figured out where I can work on those financial records?" Callie asked.

"Not yet. That's my project for this afternoon. Once I figure it out, then I'll have the banker's boxes moved there."

Callie checked the time on the dash and saw it was only midafternoon. "Sounds like a plan. Let me know if you need any help."

Callie needed to check her work email. It had been two days since she'd opened her laptop because she'd been so preoccupied with what was going on around her.

She smiled. Especially with Tyler.

AFTER GETTING THE chairs unloaded and put away, Callie went upstairs and Tyler headed out in his truck for the police station to find an office space for Callie.

There wasn't a large enough room in the small building that would accommodate Callie and all the boxes that were involved.

Then he remembered the Lincoln Hotel. After listening to Aunt Poppy's unhappy account of her argument with Gino last night, he knew that Gino was restoring the building. If work hadn't begun yet, using a space in there might be a possibility. Callie would only need a week or two at the most.

And if Gino agreed, he might make points with Aunt Poppy.

When Tyler pulled up to the house, he'd hoped to speak to Gino, but his car wasn't out front. He made a U-turn and went back into town, thinking he'd find Gino at the hotel.

Sure enough he located the man's car in the

small parking lot behind the old building. Tyler parked his truck and went around to the front door of the hotel, which was locked. He knocked loudly, hoping Gino could hear him. No answer. He knocked again and then he heard movement right inside the door.

The lock clicked open and the large wooden door opened. Gino's eyes widened and he smiled, but not as heartily as he normally did. "Come in, Ty, come in." The older man held the door open wide for him and then locked it again when Tyler was inside.

The two men shook hands and Gino spread his arms. "So, what do you think? Can this old building become grand again?"

Tyler nodded as he looked around at the lobby that had been used hard by groups over the years. "It'll be a lot of work, but I definitely think it's worthwhile." There were bulletin boards and posters half-torn down on the walls where plaster was either cracking or coming off completely. Beyond that, Tyler saw the intricate woodwork, the oak floors that needed refinishing and all the other bits of personality that would require some loving care.

They spoke for a few minutes about Gino's plans for the building before he said, "I suppose you're here to tell me you're taking Poppy's side and that I shouldn't have bought the property."

"Actually, no. I'm here for a different reason, although I'm not happy that you've hurt Aunt Poppy."

Gino nodded vigorously. "I know, I know. But you have to believe me that I had no idea that she was planning to go from boardinghouse to B and B."

"I think that was always her plan," Tyler said. "She just didn't want so many strangers coming in and out of the house while the girls live there. Give her some time and she'll come around. Maybe the two of you can somehow collaborate and make things work for both of you."

Gino seemed to consider the idea.

"Anyway," Tyler continued, "I think I might have a way for you to make points with Aunt Poppy."

Gino's eyebrows rose. "Go on."

"I need a work space for Callie to go through financial records and wondered if you might have room here. The police station is already way too cramped."

Gino looked around the lobby. "Come with me. I have the perfect spot." He led Tyler down a long hallway, past restrooms and other doorways. He stopped at a large room at the end of the hall. "Would this work?"

There were no lights on since the electricity was probably turned off, but some natural light came through the large windows. Tyler could see the room would be more than adequate for Callie's needs.

"This would be perfect. What about construction? Will Callie be in the way if she's working in here?"

Gino shook his head. "I'm still getting permits and working with an architect. Anyway, we're only talking a few days or weeks, right?"

Tyler nodded. "I hope it won't be more than two weeks tops."

"Then the room's all yours."

"Electricity?"

"Supposed to be turned on by tomorrow. This room gets plenty of light from the windows, but I can't guarantee that'll be enough light."

"We can work around that." Tyler hesitated. "How much?" He had no idea where he'd find money in the budget, but this work needed to be done, and the person responsible—if there was a problem—held accountable.

Gino put his hand out. "No charge." The men shook hands and Gino added, "Better chance of making points with Poppy if I don't charge her nephew."

The two men went over specific details and Gino gave Tyler a key to the front door.

"I'll move the boxes over in the morning," Tyler told him.

When he left, he felt like he'd accomplished something and almost dreaded the next thing he needed to do.

Call his sister, Isabelle.

It wasn't that he didn't want to talk to her. They spoke every few weeks or so.

He was more worried about what she might tell him about Callie and her stepsister. If he trusted what Isabelle had told him when they were teenagers, back when he'd had a crush on Callie, then Callie had a bad temper and was mean to Wendy.

But if he believed what he'd witnessed since Callie returned to town, he'd guess his sister hadn't told him the whole truth.

He pulled into his parking space at the police station and walked in the front door of the building. Making the call from his office would be more private than making it at Aunt Poppy's. The last thing he wanted was Callie overhearing him talking about her.

He waved to the officer, reading a book at Donna's desk, who was covering the phone that rarely rang. Then Tyler unlocked his office door and turned on the lights. Before he called Isabelle, he checked his email then wrote an email to his staff asking for help moving the financial records from the storage space to the Lincoln.

Finally he pulled his cell phone from his pocket and called his sister.

"Hi, Izzy," he said when she answered.

"Hey, Ty," she responded. "What's up?"

"Why does something have to be up for me to call you?"

She harrumphed dramatically. "Because I'm usually the one who calls you."

He chuckled. "You're right. I'll try to do better." He paused. "So what's going on with you?" He'd do the chitchat thing before getting into the real reason he called since she was already suspicious.

"Not much. Work is busy, so I don't have much free time. I'm hiring a new assistant manager and several of my servers left for college." Isabelle managed a chain restaurant.

"What about that guy you met online?"

"Oh, Barry and I have been talking a lot. At least by email and text."

"No phone calls?"

"No. We never seem to be free to talk at the same time. You know how my hours are at the restaurant."

"And remind me what Barry does."

"He's a firefighter. So his hours are crazy, too."

"Doesn't he have days off at a time?" Something wasn't sounding right about this Barry.

"True. But they never coincide with mine. Besides, his schedule is always getting changed. You know, people taking time off and needing to switch. He's just a really nice guy who says yes."

Again, warning bells went off in Tyler's head, but he decided to keep his suspicions to himself. For now. Maybe Barry really was the perfect guy Isabelle thought he was.

"What about you? What have you been up to and how are my nieces?"

"The girls are good. You should come down to visit before school starts."

"I can't believe Alexis is going into first grade already."

"I know. Time flies."

"You're still at Aunt Poppy's?"

"We are. My house is coming along slowly." He needed to get to the reason he called. "Speaking of Aunt Poppy, a new tenant moved in last week. Callie James."

"Oh." A less than enthusiastic response. "Why is she back in town?"

He didn't want to betray Callie's confidence by telling his sister what he knew, but he didn't want to lie, either. "She's taking care of some family stuff." Not a lie, just not the whole truth. "I doubt she'll be here more than a few weeks."

"Family stuff, huh? That family will need more than a few weeks to straighten itself out."

She'd piqued his interest. "How's that?"

"They're just all pretty screwed up from what I've seen."

"That's right. You and Callie's stepsister hung

around in high school. Do you still keep in touch with Wendy?"

"I haven't spoken to her since I left for college. I heard through other friends that she went a semester to community college and then dropped out when she got pregnant."

"She has a kid?" Where had the child been every time he'd run into her?

"I guess so."

"Is she married?"

"From what I've heard, her marriage has been rocky. He's got an alcohol problem and maybe drugs, too. But that's just what I've heard from other people."

"Are they living in Whittler's Creek? There haven't been any incidents involving Wendy's husband since I've been on the force."

"I think they're living right there in town." Isabelle paused. "Why are you so interested in Wendy?"

He decided to be honest. "Because I've run into her several times over the past week and she's been downright nasty to Callie. Didn't you tell me Callie was the one with the temper?"

"That's what Wendy told me. She'd go on and on about how Callie would scream at Wendy's mother and belittle Wendy. So I always kept my distance. I didn't want Callie turning on me, too."

"So Callie had a bad temper. Did you ever witness it?"

"Honestly, no. I only heard about it from Wendy. Why? Has she done something? Did she do or say something to the girls?"

"No, no. Nothing like that. I'm just curious. Callie's been extra calm around Wendy and I'm trying to wrap my head around it. Even when Wendy has been downright rude and aggressive to her, she's kept her cool. I've seen no sign of this supposed temper."

"Maybe Callie has grown up and learned to control her temper," Isabelle suggested.

"Maybe." But he didn't quite believe it. "Can you think of any reason why Wendy might have lied about Callie's temper?"

Isabelle didn't say anything at first. "No."

Now that he'd spoken to his sister, Tyler was more confused than ever.

CHAPTER TEN

MONDAY MORNING CALLIE rose early and was surprised by her good mood. She was actually looking forward to the day. That feeling was a first in the week since she'd returned to Whittler's Creek.

Last night, Tyler had told her about the space at the Lincoln Hotel that he found for her to go through the financial records. She couldn't wait to get started. She loved a challenge.

"I'd give you a ride this morning," Tyler said when they ran into each other in the kitchen a little while later. "But I don't want to strand you at the hotel if I get called somewhere."

"That's okay. I don't mind getting myself there. There's parking in the back, you said?"

He nodded. "I've got the boxes being moved there this morning, so I'll go unlock the building. After they're all moved, I'll give you the key to hold on to so you can come and go as you need to."

"Sounds like a plan." She helped herself to coffee. "Oh, one other thing. Can you forward me the email you received about the embezzlement?" She pulled out a business card she'd stuck in her jeans' pocket and took a pen from the container on the counter. She wrote her personal email address on the back and held it out to him. "I won't bother taking my laptop. I can do everything from my phone. I'd love to see specifics, if the person provided any."

"I'll do that as soon as I get to the office." He took the card from her and put it in his wallet.

She felt a spark when their fingers touched and she couldn't help being disappointed that Tyler hadn't made any more mention of that short-term affair they'd talked about having. She understood about him dealing with Poppy and then his daughters, but why hadn't he even hinted at it since?

"Where are the girls?" she asked instead of the question burning her tongue.

"They're outside already, riding their bikes on the sidewalk. Aunt Poppy's with them, enjoying her coffee on the front porch." He looked over at the clock on the stove. "I better get going."

Callie nodded. "Okay, then. I'll see you soon."

She watched him walk out the door in his uniform, her body heating, and she wondered why men in uniform had never affected her quite like this before.

Maybe it was because he was more than just a man in uniform. He had a warm and giving soul, a great personality, and he was a pretty terrific kisser.

She grew warmer as she remembered his mouth on hers. She had to blink several times to clear her head. She had no time for thoughts like that today. She had work to do.

About an hour later she parked next to Tyler's truck in the Lincoln Hotel's parking lot. She'd passed a van parked at the front door. The vehicle had a Whittler's Creek logo on the door and had probably been used to transport the files to the hotel.

She'd visited the hotel once as a teenager to attend a sixteenth birthday party in the lobby. She remembered it had been catered and there had even been a DJ. The birthday girl's parents had gone all-out.

Unlike any of Callie's birthdays, which had usually passed as normal days. Her dad would either be on a long-haul trip or he'd forgotten her birthday altogether. The most recognition she'd gotten were more chores from her stepmother and bruising punches in the arm from her stepsister.

Callie straightened. That was the past. She didn't allow herself to be hurt physically or emotionally anymore.

Tyler strode down the hall toward her, a welcoming smile on his face. "Come with me. I'll show you to your new digs."

She followed him down the hallway and into what appeared to be a small conference room.

"This is perfect," she said and then looked to the wall for a light switch. She flipped it with no result.

"Gino said the electricity should be on this morning." Tyler pointed to the windows. "It's pretty sunny right now. But if that's not enough light to work, then you can come back when the power's on."

Callie shook her head. "No, I'm anxious to get started. I can get organized and see what we've got." She glanced at the half dozen or so boxes piled by the wall. There was a scratched conference table and some sad-looking rolling arm chairs. Nothing like her ergonomic leather chair, glass-and-metal desk, and the park view she had in her office back home. But she could make do here. She was up for the task.

"Then I'll leave you to all this," he said, gesturing to the boxes and the room, "and I'll get to work." He turned to go but then spun around to face her. "I could pick you up a sandwich for lunch."

"Is that your sneaky way of checking up on me?" She couldn't help teasing him.

"Hey, if you don't want me to bring lunch, just say so." He grinned. "Maybe your question is your way of saying you'd rather not have lunch with me."

She made a goofy face at him and then their

gazes locked. She took the few steps to the doorway where he stood. She stopped before their bodies touched but close enough that she felt the heat coming off him. There was also that distinct physical pull, like a magnet to metal. She put a finger to his lips. "That's not at all what I was saying. I'd love a sandwich." She ran her finger over his lips, down his chin and neck until she reached his breastbone. "So where are you going?"

She almost laughed aloud at his look of confusion.

"I'm going to work," he said.

Then she did laugh, enjoying the sexual power she had over him. "I meant, where are you going to pick up lunch so I can tell you what I want to eat?"

He didn't answer. His arms were around her and she was plastered against his body before she could register what was happening. Then he kissed her with abandon.

Exactly what she'd been hoping he'd do all along.

TYLER NEVER MADE it back to the hotel for lunch.

Instead his admin assistant, Donna, delivered Callie's requested sandwich.

"Here's your tuna wrap," Donna said as she came into the conference room, making Callie aware of the mess she'd created with the files.

"The Chief said he's sorry he couldn't bring it himself. He and the boys got called to a domestic disturbance." Donna set a paper bag in front of Callie, careful not to place it on any files.

"I completely understand." That was true but it didn't mean Callie wasn't disappointed. "They all had to go?"

Donna nodded. "Except for Jim—Officer Franklin. He stayed behind in case something else came up. He's also covering the phones while I take lunch." She stopped to take a breath. "This is the third time they've been called to this particular address and last time there were weapons involved. It could be pretty serious."

Callie was reminded of how dangerous Tyler's job could be. "And Tyler—Chief Garrett—felt the need to be there himself." A statement not a question.

"Exactly." Donna surveyed the room. She appeared to be in her midthirties or close to forty. She had a few stray grays in her dark brown hair that she'd pulled back into a low ponytail. She wore dark-rimmed glasses that framed her huge brown eyes.

"So you're going over those files that were moved in and out of the Chief's office?" Donna hitched up her black pants and checked the tuck of her white button-down shirt.

"I am." Callie hadn't expected Donna would

hang around, but she appeared to not be in any hurry to leave. "Would you like to sit down?"

Donna hesitated, as if deciding. "Sure," she finally said, rolling a chair out from under the table and taking a seat. She stopped suddenly and looked at Callie. "Unless you'd rather I leave?"

"Oh, no, sit. Keep me company. Have you eaten yet?"

She nodded. "I did. I brought my lunch from home, so I ate before picking up yours."

"That was very nice of you. Thank you." Callie reached for her purse. "How much do I owe you?"

Donna held up a hand. "No need. The Chief took care of it."

Callie left her purse where it was. "I guess I'll have to take it up with him."

"Go ahead and eat." Donna pointed to the bag of food.

"Are you sure you don't mind?"

"Not at all." She patted her stomach where her white shirt pulled at the buttons. "I'm stuffed. I brought some leftovers to heat up and ate too much."

Callie laughed as she unwrapped her food. "I need to make sure I don't do the same thing. This wrap is huge!"

"The portion size at the new deli is certainly generous," Donna said and then changed subjects. "So you used to live here?"

Callie had the distinct feeling during their mundane conversation that Donna had been looking for an opening to get information on Callie.

"Yes, born and raised. I left when I went to college and now I'm living and working near the Maryland side of the DC beltway. What about you?"

"I moved here almost five years ago. I can't believe it's been that long already."

The fluorescent lights in the ceiling suddenly came on. "Oh, good! We finally have electricity." At Donna's questioning expression, she added, "It's been turned off until now—the new owner had to get it turned back on. It's not as warm as I'd expected in here because of the high ceilings, and the sun coming in the windows has made it light enough to work in here. But using the ladies' room with no windows was tricky with just the flashlight on my phone."

The two women laughed and Callie relaxed a little. "So what brought you to Whittler's Creek?" She took a bite of her wrap.

"Actually it was a friend of your sister's suggestion."

Callie nearly choked on her food. "My stepsister? You know Wendy?" Callie's guard was back up.

"Not until after I moved here. We met through a mutual friend who raved about how nice this town was. She even gave me a heads-up about the job opening as assistant to the Chief of Police when I was looking for a fresh start. As for your stepsister, I've seen her in passing, but we really haven't talked in a while. How's she doing?"

Talking about Wendy made it impossible for Callie to eat. She set her sandwich on the wax paper it had been wrapped in. "I haven't seen her much since I've been back. I guess she's okay." She pulled a bottle of water from her things and took a long drink.

"So you're not close?"

Callie was hesitant to continue the conversation about Wendy because she wasn't sure how close Donna and Wendy might actually be. She wouldn't put it past Wendy to have Donna interrogate her.

"You said you haven't been in touch with Wendy in quite a while?" At Donna's nod, Callie asked, "She seems down on her luck." Callie wondered how Wendy had fallen so far that she needed free food.

Donna leaned closer and lowered her voice, even though they were the only two in the room. "I only know what I've heard, but supposedly she and her husband have been having problems. He's got alcohol and drug issues and he also lost his job a while back. But I don't know how much of that is true."

"What about Wendy? Is she working?"

Donna shrugged. "I really don't know. The last I talked to her, she was applying for jobs after getting laid off at the cheese factory. But that was quite a while ago. Maybe even a year or more."

"So you've worked for Tyler since he took over as Chief of Police?" Callie needed to steer the conversation away from Wendy.

Donna nodded. "That's right. I worked for his predecessor before that. The Chief was nice to let me stay on."

"I'm sure it's because you're good at what you do." Callie tried taking another bite of her sandwich.

"I hope so. I really like my job." Donna looked at her watch. "Oh! I need to go. Officer Franklin is waiting for me to get back with his lunch. He's probably starving." She rose from her chair so quickly that it rolled backward a foot or so.

"It was nice talking to you," Callie said.

Donna hesitated at the doorway. "Same here." She sounded surprised, making Callie wonder what horrible things Donna had heard about Callie from Wendy. Interacting with people in this town was like walking through a minefield. Callie never knew who'd heard Wendy's lies.

TYLER RETURNED TO his office midafternoon, ready to go home for the day, but he knew he still had things that needed to be done.

"Everything work out okay?" Donna asked as he came by her desk.

He ran his hands through his hair. "Yeah. After we got Mr. Dalton to let Mrs. Dalton come out of the house, we arrested him without incident. He's at county lockup. It always takes forever to get someone processed there."

Donna nodded.

"You got lunch for Callie?" he asked, knowing Donna would do anything he asked of her. He was actually more interested in whether Callie was disappointed that he couldn't have lunch with her. He just didn't want to come right out and ask.

"I did. She seems nicer than I expected."

Odd thing for Donna to say. "She is." He paused. "Why did you expect her to not be nice?"

"Oh, you know. Things her sister told me about how nasty she can be."

"Really? I didn't know you knew Wendy." He hadn't seen even a hint of nastiness in the past week. Even when Callie had wine poured on her or when her stepsister had pushed her to the ground and belittled her. "What kind of things?"

Donna's eyes widened. She was probably surprised he'd want details. "I shouldn't be gossiping."

"This isn't gossiping. It's telling me what kind of things Wendy has said about Callie. You know she's under my supervision—which is confidential, by the way—so I should know what I'm dealing with."

"I wouldn't share anything I know with anyone outside this office, Chief." Her voice trembled with emotion.

"And that's why I trust you implicitly. Now, what has Wendy said about Callie?"

Donna hesitated, her gaze going to the ceiling as if trying to remember. "She would say things like how Callie would yell at her for no reason and tell lies about her to Wendy's friends. Things like that. Oh, and she'd get Wendy into trouble with her teachers, too."

Tyler nodded. "Anything else?"

"Just how Callie treated Wendy's mother."

"And how was that?" He recalled the night he'd witnessed the two of them arguing and how Callie had told him things weren't always as they seemed.

"Callie would yell and throw things at her. Wendy made Callie seem like an unstable and dangerous person to be around." Donna paused. "Not at all the impression I got of her today."

Not Tyler's impression, either.

"Thanks, Donna. If you think of anything else Wendy told you, let me know."

The phone rang and Donna needed to answer it, so Tyler headed to his office to do the paperwork on the domestic disturbance. He needed to confront Callie about what Donna had said about her, but he was conflicted. On one hand, he needed the truth for the sake of his daughters' safety. On the other hand, things were going well with him and Callie and he didn't want to ruin that by bringing up her past.

It was after five when he finally finished up for the day. He headed over to the Lincoln Hotel to see how Callie was doing. There were workmen leaving the building as he came in.

He stood in the doorway a few seconds, watching Callie as she concentrated on some papers. "Making any progress?"

Her head jerked in his direction, as if he'd surprised her. Then her expression softened into a smile. "If you call making a mess progress, then, yes."

He stepped into the room. "This all makes sense to you?" The pages of numbers and words were just that to him.

She grinned. "This is my life. Making sense of numbers." She straightened a pile of folders. "I like how numbers can tell a story."

"A story?"

"Yes. Here, let me show you." She picked up a file and opened it. "This is a record of the city employees and their salaries. By the way, these should really be computerized."

"I know. Budget issues. Tell me more about this story."

"Okay." She looked down the list. "This tells us not only who was working for the town, but what their jobs were and how much they were paid for doing those jobs during that time period. Then, if we compare this list to the one from previous years, it will tell who was hired, fired or retired, as well as if there were new positions created or any that were no longer needed." She looked up at him. "To me, that makes quite a story."

He grinned, enjoying her enthusiasm. "If you say so. I prefer my stories with some sex and violence."

They both laughed.

He became serious, knowing he had to broach a sensitive subject. "I need to talk to you about something. I've been hearing things. About you."

"About me?" Her eyes widened.

He nodded. "I'm not saying I automatically believe everything I've heard, but I think you should know what's being said."

She visibly swallowed. "Go on."

He stumbled over his question. "Did you mistreat your stepsister when you were growing up?"

Callie glared at him, obviously fighting to keep control of her emotions. "Did *I* mistreat *her*? You're kidding, right?"

"Bullying isn't a subject I'd kid about. You hitting Wendy and yelling at her seems to be the consensus according to a couple of people who've known both of you."

Callie rose from her chair and walked to the other side of the conference room. She faced him, not saying a word.

"I'm just repeating what I've heard."

"What do you want me to say, Tyler? Do you really think I'm guilty of bullying?"

"Of course not." He shook his head. "I don't know what I want you to say. Maybe I just need you to deny the allegations."

Her shoulders slumped. "I thought we knew each other better than that. You should already know the answer." She paused. "Even if I tell you the truth, will you believe me?"

He blinked. "Of course I will. Why would you ask that?"

"Because that's how I ended up back in town. My ex-boyfriend didn't believe me when I said I didn't break his stupid vase. And now you're here wondering if I bullied my stepsister. How do I know that you'll trust that I'm telling the truth?"

"By looking in my eyes."

She did just that. The glassy appearance of her eyes spoke volumes about her emotional reaction to their conversation. She finally spoke, clearly and succinctly. "I have never bullied Wendy or anyone else."

He took a step in her direction and she put up her hand to stop him.

"Callie. Please don't be angry. I told you I didn't believe what people were telling me, but I needed you to know the rumors were out there." He paused. "If I believed one word of it, I wouldn't allow you to be within fifty feet of my daughters."

She had to know he was speaking the truth. His daughters were precious to him and he'd never put them in harm's way.

"Who's been spreading these lies about me?" she asked, wiping at a single tear that had escaped.

"That's not important. The next time I hear something like that, I'll make sure I let people know they should check their facts."

"Is Wendy one of the people who spoke to you?"

He shook his head. "No. Just a few people who knew both of you when you were kids." He hesitated then decided she deserved to know who was talking about her behind her back. "My sister and my admin, Donna."

Callie nodded. "Wendy has always been persuasive and an outstanding liar, so I'm not surprised, since she knows your sister and Donna. Your sister has never been a fan of mine."

"I didn't mean to upset you."

"I know," she said quietly. "Sometimes the truth is difficult to hear, especially when it involves lies being told about yourself."

He furrowed his brow. "That's a convoluted way to look at it."

She shrugged. "I should have known that rumors take on a life of their own in this town. Forewarned is forearmed. Isn't that what they say?" She turned her attention back to the conference table, essentially ending the discussion.

She was about to close a file folder when she suddenly quieted and stared at the record.

"What is it? What's wrong?"

She slowly looked at him. "Did you know my stepsister works for the city?"

"Really?" She handed him the evidence and there was Wendy's name. He ran a finger from her name across to her salary. "If she has a job with the city, then why was she taking advantage of free food Friday night?"

Callie nodded. "And why does she look like she's been living on the streets?"

CALLIE LOOKED CLOSER at the file she'd randomly chosen to make her point about numbers, glad for a change in subject. "From what I see here, she was hired a little over a year ago."

"Can you tell if she's still working for the town?" Tyler asked.

Callie shook her head. "No. This is just a list of employees." She skimmed through the file, but there was nothing else related to Wendy's employment. "I'll see what else I find as I go through these files," she said. "I'm finding a lot of them have little or nothing to do with the town's finances." She gestured with the file in her hand. "Like this one. So going through each file is what's taking up most of my time so far."

"Sorry about that. I didn't realize when I asked for financial files that they'd box everything else with it."

"That's okay." She smiled, admiring his erect posture in that darn sexy uniform. "This is *so* much better than cleaning built-up grease on stoves or picking up disgusting trash."

He winced. "Sorry again. I had nothing else for you to do. You should have mentioned your day job sooner."

She shrugged. "I wasn't sure what to expect when I arrived in town, and I didn't want to make waves. If I'd known about the email you received concerning the town's finances, I would have spoken up right away."

"Speaking of the email, did you get it? I forwarded it earlier."

She nodded. "I did. There's not much to it, is there? Just the person claiming that the records needed to be audited because funds had been misappropriated."

"Do you feel you're making progress?"

"I'm only into my second box of files, and so far I haven't seen a problem, but it's a slow process."

A thought came to Callie. "Don't town employees work at City Hall?" At his nod, she continued. "So if Wendy worked for the town, then why didn't you know? Wouldn't you have run into her occasionally while working in the building next door to City Hall?"

"Good question," he replied. "I'm not that familiar with what positions are at City Hall, but I do know there's also an annex where some town employees have offices."

"So she probably works there?"

He nodded. "I have to wonder if she still has a job with the way she's looked recently."

"Me, too." Callie was becoming more and more interested in what was going on with Wendy, even if she didn't want to be.

"I keep hearing bad things about her husband, like he's abusing alcohol and drugs, but nothing's been substantiated."

"I wonder—if she's as hard up as she's appeared—why she hasn't gone to my dad for help."

He nodded. "You said her mother is having health problems, but, yeah, you'd think it would be a given that she'd go to your dad for help since he raised her, too."

"Maybe she did," Callie said. "And maybe he said no. Or maybe he *has* been helping her, but not enough." Her dad hadn't appeared to be financially well-off by the look of their home and furnishings, so maybe he was unable to provide for Wendy at the same time he obviously had medical bills for his wife.

Which made her wonder if he had been able to manage financially even before the medical bills.

"I think I need to see my dad again." She even surprised herself with the idea. "I have questions I need to ask. And not just about Wendy."

"You're concerned about your dad?"

"More about his financial stability than anything else." She paused. "I'm pretty comfortable financially, so if he needs help with medical bills…"

"It's nice that you'd help them out like that."

"I prefer to look at it as helping my dad. Period."

"Whatever. I think it's admirable either way."

"I'm not trying to be," she said honestly. "I just don't want him to suffer financially because of my stepmother. He's worked hard his entire life."

"Is he retired?" Tyler asked.

"I'm not sure. I never asked. He's sixty-eight, so it's probable. I don't know how he could leave my stepmother alone in her present condition otherwise. He was an independent long-haul trucker and is probably living on social security. I doubt he has much saved to supplement his income." She hadn't felt poor growing up, but there was never extra money for luxuries. Especially for Callie.

"You don't think Medicare is covering your stepmother's medical bills?"

"Probably the majority, but he's liable for a percentage of the deductible."

"Don't they own the house they live in?"

She shrugged. "As far as I know. I guess a reverse mortgage is a possibility if they haven't gone that route yet. Or maybe they're carrying a hefty mortgage. I don't know." She straightened the files on the table and turned to Tyler. "These are all good questions that I need to ask. Maybe I'll give my dad a call to see if he's available tonight."

Tyler nodded and reached for her hand. She met his gaze and smiled. He smiled back and asked, "I know I'm totally switching topics here, but are you still interested in that plan we spoke about earlier?"

"Plan?" She widened her eyes to play the innocent. She knew full well what he was talking about. In fact, she thought she'd have to be the one to bring it up.

He grinned even wider. "So you're not interested?"

"I didn't say that."

"Then you'll let me know when you're back from your dad's, so I can come to your room and—"

"And?" She batted her eyes.

He paused. "And hear all about what you learned."

"Oh!" She playfully slapped at his arm.

He laughed aloud. "You are so easy to tease."

She grew serious. "We'll see who can tease better when you come to my room tonight."

He opened his mouth but no words came out. Merely a groan.

CHAPTER ELEVEN

POPPY OPENED THE oven door to check on the progress of her dinner casserole. "Not quite," she said aloud to her empty kitchen and shut the oven door.

Meanwhile she washed the frying pan she'd used to brown the sausage and had the rest of the kitchen cleaned up when she heard the front door open and close. From the conversation she could hear, Tyler and Callie had arrived home simultaneously.

"The girls are in their room playing," Poppy told Tyler when he came into the kitchen. "Did I hear Callie?" She checked the casserole's temperature again and decided it was done.

"You did. She had a phone call to make. She'll be down in a few minutes." He peeked at the casserole covered with foil that Poppy had removed from the oven and set on the stovetop. "Smells great."

Poppy put the cornbread she'd mixed up earlier into the oven. "Dinner will be ready as soon as the timer goes off."

"I'll get cleaned up, and the girls and I will set the table."

Poppy nodded. "I'd appreciate that."

"How are you?" he asked.

She shrugged. "I've been better."

"Have you talked any more to Gino?"

"No." Her answer was sharper than she'd intended. "We have nothing more to say to each other."

"Will he be here for dinner?"

"No idea," she said. "And I don't care one way or the other."

"Yeah, right," Tyler mumbled as he left the kitchen, leaving her no chance to reply.

As if they'd willed him to appear by talking about him, Gino came through the front door. She'd recognize the sound of his walk anywhere. He was heavy-footed and couldn't tread lightly if he tried.

She pursed her lips, reminding herself that she was angry with him. He'd betrayed her by becoming her competitor. Unless he stopped working on the Lincoln Hotel, she had no time for him. She busied herself by getting out plates for dinner.

"Hi," he said when he entered the kitchen.

"Hello." She replied stiffly without turning around. She opened the silverware drawer and counted out the necessary utensils. "You're staying for dinner?"

"If that's okay." He remained in the doorway.

She shrugged, pretending not to care. "You pay for your room and meals come with it."

"Smells great." He stepped closer to her. "Poppy?"

She turned to face him. "What?"

"I hate that we're not speaking." Even in work clothes—jeans and a T-shirt—he looked good. Better than good.

She decided to act flippant. "What do you call what we've been doing just now?"

He scowled. "I mean really talk about what's going on with us."

"I don't have anything more to say. You've made your decision and I'm the one who's left hurting."

He took a step closer and her heart sped up.

She raised her hand to stop him. "Stay back."

"We have to talk."

"What else is there to say?"

He hesitated. "First of all, I'm sorry."

She didn't respond. A simple apology wasn't what she was looking for.

He continued. "I had no idea what you had in mind for your house."

She opened her mouth to answer but this time he was the one who held up a hand to stop her from speaking. "I know, it's completely my fault. I didn't pay close enough attention to what you were saying."

"Thank you for acknowledging that you didn't listen to me, but it doesn't change the fact that you're going to be taking away my business." Her demeanor was ready to crack but she held it together.

"I've been thinking about that, and I have a question for you. Why are you interested in running a B and B? Is it the money?"

She was about to answer when he continued speaking.

"If it's the money, I can help you out. You don't need to run a business to pay your bills."

She stared at him in shock. "You really haven't been listening to me, have you?" She turned away so he wouldn't see her eyes welling up. "I don't need the money. That's not why I decided to do it."

Before she could say more she heard Tyler and his girls coming downstairs. "I can't get into this now."

Gino reached for her. "Can we talk later?"

She pulled away, unable to allow his touch when he so obviously didn't understand where she was coming from.

Soon Callie joined them, too. The table was set, glasses were filled and the timer for the cornbread went off. With everyone at the table talking about their day, there was no need for Poppy and Gino to say another word to each other.

She tried to ignore him at the other end of the

table, but it was harder than she'd anticipated. At one point she glanced at him and their eyes met. He smiled at her—that smile that got to her every time. She guarded her feelings, looking away without acknowledging him.

"Did you arrange a time to see your dad?" Tyler asked Callie.

She nodded. "He couldn't do tonight, but he invited me for dinner tomorrow night."

"That'll be nice," Poppy said. "I'm glad you're spending time together."

Poppy caught the look between Tyler and Callie but she didn't want to ask what was going on in the midst of dinner.

When dinner was over, Tyler and the girls offered to do the cleanup, leaving her time to hear what Gino had to say.

Before discovering his plan for the Lincoln, Poppy would have welcomed the time alone with him. Now she wanted nothing to do with him.

At least that's what her mind kept telling her. She refused to hear what her heart had to say.

CALLIE CLOSED HER laptop and sat back on the love seat in her room. After dinner she'd come up to change into shorts and a T-shirt before checking her work email. She ended up doing some research online regarding a clothing company whose owner recently passed away. She suspected a competitor would buy the company, which could either be a good or bad thing for investors looking for a quick return.

A quiet knock on her door had her checking the time. It was close to ten. She hadn't realized she'd been working so long. She rose to let Tyler in and smiled when she saw him.

"Hi," she whispered, her voice sounding a little rough after not speaking for a few hours. The sight of him and his broad shoulders and sexy mouth made work and everything else slip from her brain. They were replaced by thoughts of being naked with him.

He grinned. "Hi, yourself." He held two bottles of beer, one in each hand. He put them both in one hand and pulled a bottle opener from his back pocket. He popped the top of one bottle before handing it to her.

She took it, loving the slight spark of electricity when their fingers touched. "I love a man who brings presents. Especially alcoholic ones." She stepped back so he could enter her room completely and she shut the door behind him.

"I didn't know if you'd be up for company." He opened the top of his own bottle and pocketed the opener and both bottle caps.

"I got caught up in work and didn't realize how late it was getting." She took a long swallow of the cold liquid, loving the cooling effect it had on her throat.

"I've been reading with the girls and trying to get them settled down enough to go to sleep."

Callie grinned. "I'm sure you instigated something that got them riled up in the first place. I've seen you in action."

He shrugged, his complexion darkening slightly at being caught. "I might have done something to set them off…perhaps reading in a British accent."

Callie's eyes widened. "You're so talented. Do you do other accents?"

"Let's put it this way," he said after taking a long swallow of beer. "Accents and voices are for my daughters only. I'm not a public performer by any means."

She gestured to her room. "This seems as un-public-like as possible."

"Un-public-like?" He grinned. "Is that even a word?"

"You're changing the subject." She raised her eyebrows and pursed her lips. "Maybe I need to do some eavesdropping when you're reading with your daughters." She pointed to the love seat. "Want to sit?"

He followed her and said, "I guess I'll need to watch out now to make sure I'm not overheard."

They both laughed as they got comfortable on the love seat, each turning to face the other.

Callie set her bottle down on the end table and looked at Tyler, who was looking back at her. "What?" He looked like he wanted to say something.

He put his bottle on the floor next to him since there wasn't a table nearby.

"You've changed your mind," she said before he could speak and before she could edit herself. "You think it's a bad idea for us to go through with this plan of ours."

He chuckled. "Not even close."

"Then what is it? I can tell you want to say something." She wiggled in her seat a little, hoping he was telling the truth about not changing his mind. If he jumped on top of her right this minute, he still wouldn't be fast enough.

"You're right. I do." He ran a hand through his hair. "I want to make sure you're okay with this 'arrangement' we've talked about." He halfheartedly used air quotes to make his point.

"You mean sex with no strings?" She decided one of them had to be frank and he seemed to be skirting the issue.

His eyes widened and he grinned. "Yeah, that's the one." He squirmed slightly in his seat, changing positions to put one foot on the opposite knee.

"So you're backing out?" She didn't think so, but she wanted everything out on the table. Or on the bed, on the floor, against the wall...

"No! Not at all." He ran his fingers through his short hair. "I just don't want you to have any regrets."

How could she regret being with him? She'd been attracted to him since they were teenagers. Now she was practically drooling at the mere thought of it. "Are you saying you won't live up to my expectations?" she teased. If she had wanted to draw on any insecurity he might have, she could have recited a list of any number of factors that might make their experience less than ideal. His reaction to her question was humorous enough.

His eyes widened and his jaw dropped momentarily before he could process her words. "Is that a dare? I'll show you how I can meet and exceed your expectations." His words were nearly a growl as he pounced on her, his mouth covering hers while he pulled her across the cushion to sit on his lap. He deepened the kiss and, just like the other times he'd kissed her, she was overcome by the heat they produced in her. Enough to cause her core to flare into a full-out firestorm and make her toes curl.

She ran her fingers through his thick hair. Then she grasped his head so he couldn't do anything but continue his erotic assault on her mouth.

She heard a moan but she wasn't sure which one of them produced it.

She was about to complain when he removed

his mouth from hers until it landed on her sensitive neck where his skill took her to another level of pleasure. This time she was sure she was the one who moaned.

He slowly laid her back so her head rested in the crook of his arm and he lifted the bottom of her T-shirt enough to run his hand over her bare midriff. He raised goose bumps at the same time he heated her insides to a boil.

She was dying for him to move his hand to her breast. So much so that she was tempted to shove his hand in that direction but she didn't. He'd get there eventually, she was sure, and his roving hand at her waistband was more than enough to keep her interested in seeing what came next.

Meeting his gaze, she leisurely ran her hand up his arm, enjoying the strength and solidness of his muscles, until she reached his neck. She lightly touched the shell of his ear and then continued across his slightly bristly cheek to his mouth. His lips suddenly parted and he sucked her index finger partway into his mouth to roll his tongue around it.

She chuckled, craved his mouth on hers, longed for his tongue to parry with hers again.

Turning onto her side, she lifted herself to do just that. She pulled his mouth to hers, and it was as hot and sexy as she'd expected. So intense that she became dizzy with wanting him.

As if reading her mind, she was suddenly floating across the room because Tyler had picked her up without removing his mouth from hers. He carried her easily. As if she weighed no more than a bird.

He placed her on the bed, only disengaging their mouths long enough to whip off the bedspread and reveal the fresh white sheets.

Propped on her elbows, Callie watched as Tyler stripped off his T-shirt and threw it on the love seat. Her eyes followed him to the door. His broad chest with a smattering of hair, his narrow waist and hips where his shorts hung low. Just as she was about to ask where he was going, she heard the click of the lock.

She smiled and he smiled back. "Good idea," she remarked.

Before she could register his movements, he was on top of her and his mouth had seized hers again. Without his shirt, she was able to run her hands over his bare back. She loved the play of his muscles as she touched him, memorizing every inch of him. Even the indentation at the base of his spine when her hand wandered inside his shorts and briefs to his firm butt.

This time he moaned. The sound and vibration, while his face was buried in her neck, made her tremble with need.

His rock-hard erection pressed against her

upper thigh. So close but so far away from where she needed him.

With both hands on his hipbones, she urged him up to release her from beneath him so she could wrap her legs around his upper thighs, enabling her to position her throbbing epicenter against his still-concealed erection.

She rubbed against him ever so slightly.

"You're killing me," he mumbled into her ear before nipping at her lobe.

Before she could respond with more than another slight movement against him, he rose up and drew her T-shirt over her head. Without hesitation, she held his gaze and unhooked her front-closing bra, but kept it in place over her breasts.

He ran his index finger so slowly down her sternum to between her breasts that she thought she'd explode. Centimeter by centimeter, he moved one bra cup to the side to reveal her breast until his finger touched her exposed and highly sensitive nipple. She jerked in response, never wanting the pleasure to end.

With one breast bare, Tyler repeated the torture on her other breast. She braced for the sensation this time but still shuddered slightly when he got to her nipple.

His mouth was on her breast without her needing to beg for it. His large hand grasped her breast so he could suck on her nipple and his tongue did delicious things to it that stirred her throbbing core and intensified her need for release.

Replacing his mouth on her breast with his skillful thumb and forefinger, he explored her chest and abdomen with openmouthed kisses. When he got to her waistband, he removed his hand from her breast to undo her shorts and she nearly cried out from the loss of his touch.

She watched his eyes take in her nakedness as he slowly pulled her shorts down to below her knees to reveal her red boy shorts with the lace trim. She gave a little kick and her denim shorts fell to the floor.

She ran her foot along the back of his calf, the hair on his leg slightly rough against her sole. Feeling the unrelenting need to have his erection press into her again, she wrapped her legs around his butt to hold him in place. She wiggled a little, enjoying the pressure and movement against her sensitive apex. She was so turned on that she could have climaxed with only a few strategic brushes of his penis against her.

But that wasn't going to happen because he apparently had other plans. His hand reached deep inside her underwear, moving immediately to her crotch.

She arched her back when he promptly slid his fingers inside her and began moving in and out rhythmically and doing an even better job of bringing her close to climaxing. She heard herself pant as she came closer and closer to that point of release until she felt a scream build. Before she uttered more than a squeal, Tyler's mouth covered hers.

There was no time to recover completely before Tyler slid down her body and removed her underwear. Then he repeated his ministrations with his very capable mouth. This time she grabbed a nearby pillow to contain her vocal reaction when she climaxed. Which she did in spectacular fashion.

TYLER RESTED HIS face on the inside of Callie's thigh while she came back down after that last orgasm. He kissed the delicate skin on the inside of her upper leg and then stood next to the bed. He couldn't wait any longer to be inside her. His painful hard-on needed release. He pulled a condom from his pocket and stripped off his shorts and briefs in one fell swoop. He kicked them out of his way. At the same time, he fumbled with the foil packet in anticipation of being intimate with this beautiful woman.

Callie scooted up on the bed, tossing her bra out of the way. She was gorgeous, so perfect. The virginal teenage body he'd lusted after all those years ago had become the body of a sensual woman without inhibitions.

He positioned himself over her spread legs and thrust deep inside her. She brought her knees up to her chest and flattened both palms on his butt. She urged him on until this time they both reached the summit together.

He collapsed on her long enough to catch his breath. Then he rolled onto his back, bringing her with him to cradle her head on his shoulder. She placed her hand on his solid abdomen and bent her leg to rest it on his upper thigh, tightly pressing her still-hot and tempting focus of his desire against his hip.

He turned his head in her direction. "Give me a few minutes," he mumbled into her hair. "I'm not done living up to your high expectations."

Her body shook slightly when she giggled.

That was the last thing he remembered until his bladder woke him. The clock on the nightstand said it was almost two. He padded naked to use Callie's bathroom, wondering how prudent it would be to wake her for round two.

She answered the unasked question when he came out of the bathroom to find her snuggled under the sheet. He picked up his shorts, intending to put them on to go down the hall to his own bed so the girls wouldn't wonder where he was when they woke in the morning.

He paused. Maybe he could just lie next to Callie for a few minutes. No, he'd never get up if he got back into her bed. She had a magnetic pull that made it difficult to withdraw.

"Are you going to stand there all night or what?" Callie pulled the sheet back in invitation, giving him an instant hard-on.

He didn't question his next move. He'd brought a second condom for just this situation, and he didn't hesitate to grab it so he could put it to good use.

He climbed into bed and reached for her, but this time she straddled him, taking charge. She slowly and sensually rubbed against his erection, back and forth, back and forth. He grasped her breasts, one in each hand, teasing her hardened nipples with the pads of his thumbs.

She began trembling, so Tyler lifted her hips to slide into her. He groaned at the instant pleasure being inside her produced.

She collapsed onto him, her breasts pressed into his chest. He ran both hands down her shapely back and grabbed her ass, loving the firmness of it as he guided her movements along his insistent shaft until they were both satiated.

A little while later, reluctantly moving a sleeping Callie off him, he got out of bed, pulled on his shorts and gathered his clothes. As he crept quietly down the hall to his room, he couldn't help thinking about how he and Callie had caught Gino sneaking back into his own room after being with Aunt Poppy.

The next morning his phone alarm went off way too early for his liking. As his brain cleared, he remembered it was Tuesday. A workday. Then he recalled why he was so tired. He grinned like a crazy person and looked forward to seeing Callie.

He showered and dressed, whistling as he did so. Something he hadn't done in a very long time. As a single father, enjoying the company of women wasn't something that came easily. And he'd certainly enjoyed Callie's company last night.

Several times.

He grinned, glad he was alone in his bedroom before someone accused him of acting crazy.

Callie's bedroom door was closed. He raised his fist to knock but decided against it. There was no time this morning for what he'd like to do to her.

Practically skipping down the stairs to head to the kitchen, he greeted his daughters and Poppy.

"Aunt Poppy made waffles this morning, Daddy." Madison lifted a bite to show him before stuffing it into her mouth.

"Looks delicious," he remarked. "Did you thank Aunt Poppy?"

He grabbed a plate from the counter and helped himself to a waffle in the warmer.

"There's bacon there, too," Poppy told him from where she sat with the girls at the table.

"Th-thanks," he said to his aunt, becoming tongue-tied when Callie entered the kitchen.

It was as if she were surrounded by an angelic glow. She couldn't be more beautiful at this moment if she tried. Her blond hair flowed down in waves, nearly covering her perfect breasts that he hadn't been able to get enough of a mere few hours ago. Her white-denim skirt was short but still decent, and her formfitting, bubble-gum-pink top matched the hint of lip color she wore.

"Good morning, Callie." His body immediately reacted to her. He needed to take control of his brain and think about something other than jumping her bones.

"Good morning." The edges of her mouth turned up and he saw from the look in her eyes that she was thinking about last night, too.

Thankfully his daughters began chattering to her about breakfast and he just watched, enjoying how the three of them got along.

He ate mindlessly, not even hungry but knowing he needed sustenance to make it to lunchtime. Especially after all the energy he'd expended in Callie's bed.

And as he sat there he decided that lunch with *her* was what he wanted. Her company while they ate, hearing her laugh, watching her tuck her hair behind her ear. He wanted so much more than sex with her.

Their eyes met as she put a bite of food to her mouth. He shot to his feet.

"I have to go." His panic at his sudden revelation was bound to show but he didn't have the words to explain. "Work," he said unnecessarily and put his dishes in the dishwasher.

"O-kay," she said in a questioning tone. Then she paused before slowly adding, "Have a good day."

"Um, you, too." He kissed the girls quickly while Aunt Poppy recited their plan to go to a water park that afternoon. "Have fun today."

As soon as he left the kitchen to head for the front door, he took a deep breath to calm his heart rate.

He had agreed that he and Callie would only have a short-term affair. So now what was he going to do? He hadn't had feelings for a woman since his marriage ended.

And he definitely felt more for Callie than sexual desire.

CHAPTER TWELVE

CALLIE COULDN'T STOP SMILING. Even while driving to the Lincoln Hotel, she found people smiling at her because she was grinning uncontrollably.

All because of Tyler.

Their relationship—she had no other word to describe it—had taken a dramatic turn last night, and she didn't regret it for a moment. She'd had doubts beforehand, but now she was sure making that leap to the next level was definitely the way to go.

And she needed to make sure she kept asking him to prove that he could live up to her high expectations. Her face heated at the memory of him doing just that.

Tremendous disappointment didn't come close to what she felt when she'd woken to him gone, but she certainly understood. His girls weren't the best at sleeping through the night and they'd probably panic if they woke up and he wasn't in his own bed.

When she entered the conference room at the hotel, she immediately got to work on the town's

financial records. As she went along she began to
have questions that needed answers, so she started
a list for Tyler to answer or at least to point Callie
in the right direction to obtain the answers.

She became so engrossed in what she was doing
that it was close to one o'clock when she paused
because of hunger pangs. She hadn't heard from
Tyler, so she decided to text him to see if he'd
eaten or if he wanted her to bring him lunch this
time. She would have liked to surprise him, but
he could be out on a call and the gesture would
be pointless.

His response to her text was:

Thanks for thinking of me. In a meeting, lunch provided. Have a nice dinner with your dad and I'll
see you later. ;-)

Callie hoped that winking emoticon meant what
she thought it meant. Her pulse sped up and she
replied.

Looking forward to it. ;-)

Couldn't be any clearer than that. She needed a
repeat performance of last night and wasn't afraid
to let him know.

She ran across the street to the deli, bought a
salad and brought it back to the hotel to eat while

she continued to work. The afternoon flew by and, if not for Gino popping in and prompting her to check the time, she would have been late for dinner with her dad.

After such a good experience the last time she'd gotten together with him, she was much more relaxed when she rang his doorbell.

"Hi, Dad," she said when he opened the front door. He moved back so she could enter. She gave her dad a hug and glanced around the living room. Her stepmother was nowhere to be seen. "Will Ellen be joining us?" Callie wanted to be prepared.

"No, she's taking a nap. I'll fix her some dinner when she gets up." Her dad ushered her to the kitchen.

"Oh, okay." She had no idea how dinner would taste since her father had rarely cooked when she was growing up. Sometimes he would open a can of soup or scramble an egg, but that had been the extent of his culinary skill.

"This looks great," Callie said, trying not to sound surprised when she saw the lasagna and salad and bread on the small maple kitchen table with mismatched chairs. The table was set with the same inexpensive dishes she remembered, but with even more chips on them now. "When did you learn to cook?"

His color deepened. "I've learned how to make

a few more meals out of necessity because of Ellen's health issues." He lowered his voice as if telling her a secret. "To be honest, I can't take credit for this meal. One of our neighbors made it when she heard you were coming for dinner."

"Oh! How sweet of her. I'm sure it's delicious." She sat at the place her dad pointed to, more confident she'd be eating a palatable meal. "I'm glad you've got at least one good neighbor."

Her dad nodded, fixed two glasses of ice water and took his seat. "It wasn't until Ellen got so bad that the neighbors began coming around to see if we needed anything."

"You didn't know them before that?" They'd lived in this house since Callie was just over a year old. She knew Ellen had kept a tight rein on the family, making excuses for not attending community activities, but Callie never realized her dad hadn't even known the neighbors.

He shook his head. "Not really. Only to wave hello. Ellen didn't like them much, said they weren't very nice to her, so we didn't go out of our way to spend time with them. And I was gone a lot." He cut a portion of lasagna and held it up to put on her plate. "Turns out they're pretty nice, after all."

She offered her plate. "That's good. I'm really glad you have some support." That wasn't a lie.

She suspected her dad had more responsibility than he could handle on his own.

Callie had questions she wanted to ask—questions she'd held on to for so long—but that seemed too serious a subject to broach while eating dinner. Instead she asked, "Does Wendy come by very often?" After all, Ellen was Wendy's mother. Wendy should be taking some responsibility for her. Callie was also interested to know what Wendy's story was. Why was she dressed in dirty and torn clothes and eating free meals at the community center?

Her dad chewed his food slowly as if trying to come up with an answer. Finally he said, "Wendy comes by once in a while. Usually on holidays. I guess the last time was when she stopped by for a few minutes on Mother's Day."

Callie's eyes widened. "Mother's Day? That was three months ago. You mean she doesn't help out with her own mother?" Callie was flabbergasted.

Dad shrugged. "She's got a lot going on what with that boy of hers and her no-good husband, plus a full-time job."

Callie nodded, taking in the information. *Not the first time someone's spoken poorly about Wendy's husband.* "So her husband is having problems?"

There was a noise just outside the kitchen and

suddenly Ellen was in the doorway, gripping a wooden cane. She wore a sleeveless nightgown that had seen better days, and her feet were bare. Her expression was downright ugly, reminding Callie of her childhood.

Raising the cane threateningly, Ellen yelled, "What do you think you're doing, asking about my daughter's husband?" She ran her forearm over her mouth to wipe it. "That's none of your business, you bitch!"

Callie automatically slid her chair back to face Ellen full-on.

Her dad rose from his seat and stepped toward Ellen. "We were just catching up," he told her calmly. "Nothing to be upset about. Why don't I bring you some dinner?"

Ellen screamed, "I don't want any stinkin' food that your whore made. I know you've got a thing for that trashy neighbor."

Callie automatically cowered, feeling like a ten-year-old again.

Ellen continued her rant. "You think I don't know you've been going over there every chance you get?"

"Ellen. You know that's not true."

Her stepmother glared at Callie. "And you! Trying to snare my daughter's husband, are you?" Her lip curled. "Just like you were in high school. Always stealing her boyfriends."

Callie had no idea what Ellen was talking about. She opened her mouth to speak, but no sound came out.

"Nothing to say?" Ellen sneered. "Maybe you need some time alone to come up with a response."

Callie shuddered, memories of her childhood haunting her. She fisted and relaxed her hands several times, keeping herself calm.

She was a grown woman and Ellen was an invalid. There was no way Ellen could hurt her, either with words or actions. She repeated it silently multiple times.

Ellen suddenly took a few awkward steps to the kitchen table. Her dad reached for Ellen, but he was too late. With unbelievable strength in her current condition, she upended the table. Dishes and food went flying onto the floor, splashing on all three of them.

"Ellen! Calm down!" Her dad's volume rose. He reached for Ellen, but she had already moved the few steps to the kitchen sink. She picked up a glass and threw it at her dad, barely missing him.

"I'm going to call for help." Callie took a few steps toward the kitchen doorway. She'd left her purse near the front door. She had no idea if they had a landline and now wasn't the time to ask.

"No!" Her dad's voice stopped her midstep. "Don't call anyone. I can handle her."

"But, Dad—"

"I said no."

His attention was on Callie, his back to Ellen, who reached back and pulled a large knife from the block on the counter. She raised it over her head, her eyes trained on Callie.

Callie's surprised expression must have served as a warning to her dad. As if in slow motion, he turned to see what Ellen was doing. "Look out!" he yelled to Callie, putting an arm out to block the blow. At the last second, Callie lurched to the side to avoid Ellen.

Due to his effort to protect Callie, her dad lost his balance and teetered to his right, grabbing for a chair to keep himself upright.

Meanwhile, Ellen had apparently expended her meager energy and leaned against the counter, using her cane for support.

Callie needed to do something before her stepmother reenergized.

Keeping an eye on Ellen, she told her dad, "We have to get help. I'll be right back." She gasped and froze. "You're hurt!" There was a tear in the short sleeve of his gray shirt and blood was beginning to soak it.

Her dad glanced at the arm and said, "I'm fine, just a glancing blow. Why don't you come back another time and let me handle this."

"There's no way I'm leaving you alone with her."

Ellen turned her head to glare at Callie. Her expression was one Callie was extremely familiar with. One she knew forecast what was to come. Ellen's physical and verbal attack wasn't over. She still held the knife at her side.

"Keep an eye on her and stay back," Callie told her dad while backing into the doorway. "She still has the knife."

"She's going to put it down," her dad said calmly, keeping eye contact with her stepmother. "Aren't you, Ellen?"

Her stepmother sneered and echoed his question in a singsong tone. "Aren't you, Ellen?"

Callie ran to the front door, grabbed her purse and dumped it on the floor to get to her phone. She hurried back to right outside the kitchen while at the same time punching in 9-1-1. She could hear what was going on in the kitchen without her stepmother seeing Callie.

A female dispatcher answered on the second ring. "Nine-one-one, what's your emergency?"

Callie slowed her breathing and kept her voice low. "We need help. My stepmother is having some kind of psychotic episode. She's wielding a knife and she cut my father. Please send help to 438 Oleander Drive."

Callie heard a series of clicks on the line and then the dispatcher spoke again. "Help is on the way. Please stay on the line and tell me what's happening. How bad is your dad's cut? Is he conscious?"

"Yes, he's conscious. He was cut on the upper arm, but I don't know how bad it is. His sleeve was sliced and blood is soaking it." Callie's heart raced. Not a life-and-death injury—yet. "My dad's trying to get my stepmother to give up the knife, but she's not cooperating."

The 9-1-1 operator said, "Can you ask your dad to step back and wait for help to arrive?"

"I tried, but he didn't even want me to call you." She heard yelling in the kitchen. "Please hurry." She peeked around the corner to see her dad and stepmother on opposite sides of the room.

"We have a squad car less than a minute away," the dispatcher told her.

Police. She leaned back against the wall outside the kitchen and prayed that one of Tyler's officers would arrive and not Tyler himself. She didn't want him to observe this unpleasant side of her family. He'd inadvertently witnessed that incident between Callie and her stepmother when they were teenagers. Once was enough.

Just when she was beginning to feel welcomed back into the community, Ellen had to ruin it. As soon as the news got out about tonight, Callie would become a pariah once again.

There was a sudden loud crash, followed by a thud from around the corner in the kitchen. She immediately went on high alert and peered around the corner to see what had happened, berating herself for her concern about what others would think of her.

"Dad!" He was on the floor, facedown, and the toaster was next to his head. Ellen was nowhere to be found, but the kitchen door that led to the backyard was wide open.

Callie ran over to her dad, her phone in one hand, and she checked for a pulse at his neck with the other. His chest expanded and she let out a sigh. He was so still, but alive. Right now he was only unconscious.

"My dad's unconscious but breathing," she told the 911 operator.

"It shouldn't be long now," the woman said calmly.

Sirens screamed as help was on its way "I can hear the ambulance now," she said into the phone.

"It's okay, Daddy," she whispered close to his ear, even though she knew he couldn't hear her. "Help is coming."

TYLER SLAMMED ON his brakes and his truck screeched to a halt in front of the Jameses' house. Driving to Aunt Poppy's for dinner, he'd heard the address come over the radio and recognized it immediately. He also knew Callie was probably still there. So he'd slapped his flashing light on his truck's dashboard and sped to the scene.

The engine barely stopped before he was out of

the vehicle and booking it to the front door. The sirens from an ambulance and a patrol car were getting closer. He couldn't wait for backup. He needed to make sure Callie was okay.

His baton and Taser were secured on his belt and his gun was holstered. He hoped they wouldn't be needed.

He got to the front door and pounded. "Police!" The door opened immediately.

His stomach lurched when he saw Callie.

"You're bleeding," he said.

She shook her head. "Not me. I'm okay." Her quiet words were close to robotic.

"Are you sure?" He wanted to pull her close but now wasn't the time.

She took his hand and quickly pulled him through the house to the kitchen. "It's my dad. Please help him."

The man was facedown on the kitchen floor, a cut in the back of his head that had bled onto his neck and face, as well as the floor. Tyler bent to check the man's pulse. "EMTs are right behind me," he said to Callie over his shoulder. As soon as he got the words out, a shout came from the front door. "Back here," he called to the paramedics then moved out of their way.

"What's the patient's name and age?" one of the paramedics asked Callie.

"Bart—Bartholomew James." She paused as if trying to remember his age. "Sixty-eight."

"Does he take any medications or have any other health issues?"

Callie's eyes widened. "I'm sorry. I don't know anything about his health."

Tyler's officer, Joe Mansfield, trailed behind the EMTs and Tyler guided Callie to him once she'd provided as much information about her dad as possible. "Can you tell us what happened?" he asked her gently, maneuvering her to a living room chair. He knelt next to her, his officer standing close by.

"It was Ellen. My stepmother." Callie paused. "My dad and I were having dinner and she suddenly appeared in the kitchen doorway. She'd been taking a nap, according to my dad." Callie stared at the far wall as she spoke, obviously reliving the incident in her mind. "She was angry. About everything. Dinner. The neighbor. She even thought I was trying to steal Wendy's husband. Nothing she said made sense. I've never even met Wendy's husband."

"Where is she now?" He looked around.

"I think she took off outside. The back door was open when I found my dad unconscious on the floor."

"Can you tell us what she's wearing, what she looks like?"

"She's a few inches shorter than I am, probably five-four, with long gray hair. She was wearing a sleeveless blue nightgown and she was in her bare feet," she said. "And she's probably got her cane." Callie stiffened. "She might still have the knife, too. I don't remember seeing it in the kitchen."

Tyler spoke to his officer. "Call for backup, then check the kitchen for the bloody knife. As soon as backup arrives, go out and look for her. Be careful, especially if you don't find the knife." Tyler turned to Callie. "How did your dad get hurt?"

"He…he was talking to Ellen calmly after she flipped the kitchen table over." Callie turned her head and looked straight into Tyler's eyes. "I don't know how she had the strength to do that. She's had several strokes and even walks with a cane. She can barely stand on her own."

"What happened after she flipped the table? Is that how your dad got hurt?"

Callie shook her head. "No, she grabbed a knife from the counter. I yelled to warn him, but he blocked her to protect me. That's when Ellen cut his arm." She took an unsteady breath. "He said he could handle her, but when I saw him bleeding, I knew we needed help. That's when I called 9-1-1." She paused. "I was still on the line with the dispatcher when I heard a loud crash in the kitchen. So I went back in and…and found him unconscious on the floor with the toaster next to his head, and she was gone."

Tyler nodded. "Anything else you can add?"

She shook her head, very calm for what she'd just been through. But then her eyes widened.

"Tyler!" Her tone was urgent.

"What is it?"

"You need to check the neighbor's house. That might be where Ellen went. She spouted all this nonsense about my dad and the neighbor, just because the neighbor made lasagna for my dad and me. Ellen might have gone after her next."

"Good idea. Do you know where she lives?" At Callie's violent shake of her head, he called over his radio. "Joe, go door to door and make sure Ellen James isn't there." He paused. "And ask at each house if they made lasagna for Mr. James."

Callie nodded her approval.

"Lasagna?" came over the radio from his officer.

"Correct. And if you find the right person, ask permission to search her place, and then be sure to have her secure her house until we find Mrs. James."

"Right, Chief."

Tyler turned his attention back to Callie. She was pale but holding her own. He took her hand. "Are you sure you're not hurt?"

She nodded. "I'm sure." She moved to get up and he stopped her.

"Where are you going?" he asked.

"I need to check on my dad."

He held her in place. "Let the EMTs do their job. I'm sure they'll transport him to the hospital and we'll know more when we get there."

"We?"

"You don't think I'm abandoning you, do you?"

"But you need to find Ellen."

"Officer Mansfield is going door-to-door and backup has probably already arrived."

The noise of a stretcher being wheeled in through the front door caught their attention. "We'll be transporting Mr. James to Lewisburg Hospital," the paramedic told Callie.

She nodded. "Thank you. How is he?"

"You'll have to talk to the doctor about specifics, but he'll need stitches on his head and his arm."

"Is he conscious?" Callie asked.

"He's in and out, probably a concussion, but tests will confirm or deny it."

"May I talk to him?"

The paramedic seemed to consider her request. "For a minute. I want to transport him quickly since we have no prior medical information on him."

Tyler squeezed her hand before letting go.

She had barely walked into the kitchen to speak with her father when his radio sounded.

"Chief, we found her. She's holed up in a bathroom in the neighbor's house, the one who made the lasagna. It's two doors south of your location."

"Is the neighbor okay?"

"She got out of the house uninjured. She's safe in my patrol car right now."

"Good work. I'll be right there." He ran into the kitchen to tell Callie what he was doing and then left the house.

He hurriedly jogged to the house in question where Joe met him at the front door. "Gary is trying to get her to open the bathroom door."

"Is there a window?" Tyler asked.

"I was just about to go around to check."

"I'll go," Tyler told him. "You stay here in case Gary needs you. Where's the bathroom located?"

Joe pointed to Tyler's right and he headed that way around the house. There were two identical windows on the side of the house and one smaller one. It was almost above his eye level, but he stood on tiptoes to see it was the bathroom window. At first, he didn't see Callie's stepmother. But then he saw her leg and realized she was sitting on the floor and leaning against the outside wall under the window.

"Go away and leave me alone," Ellen yelled. "I don't need to be harassed by some stinkin' cops."

Tyler couldn't hear what his officer said through the door except for Ellen's snicker. Then she began to talk to herself. He could barely understand her, but the phrases he heard in relation to Callie—like "lock her up in the basement" and "teach Callie a lesson"—were unnerving. Had Callie endured the same kind of treatment his daughters had? He pushed aside those thoughts. Right now he had to form a plan to subdue Ellen.

He went around to the front to talk to Joe and Gary. "I want one of you to pick the bathroom lock while I grab her attention at the window. When you have it unlocked, knock on the door three times and give her a chance to open it. If she doesn't, then I'll get her attention again and you come in and subdue her. Be sure to go after the knife first so no one gets hurt."

Both officers reentered the house and Tyler grabbed a chair from the small, metal table-and-chair set on the neighbor's front porch. Then he ran around to the bathroom window and positioned the chair so he could stand on it to see into the bathroom. Callie's stepmother was still sitting on the floor under the window.

Tyler knocked on the closed window. "Mrs. James?" He yelled so she could hear him.

Her legs moved and now he couldn't see her. "What the hell do you want?" she yelled back.

"It's Tyler Garrett. You remember me, don't you?"

Mrs. James slowly stood and faced the window. She leaned on her cane and the knife was on the edge of the sink. He could have radioed his officers its location, but he had her attention and didn't want to break their contact.

"Tyler?" She squinted at him. "What are you doing here?"

"I'm here to help you, ma'am."

"I don't need help."

"You know this isn't your house?"

Her face scrunched and her lips pursed. "I know. This house belongs to that whore of a neighbor who's after my husband." She switched the cane to her other hand and shifted her weight, looking as if she might topple over at any moment. "She's just like that stepdaughter of mine. Goin' after men that don't belong to her." Her eyebrows rose. "You were supposed to be Wendy's boyfriend. That girl's been in love with you forever."

News to Tyler. He'd never had any interest in Callie's stepsister.

"But Callie kept getting in her way."

"Callie? How's that?" he asked, wondering how long it would take his officers to pick the bathroom lock.

"Wendy knew Callie had the hots for you, always distracting you with one thing or the other."

In Tyler's mind, this was crazy talk. Yes, he'd had a crush on Callie when they were teenagers, but he'd never had any idea Callie had felt the same way. He also hadn't known about Wendy's feelings for him, but it did make Wendy's nasty comments to Callie and her hatred of Callie much easier to understand.

There was a loud knock on the door. This was it.

"Go away. I'm not coming out," she yelled.

The plan turned back to Tyler then. "I don't blame you, Mrs. James. Why don't you open this window so we can continue to talk about Wendy?" She couldn't move quickly, so his officers would have the advantage if he timed this right.

She hesitated but he had her attention. She reached up and while she was fiddling with the window he said into his radio, "Now!"

His officers came rushing into the bathroom. Gary grabbed her around the waist and lifted her as she flailed her arms and legs and batted at him with her cane. Joe snatched the cane from her but not before being hit with it.

"The knife's on the sink," Tyler yelled through the window. Joe procured it and the three of them moved out of the bathroom. Tyler met them as they came out of the house, Mrs. James still kicking and screaming.

"Put her in the backseat of your squad car until another ambulance gets here to secure her and take her to the hospital for an eval."

The last thing he heard Mrs. James yell as she was put into the car was aimed at him. "You'll pay for this, Tyler Garrett, you son of a bitch!"

CHAPTER THIRTEEN

EVEN THOUGH SHE'D halfheartedly resisted, one of Tyler's officers drove Callie to the hospital. She remained silent during the ten-minute drive and the officer—Gary, she thought he said his name was—didn't push her to speak. She vaguely registered that she was probably in shock. She'd never been in the middle of anything as dangerous as what had transpired in her dad's house.

"I'm Bartholomew James's daughter," she said to the young woman behind the desk in the emergency room. "He was just brought in by ambulance."

"He's in Curtain 2," she told Callie after checking the computer. "Have a seat in the waiting room and I'll have someone come out to update you."

"Thank you." Callie headed in the direction the woman had pointed. There was one other person in the seating area, a middle-aged woman concentrating on her cell phone while a television on the wall presented a twenty-four-hour news station.

Callie took a seat off by herself. She wasn't in a talkative mood.

She'd only been sitting for a few minutes when she heard Ellen's distinct yelling and carrying on as the EMTs rolled her into the emergency room. Callie crossed her arms over her chest and hunched over. She'd thought being tormented by Ellen had ended years ago.

She'd been dead wrong.

"How are you doing?" Tyler appeared in front of her with no warning.

She must have been deep in her own nightmares to have missed him coming into the ER.

"I'm okay I guess." She cleared her throat, embarrassed that her voice came out so weak. She was a capable woman, had made a career and a good life for herself. She needed to snap out of this weak persona.

"How's your dad?" Tyler settled into the seat next to her.

"They haven't told me anything yet. They're sending someone out to fill me in."

Tyler took her hand. "I'm sure he'll be fine."

Callie nodded then asked, "Where are your daughters? Shouldn't you be with them?"

"I was on my way home when I heard what was happening at your dad's house on the radio. I called Aunt Poppy and she had nowhere she needed to be tonight."

"You can go home now if you want," Callie told him.

He squeezed her hand. "I'm not going anywhere until you're ready to leave."

That was exactly the answer she'd hoped for but never would have asked. "Thank you."

He squeezed her hand again, just as a medical professional in scrubs came toward her.

"Ms. James?" he asked.

"Yes." She and Tyler stood.

"I'm Dr. Martin." He shook her hand. "The cuts on your father's head and arm have been cleaned and sutured, and I've sent him to have a CT scan since he lost consciousness. From his evaluation, I suspect he has a slight concussion, but the scan will tell us if there's hemorrhaging. Either way, because of his age, we'll keep him overnight for observation." He paused. "Do you have any questions?"

"He'll be okay?"

"That would be my best guess. I'll have someone come get you when he returns."

"Thank you."

The doctor turned to go.

"Wait. What about my stepmother? She was brought in, too. What's going to happen to her?" Ellen's yelling from her bed somewhere down the corridor had finally stopped.

"I don't know anything about her case, but I can check for you."

"She'll probably need a psych eval," Tyler told the doctor. Then he turned to Callie. "She'll be facing charges if they find her competent to stand trial."

The doctor left them and they sat back down.

"Sounds like good news about your dad," Tyler said.

She nodded. "I was terrified," she blurted out. "I thought she'd killed him."

Tyler put his arm around her shoulders. She allowed him to comfort her. She'd always stood on her own, but right now it felt unbelievably good to lean on him.

Although it seemed like hours before she was able to see her dad, in reality it was much less than that.

"We're going to admit your father," the doctor told her when he got her dad's test results. "Like I said earlier, he has a slight concussion, but the CT scan shows no bleeding. He'll be taken to the second floor when his room is ready. You can go in and talk to him for a few minutes."

"Thank you," she murmured.

"Where's Ellen?" was the first thing her dad asked when she reached his side. "What happened to her?"

Callie tried to not feel hurt that concerned questions about her stepmother were the first things out of his mouth.

"She's well cared for." Callie didn't have much more information than that.

He seemed to accept that answer. "I'm sorry our dinner was ruined." He was pale, lying in the bed, hooked to an IV. A machine next to his bed blinked numbers.

Her legs became shaky as she remembered how close he'd been to not making it to this hospital bed. "Don't worry about it, Dad. It's not your fault."

"But I ought to have known it might happen again. You and I should have gone out for dinner, but I don't like leaving her alone for very long." He ran a hand through his shaggy gray hair.

Callie honed in on the word *again*.

"So this has happened with her before?"

"A few times. Nothing quite this bad. I'm usually able to calm her down before she gets out of control."

This was not the time or place to insist her dad get help for Ellen. Hopefully, Callie wouldn't have to get in the middle of this now that Ellen was being evaluated by professionals. But first she would speak to Ellen's doctor to relay the message that this was not the first time Ellen had been uncontrollable.

And that didn't even include the way Ellen had behaved while Callie was growing up.

SHORTLY AFTER SPENDING a few minutes with her father, Callie met Tyler in the waiting room. He'd planned to take her to get her car. She hadn't wanted him to, at first, preferring to make sure her dad was settled in his room, but Tyler had insisted. He was worried about her. "There's nothing more you can do for him. The staff will take good care of him."

She nodded. "I know. I guess I feel guilty for not being able to prevent this."

They were walking out the door to head to the parking lot where he'd left his truck. "How could you have prevented it?"

She shrugged. "I should have been prepared."

"But how could you have known she'd become violent?" He thought back to earlier when Callie's stepmother was ranting about Callie.

She didn't answer right away. "I just know how she is." Her words were barely audible.

They reached his truck and he turned the key in the ignition. "You can't blame yourself, Callie," he said as he pulled out of the parking space. "You're not psychic."

She didn't say anything more and he didn't push her on the drive to her dad's house to pick up her car.

"Thank you for the ride." She exited his truck.

He expected her to get into her car and pull away, but instead she headed to her dad's front door. She must have grabbed a house key on her way out earlier because she unlocked the door and entered. Thinking she must have forgotten something, he waited for several minutes but she never exited the house.

He shut off his truck and went to make sure she was okay. "Callie?" he called as he entered the house. "Are you all right?"

There was no answer, so he walked around to investigate. He heard a noise in the kitchen and found her on her hands and knees, scrubbing the kitchen floor with a brush. A bucket of soapy water was nearby.

"Let me do that," he offered and then tried to help her to her feet.

"No, I need to do it." She shouldered him away and continued to scrub at the darkened bloodstain on the yellowed vinyl flooring. "It's my job. I have to do it."

"Your job?"

She nodded vigorously. "I'll pay for it later if this floor isn't clean."

He was confused. "Why would you think that?"

She rubbed the brush furiously on the stain. "Because I know what happens when I don't do my chores the way she expects."

"She?" As soon as he spoke, he knew the answer. "Are you talking about your stepmother?"

Callie nodded, intent on her job. "Of course. She demands perfection."

He was beginning to think Callie was having a break from reality and wasn't sure what to do about it. She obviously wasn't going to snap out of it at least until after the house was back in order. So he went in search of a broom and trash bags to clean up the broken dishes and food.

When Callie deemed the house clean, he asked, "Are you ready to go?" He followed her around as she made sure everything was in order.

She finally said, "Yes, we can go now."

"Not yet." He needed to make sure she was okay before she drove herself to Poppy's, even if it was only a short trip. He guided her to the living room sofa. "Sit down a minute." He sat across from her.

"I thought you wanted to go home," she said.

"I do. But there are things we need to talk about first."

She stared at him without speaking.

"Where were you when you were scrubbing that floor?"

She cocked her head. "What do you mean? I was in the kitchen. Where else would I be? That's where the mess was."

"I mean where were you in your head? You talked about doing your chores correctly. Were you worried about getting in trouble with Ellen?"

Callie went pale, covering her mouth with a shaky hand. She nodded.

He reached out and put a hand on Callie's knee. He needed to know the whole story after he'd heard her stepmother's comments. "Did Ellen punish you when you were growing up here?"

Callie nodded, her eyes huge and glassy. "I—I don't want to talk about it."

He debated not pushing further, but he couldn't help her if he didn't know what happened. He repeated what he heard Ellen say. "Did she lock you up?"

Callie gasped. "How…how did you know that?"

He took her question as an affirmative and moved to sit next to her on the sofa. He reached out and she willingly came into his embrace. "I heard Ellen talking to herself when she was locked up in the neighbor's house," he said softly into her hair. "She talked about punishing you and locking you up."

Callie's head moved in the affirmative.

"She threw the chair that night I overheard you two fighting when we were teenagers, didn't she?" The revelation nearly knocked him over. "She was blaming you for making her mad enough to throw the chair."

Callie nodded. "Uh-huh." She spoke quietly.

"I'd just walked you home. What was she upset about?"

Silence. He waited, not willing to push her this time.

Finally she said, "She was mad that you walked me home that night."

Not the answer he expected. Not even close. "Why is that?" He listened closely to catch every word.

"Because I wasn't allowed to be around you."

He was confused. "But she didn't even know me. What did I do that made me off-limits?"

"It wasn't what you did." Callie paused. "Wendy had an enormous crush on you all through high school and she and Ellen warned me to stay away from you. Or bad things would happen to me."

He put together everything he'd heard from people over the past few days. "So that's why you wouldn't go out with me?"

She nodded.

"But I never would have gone out with Wendy. She was just my sister's friend. I wasn't interested in her like that."

"She and her mother didn't care. They thought you'd come around, and I was warned to stay out of the way."

"You never told me this before. I could have straightened them out about my feelings."

"They never would have listened to you. They always thought they knew best and no one was right except for them." She brushed her hair back from her face. "Besides, if you had talked to them, then they would have known that I'd told you about Wendy's feelings and I would have been punished."

He didn't like the sound of that. "You were punished a lot?"

She nodded.

"Physically?"

She nodded again.

"Would you call it abuse if it was done to one of my girls?"

She nodded vigorously. "Definitely," she whispered, her voice cracking.

"Do you want to talk about it?"

This time she shook her head. "No."

He paused, considered her answer, but asked anyway. "One last question. Did your dad approve of the way she punished you?"

Callie straightened and pushed away from him. Her eyes were red when she said, "Not exactly."

"What does that mean? Did he know how you were being treated?"

She laced her fingers, placed them on her lap, and became quiet.

He sensed she didn't want to talk anymore.

"Let's get you home. If you're not okay to drive, we can leave your car here and pick it up tomorrow."

Her head moved slightly. "I can drive." She rose, grabbed her purse where she'd left it by the front door and exited the house. He followed her outside. She locked the front door with mechanical precision.

He waited for her to pull away in her car before following her to Aunt Poppy's. And he made a decision on the way. Tomorrow he would contact Callie's therapist. He was worried about Callie after what she'd been through today and the awful memories it had dredged up.

And, knowing Callie, he was pretty sure she wouldn't say a word to her therapist about tonight's events.

On second thought, he decided to stay out of it. He'd give her a chance to relate the entire story to her therapist. But he wouldn't hesitate to interfere if she didn't tell the therapist everything.

CALLIE HAD NO APPETITE, even though Tyler tried to get her to eat at least a little something. She finally appeased him by having a piece of toast.

By nine-thirty she was in bed, trying to keep images from ruining her sleep. She wasn't successful. Her bedside clock read a little after one and she decided she had to do something. So she slipped a bathrobe on over her sleeveless tank and padded down the hall to Tyler's room. Before she reached his door, it opened, startling her.

"Are you okay?" Tyler whispered.

She shook her head.

"That's what I thought," he said. "I was just coming to check on you."

She swallowed, unused to asking anyone for anything. "I was hoping—"

He reached out and pulled her into his room, closing the door behind them. He drew her into his strong arms and she went willingly. This was what she'd needed. The safety of his embrace.

"Don't get the wrong idea," she said into his neck. "I just couldn't sleep."

Without saying a word he released her and pulled the covers on his bed down so she could climb in. He got into bed and pulled her close. "I'll just hold you until you fall asleep."

In that moment she went from liking him a lot to falling a little bit in love with him.

Comfortable in his arms, she fell almost immediately to sleep. She had no idea how much later it was when she woke because of mumbled voices. The covers were over her head. Trying to orient herself, she remembered that she was in Tyler's bed. Listening carefully, she realized Tyler was out of bed and speaking to one of the girls. Madison, she thought.

"Let's get you some water and then it's back to bed," he said.

Callie lay perfectly still, hoping the room was still dark and Madison didn't notice a human-shaped lump in her daddy's bed.

"I want to sleep in your bed," Madison said sleepily.

"And I told you that you have a bed of your own to sleep in." Their voices seemed to be moving farther away, perhaps out to the hall. "You know I like to take up most of my bed and you don't want to get hurt when I roll over, do you?" Madison giggled, making Callie smile for the first time in what felt like a lifetime.

A few minutes later Tyler returned. The door closed and the lock clicked. The bed moved as he got back in.

"I should go," she whispered, even while allowing him to draw her into his arms. "What time is it?"

"Almost four. Don't go yet," he whispered. "Let Maddie have a chance to fall back to sleep first." He adjusted his position to hold her more intimately. He kissed her temple.

"Whatever you say." Thinking she could luxuriate in his embrace, it wasn't long before her hands began wandering over his body and she was begging him to make her forget everything but making love.

THE NEXT MORNING Callie awoke in her own bed to the sound of her alarm. Clearing the cobwebs from her brain, she vaguely remembered Tyler carrying her to her room while it was still dark out.

Wanting to crawl back under the covers so she didn't have to deal with anything unpleasant, she knew she couldn't.

Tyler was long gone by the time Callie made it downstairs for breakfast, but he'd texted her while she'd showered to say he'd stop by to see her at the Lincoln when he could get away.

She called the hospital before leaving Poppy's and found out her dad had a restful night and could go home anytime. Callie realized her dad was now her responsibility.

After getting Tyler's okay, she told her dad's RN that she would pick him up during her lunch break. She never asked about Ellen because Callie was afraid she'd be told that her stepmother had been released already. Although maybe she should have inquired about her since the last thing Callie wanted was to run into her, especially unawares. Tyler had said Ellen would face charges, but what if a mistake had been made and she'd been allowed to return home? She refused to consider that possibility.

By the time she got back to the Lincoln Hotel

and dug into the financial files, she was feeling a little more like herself.

At least until she had to speak to her therapist that evening.

"So tell me what's been going on," Dr. Hammond began. "You've been to see your dad?"

His question seemed too coincidental. "How did you know that? Did Tyler call you?"

"Tyler who?" he asked.

"Tyler Garrett, Chief of Police. I know you two talked when you asked him to take over my community service."

"I haven't spoken to him since." Either Dr. Hammond was a good actor or he really hadn't spoken to Tyler. "*You* told me you were going to see your dad. Did it not happen?"

She realized she was being paranoid. There was no way her therapist could know about yesterday. There wasn't even an article in the local paper about it. "I've seen him twice since last week."

"And how did it go?"

"Fine." That seemed like an innocuous enough reply.

"Just fine? What did you two talk about?"

"He asked me about work, my life. You know, the usual things." If she stuck with the first conversation they'd had, she might be able to avoid talking about yesterday or how she got him home and settled earlier today over her lunch break.

"Did he ask why you haven't been back to see him before now?"

"No."

"Did you ask why you haven't heard from him in all that time?"

She swallowed the lump in her throat. "I never had a chance."

"Why's that?"

"I don't want to talk about this anymore."

Dr. Hammond didn't say anything at first. "Let's talk about your stepmother, then."

"No!" She snapped her mouth shut, realizing she'd yelled and could probably be heard downstairs.

"That was an intense reaction to the mention of your stepmother. Would you like to tell me why?"

"Can't we forget her?" Callie nearly begged.

"She's obviously part of the problem. I don't see how we can ignore her."

It's easy, Callie thought. *Just move away and make a new life for yourself.* At least, that's how she'd handled her stepmother problem previously.

"You never told me what it was like growing up with her. Did you two get along?"

Callie clamped her lips shut. She clenched and unclenched her hands, knowing they couldn't be seen on the computer screen. "I said I don't want to talk about her."

Dr. Hammond sighed. "I understand that. But

the longer it takes you to open up, the longer it will be before I can release you as my patient."

Callie was backed into a corner. The therapist wasn't going to give up and she was about to endure something she'd successfully avoided for over a decade.

All thanks to her ex-boyfriend Andrew and his interference in her life.

"Fine. What do you want to know?" Blood pounded in her temples and nightmarish visions appeared in her mind. "Do you want to hear how she made me scrub the floors until my fingers bled because I couldn't make them spotless? Or how about the time she dunked my head in the toilet when it wasn't clean enough?" Her heart raced. She sucked in a breath. "What about the time she pushed me outside in my underwear and locked me out because I didn't fold the clothes as well as she thought I should have?" By this time the memories were coming faster and faster. Memories she'd buried deep.

"I'm sorry. That must have been awful." Dr. Hammond was probably memorizing every demeaning word she was uttering. Or maybe he was recording their session. "Did she treat your stepsister the same way?"

Callie let out a humorless chuckle. "Hardly. Wendy was the apple of Ellen's eye. She could do no wrong."

"And your relationship with Wendy?"

"We have never had one. Unless you call her hitting, kicking and spitting on me a relationship? And don't forget all the badmouthing of me she did."

"It sounds like it was the two of them against you. Where does your father fit in?"

Good question. "What do you mean?"

"Did he go along with your stepmother's punishment?"

"He never stopped her, if that's what you mean."

"Does he know what you went through?"

"No. Not really. At least not from me." She drew in a deep breath. "He was a long-haul trucker and gone a lot."

"Why didn't you go to him?"

"I did once. But he believed my stepmother's side of the story and when he was gone, she came up with a new form of torture." Callie became light-headed remembering the dark, the cold, the loneliness, the bugs. "She would lock me in a closet in the basement. Sometimes I was down there so long that I thought she forgot about me. Or maybe she'd hoped I'd die down there."

"Do you blame your dad for not stopping her?"

"How can I *not* blame him?" Tears clouded her vision as her revelation materialized. "He never did anything to protect me from them." She swallowed back tears. "Now maybe you can understand why I didn't want to come back here. Why I still don't want to be here."

"Yes, I do," her therapist acknowledged. "But you still have unfinished business with your father."

CHAPTER FOURTEEN

TYLER WAITED TO text Callie until he was sure her therapy session was over. He'd wanted to give her time to recover emotionally after she'd told her therapist about yesterday's traumatic episode.

Doing okay? He hit Send just as Alexis appeared in his bedroom doorway.

"Daddy?"

"Yes?"

"Is it okay if I say good-night to Miss Callie? I think she needs a hug." The girl was extremely observant for her age.

"Why do you think that?"

"She seemed kind of sad at dinner tonight." Alexis took a seat on the end of his bed, her expression serious as she twisted one of her braids around her fingers. She'd insisted on braids tonight so she'd have her hair kinky in the morning when she undid the braids.

The things he'd had to learn to do as a single father...

"That's probably because her daddy got hurt

yesterday and he spent the night in the hospital."
Tyler figured that was enough explanation for now.

"How did he get hurt? Did someone punch him?
Or was it in a car accident?" Alexis's eyes grew
wide.

He sometimes wondered where she got her
imagination. "No, it was in his kitchen. He hurt
his head and the doctor wanted him to spend the
night in the hospital so they could make sure
he'll be all right. Good news is that he's fine and
went home earlier today." He moved to corral his
daughter back into her room. "So if Miss Callie
seems sad, then it's probably because she's tired
from worrying about her daddy."

That seemed to satisfy Alexis and he was able
to get her tucked into bed without waking Madison.

"Daddy?" She caught him just before he closed
their bedroom door.

He opened it and stuck his head in the room.
"Yes?" She was probably going to ask for another
drink of water or one last hug. She was the queen
of stalling tactics.

"If you got hurt and had to go to the hospital,
then who would drive you home? Maddie and I
can't drive yet."

Her question nearly broke his heart. "Don't worry
about that." He walked to the bed because now he

was the one who needed that last hug. "There are plenty of people who could help me out."

"Like Miss Callie or Aunt Poppy?"

She had a point. Since he'd divorced their mother, and his dad had died, Tyler had been forced to rely on people's good nature. If not for Aunt Poppy—who had been like a second mother to him—he and his daughters would be living in a hotel room or maybe an apartment until their house was ready to move into. Who knew what stranger would be watching the girls while he was on the job or working on their house if not for Aunt Poppy? From the moment he took the police job, she'd made it clear that she would be on call to watch the girls no matter what time of day or night.

"That's right. They could help me. Or I could call a friend or even a taxi." He pulled her covers extra tight. "Now, you stop worrying and get some sleep."

When he reached his room again, he checked his phone. No reply from Callie. He couldn't imagine that her therapy session went more than an hour.

He gathered his dirty clothes, as well as the girls' overflowing hamper that he'd moved to the hallway earlier, and carried them to the basement to do a load of laundry.

He stopped outside Callie's door and listened.

No sound. He didn't want to bug her. Maybe she needed some alone time.

He continued to the basement and started his first load. He couldn't wash everything together and realized he'd be up late if he wanted to get the two loads of laundry done tonight.

Setting a timer on his cell phone to remind him when the first load would be done, he went back upstairs. Again, he stopped at Callie's door.

"She's not in there," Gino said as he came out of his bedroom.

"She's not?"

"Nope. I saw her leave out the front door earlier."

"How long ago?"

Gino shrugged. "Maybe a half hour to an hour. She looked like she was dressed for a run."

That actually made sense, although Gino's sense of time wasn't much help. "Okay, thanks."

Tyler carried the girls' hamper down the hall and set it next to their bedroom door. Then he went into his own room to check his phone. Still no reply from Callie. Maybe she hadn't taken her phone with her.

He could call it while standing outside her bedroom, but if it was on vibrate, he wouldn't hear it anyway.

He went into his room and decided to wait for

her to contact him. She knew he was there for her if she needed him.

He refused to consider that he might be more worried about her than was healthy if they were truly going to keep this relationship a casual, short-term one.

CALLIE USUALLY RAN two to three miles. She hadn't kept track, but she was pretty sure she'd gone nearly twice that length based on how long she'd been running.

Her legs complained, but she kept going. She knew the town well, which was good because the sun had set a while ago. If she had been at home, she'd want to return before dark. But here in the small town she'd spent nearly two decades exploring, she wasn't concerned about getting back to Poppy's before the light was completely gone.

She was within a block of Poppy's house, running on the side of the road, when a shadowed figure suddenly appeared on the sidewalk ahead of her. She was almost side-by-side with the person when they stepped out in front of her.

Callie stopped abruptly so she wouldn't run the person down. "What—?" She recognized the person. "Wendy?" She leaned over, trying to catch her breath. She barely had the name out when she was hit on her upper back and knocked to the ground.

"It's all your fault!" Wendy screamed. "My mother wouldn't be in the psych ward if not for you!" She must have been watching Poppy's house for Callie's return.

Callie sucked air into her lungs. She carefully brushed the gravel from her hands and gingerly stood. "I didn't have anything to do with what happened yesterday." She couldn't catch her breath. "Your mother started yelling and grabbed a knife, coming at us for no reason. She put my father in the hospital."

Wendy straightened to her full height. "No reason? Ha! You're *always* to blame!"

Callie's heart pounded. She looked around at the houses that now had lights on to see if anyone had come out to see about the commotion. She didn't see anyone. As usual, she was alone with Wendy.

Arguing with Wendy never solved anything. Callie changed her tactic. "How is your mother?"

"She hates the hospital," Wendy growled.

"I'm sure she'd rather be at home." With great difficulty, Callie kept her voice calm.

"But she won't be going home anytime soon," Wendy said. "She's facing charges of attempted murder, breaking and entering, and who knows what else."

"She did do all those things."

Wendy looked as angry as ever at Callie's statement. She wouldn't have been surprised if Wendy decided to throw a punch. Just to be safe, Callie took a few steps back.

"I need to get home," Callie told her, planning to end this encounter sooner rather than later. "I hope your mother gets the help she needs." With that she jogged away, giving Wendy a wide berth.

"You'll pay for what you did," Wendy yelled after her.

Callie was almost halfway down the block and could still hear her clearly. Probably just like all the neighbors could.

WHILE HE WAITED for Callie to return, Tyler decided to call his sister.

"Hey, Isabelle," he greeted her. "How are you?"

After a few minutes of catch-up, he got to the reason he'd called. "Do you know anything about what was going on in the Jameses' home back when Callie was living there?"

"What are you talking about now?" Isabelle asked. "What kinds of things?"

He hit the main points of Ellen's breakdown, leaving out the part about Callie admitting to being locked up by her stepmother. He wanted to know why the abuse had never been noticed or reported. He also wondered if her dad had any idea about what had gone on. "It's what I heard

Callie's stepmother say when she was talking to herself that concerned me most."

"Oh. What was that?"

"She insinuated that she would lock Callie up. Do you know anything about that?"

Silence.

"Isabelle?"

When she finally answered, her voice was so soft that he could barely make out her words. "I heard something like that, but I never believed it."

"Who'd you hear it from?" A rumor recounted by someone unrelated to the situation wouldn't be credible.

Again she hesitated. "Wendy. She's the one who told me. It was after the homecoming dance. She'd been drinking and she started spouting off about how good it felt to get Callie into trouble so she'd get locked in the basement closet."

Tyler's pulse pounded in his temple. "And you never told anyone?"

"No! Almost as soon as she said it, she claimed she was just kidding. So I always thought she was making the whole thing up. I swear she never said anything else about it."

Tyler recognized the panic in Isabelle's voice. She was definitely telling the truth. At least, the truth as she knew it.

"So she really did get locked up?" Isabelle asked in a meek tone.

"That's what I'm trying to figure out." Callie had basically admitted it, but hadn't explained further. "Is there anything else you know about that family that might help to sort things out?"

"Not that I can think of," she said. "But I'll let you know if I remember anything that might be useful." She paused. "Ty?"

"Yeah?"

"I'm really sorry I didn't say anything to anyone. I honestly thought Wendy made it up."

"I know." And he did know. He also wished he'd been the one who'd heard Wendy say it. He would have loved to have saved Callie from the abuse she'd endured.

When Tyler and Isabelle disconnected, his bedroom felt too restrictive so he went downstairs to wait for Callie. He'd no sooner taken a seat in the living room when he heard the front door open.

"Good run?" He rose from the couch and met her near the bottom of the staircase. She didn't answer. "Are you okay, Callie?" He reached for her hand but she pulled it away. He grasped her wrist and turned her hand palm up. "You're bleeding. Did you fall?" He took a step back to take in her entire body.

"Something like that." She had a trickle of blood coming from her knee that stopped halfway down her shin.

"Let's get you cleaned up." He took her elbow

to lead her to the kitchen. "Aunt Poppy has first-aid supplies in here."

She pulled away from him. "I'm fine. I can wash off in the shower. That's all I need."

"Wait a minute." Something didn't seem right. "I asked if you fell and you said 'something like that.' What does that mean?" She was keeping something from him and his police training made him naturally suspicious. Especially considering recent events.

She was halfway up the steps when she stopped and turned to answer his question. "It was just fallout from the other day." She shrugged and turned away.

"Go on."

She spoke without looking at him. "I ran into Wendy again. A block or so from here. I think she was waiting for me."

"What happened?"

Callie shrugged. "Just like last time. She caught me unawares. She shoved me and I landed on the street." She climbed a few more steps. "I'm fine. I just need a shower."

He gave her thirty minutes before he knocked quietly on her bedroom door, two bottles of beer in his other hand.

He was about to knock again when the door finally opened. She wore a deep blue tank with matching plaid pajama pants and bare feet. Her hair was still damp and her face was flushed pink. He couldn't imagine her looking any more sexy than right this minute.

But that wasn't why he was standing at her door. He was worried about her. He hadn't been this concerned about anyone other than his daughters and his dad in a very long time.

She tipped her head against the door frame. "I'm really not in the mood."

He wasn't surprised and tried to lighten things up. "You're not in the mood for a beer?" He twisted off the cap on one and offered her the bottle. "You didn't think I was here for something else, did you?" He winked and her lips twitched slightly, but her smile didn't come close to reaching her eyes.

After a two-second hesitation, she took a bottle and stood to the side for him to enter her room. She shut the door behind him.

"How are you? Physically, I mean." He opened his beer and pocketed the cap before sitting on the love seat.

"I'm fine," she said, taking a seat on the edge of her bed. He tried not to think about what the two of them had done on that mattress. "I'm more upset that she caught me by surprise again. I should have been on guard."

"You can press charges."

She shook her head. "Waste of time and that

would only make her angrier. She's going to do what she wants. And I'd rather not have anything more to do with her."

First thing tomorrow he'd go find Wendy and remind her that she could end up in jail if she continued harassing Callie, either verbally or physically. "How did your therapy session go?"

Callie didn't answer at first.

"Sorry," he said. "I shouldn't have asked. I was just concerned after what you told me you went through with Ellen."

"I know," she said softly. "It's just been a difficult night."

He couldn't agree more. "You've had more than your share of stress. First reliving the trauma with your therapist and then being surprised by Wendy. I didn't mean to add to it."

"You're not." She held up her beer bottle and gave him barely a hint of a smile. "You're actually the best stress reliever I could imagine." She took a long drink of her beer. "And it wasn't quite as stressful as you make it sound. I didn't get around to telling my therapist about the other night."

He straightened. "You didn't?"

She shook her head. "No."

"Why not?"

She shrugged. "I didn't want to get into it. I'd already lived through it once."

"Don't you think it's important to tell him? You

can't deal with your past if you don't work through it. I've learned a lot from my girls' therapist and you not talking about what happened is no different than when you were being abused as a child and you kept silent, too scared to talk about it."

She stood and faced him. "I'm only doing the therapist thing because the judge ordered it." She spoke very calmly. "I don't have any desire or need to tell Dr. Hammond every little thing about my life." She came over and sat next to him on the love seat. "Now, can we talk about something else?"

He could see there would be no persuading her at least for now. "I spoke to my sister while you were out for a run."

Callie took a long drink of her beer. "It's nice that you two are so close. How's she doing?"

"You need to work on sounding sincere."

"What does that mean?"

"I know you don't like my sister."

"That's not true. I barely know her."

"Yeah, but she was best friends with Wendy."

Callie stared at the bottle in her hand as she picked at the label.

When Callie didn't comment, he asked, "Did my sister treat you badly, too?" He wasn't sure how he'd feel if Callie said yes.

"Not exactly."

"Explain." He held his breath while he waited

for her answer. He didn't want to believe that his sister might have participated in bullying Callie.

"She didn't do the things Wendy did to me, but she never tried to stop her, either."

"You mean the physical things you told me about?"

Callie nodded, still working at the beer bottle label.

"I don't know what to say," he admitted.

She merely nodded. "Neither do I."

THE NEXT MORNING Poppy dropped the girls off at the library for story hour before heading to the grocery store. The mother of one of the girls' friends met them at the library. She was going to stay with them and then take them all to her house to play.

Poppy was in the middle of the produce section when Gino suddenly came up next to her. "What are you doing here?" she asked in an unfriendly tone, out of character for her.

"I'm buying food. Just like you."

"Why?" Again, she sounded curt.

He blinked and cocked his head to the side. "Because it's a free country and I'm allowed to buy food just like you are."

She probably deserved that. She took a deep breath. "I meant, why do you need to shop for food? You eat at my house."

"Breakfast and dinner, but not lunch. I came to get a salad to take back to work."

To take back to the Lincoln Hotel. The source of their friction.

"Well, enjoy your salad, then." She turned away and couldn't remember where she'd parked her grocery cart. She'd been wandering around the tomatoes and berries for several minutes without it.

"Is that yours over there?" Gino pointed to a lone cart by the potatoes and onions.

She clenched her jaw, disliking that he could read her mind even when she was furious with him. "Yes, thank you." Poppy marched over to it without saying another word to him.

"Poppy?"

She froze but didn't turn to him or say anything.

He continued to speak. "Can we talk about this? Please?"

She could ignore him, but she knew he would follow her through the store if she didn't hear him out. "We don't have anything more to discuss." She pushed her cart a few feet, but Gino blocked her way.

She made the mistake of meeting his imploring gaze. Damn his dark brown eyes that were almost as black as coal.

"Please, Poppy. Just hear me out."

"Why should I?"

"Because I love you." He didn't whisper it but instead spoke loud enough that a few heads turned.

"Shh!"

"Why should I be quiet?" he asked. "I'm in love with you and I want the whole world to know it."

She swallowed the emotions running through her. "If you love me so much, then answer this. Why didn't you think about what it would do to me and my business when you decided to renovate the Lincoln Hotel?"

Knowing he didn't have an answer, Poppy turned her cart to go around him and rushed away before she made a fool of herself by crying in the produce section.

As soon as Tyler got to work and had taken care of the essentials that needed his attention, he began making phone calls about Wendy.

He remembered she'd worked for the city until recently, so he was able to find out her last known address.

"I'll be back in a little while," he told Donna as he walked past her desk.

Wendy's listed address was a mobile home park on the edge of town. It was a short drive and he made it there in a few minutes.

The outside of the mobile home was badly in need of repair, not that the rest of the homes in the park were in great condition. He and his officers had been called numerous times to this area of town for anything from domestic disturbance to unleashed and barking dogs to suspected drug deals.

He parked his truck and knocked loudly on the edge of the door that wouldn't keep bugs out with the state of the screen.

There was no answer.

"Wendy James?" He remembered that her married name was Pullman. "Wendy Pullman?"

"She ain't here." A man's reply came from inside but nowhere close to the door.

"Where can I find her?" Tyler yelled.

"Why you want to know?" The man's voice came closer until he was in view.

"Are you her husband?"

"You a cop?" The man was in torn jeans and a dirty white T-shirt. His feet were bare and he appeared as though he hadn't shaved or bathed in several days.

Tyler nearly laughed at the man's question since he wore his uniform and his shield was on his breast pocket. "Yes, I am. I'm Tyler Garrett, Chief of Police for Whittler's Creek."

"Why you lookin' for Wendy? Did somethin' happen to Eric?"

"Is Eric her son?"

"*Our* son," the man corrected. "He ain't here, either. Stayin' with some friend or somethin'."

"And you are…?"

"Steve. Steve Pullman."

"Wendy's husband?"

"At least for now."

Tyler squinted at him. "What does that mean?"

"It means she left me over a week ago. Says she's divorcing me." Steve scratched his neck and then moved to scratch his cheek with its sparse growth of hair.

"I'm sorry to hear that."

"Why? She's not divorcing you." Steve scratched his head and squinted at Tyler's name-tag. "Hey, wait. You're Tyler Garrett?" His eyes widened. "Holy shit! I knew that name sounded familiar. You're the guy Wendy's always going on and on about."

Tyler stepped back when Steve made a move to exit the trailer.

The screen door slammed shut after Steve came outside. "I guess you two finally hooked up, then, if you're here lookin' for her."

Tyler held up a hand. "No, you've got it all wrong. I need to talk to her about her mother and her stepfather." He decided to avoid telling Steve that Wendy had been harassing Callie. "There was an incident the other night and they've both been to the hospital."

"That true?"

Tyler nodded. "Yes, this is official business. I have no interest in Wendy otherwise. Do you know where she's staying?" When Steve shook his head, Tyler pulled out a business card and handed it to him. "If you hear from her, please call me. It's important that I speak to her."

"Yeah, I'll bet it is."

Tyler took a few steps toward his truck and then turned back to Steve, who was still outside the mobile home. "Just to be clear, there's nothing going on between your wife and me. There never has been and never will be."

Steve made a dismissive sound that conveyed his disbelief before tossing Tyler's business card on the ground and heading back inside.

"Well, that was a useless trip," Tyler mumbled as he drove out of the mobile home park. One thing he had learned was that Wendy had left her husband, which might explain why she'd appeared as though she'd been living on the streets.

When he returned to his office, he'd have Donna get him the phone numbers for local shelters. They wouldn't give his assistant information about whether Wendy had been there, but if he called and told them he was conducting a police investigation he should be able to find out.

CHAPTER FIFTEEN

THAT MORNING CALLIE did what had always worked for her in times of stress. She engulfed herself in work, specifically the town's financial records. All her troubles left her head as she concentrated on finding the discrepancy.

And later that afternoon she was rewarded for her effort. Callie was elated. She couldn't wait to tell Tyler the good news. She pulled her cell phone from her purse and texted him.

I discovered the problem with the financial records! Come to the Lincoln when you're free.

Thirty seconds later he replied.

Good work! Be there soon.

Callie straightened the files on the conference table while she waited. Anxiously pacing back and forth in front of the bank of windows, she hadn't felt this exhilarated since she'd arrived in town.

"Hey."

She spun around to see Tyler standing just inside the conference room. The doorway framing him seemed small in comparison.

Correction. Her time in bed with this gorgeous man easily topped the exhilaration she was presently experiencing.

She couldn't help herself. She grinned at him. "Hey, yourself." She quickly pulled out a chair for him, dramatically waving an arm in invitation. "Sit. Let me show you what I found."

He sat in the proffered seat and folded his hands on the conference table, patiently waiting while she practically danced with excitement.

First, she showed him the pages of printouts she'd found with a list of checks that had been written each week over the past six months. She'd talk to him later about how the city could be so much more efficient if they went entirely electronic. There wouldn't have been a need to move these banker boxes of files around, either.

"Getting me access to the city's online bank account really helped. That way I didn't need to request copies of canceled checks." She moved her computer in front of him to show him the checks. "See this one for the Pullman Corporation?" She pointed to a spot on the screen. "There's been one written every week to them for different amounts. From two hundred to six hundred. They started about six months ago and the last one was written well over two weeks ago." The computer screen showed the backs of actual canceled checks endorsed by S. Pullman.

"S. Pullman?" Tyler looked at her. "Could it be Steve Pullman?"

Callie narrowed her eyes. "That name sounds familiar."

Tyler nodded. "It should. He's married to Wendy. I think he was a few years ahead of us in school."

"Hmm. Curiouser and curiouser. Didn't we discover that Wendy worked for the city until recently?"

"Right. I meant to look into that. I'm not sure if she was fired or quit. I also don't know exactly what she did for the city. She might have worked in an unrelated office." He scratched his head as he looked at the computer screen again. "I'm not sure I understand what the problem is. Do you have proof that the Pullman Corporation didn't deserve the money that was paid to them?"

She laughed. "Do I have proof?" She pulled up another window on her computer where she'd searched for the company. "There is no Pullman Corporation that I can find. At least, not one that has any business with Whittler's Creek. There's a Pullman *Company* that's related to railroad sleeping cars, but why would the town be paying them, especially since they were bought out mid last century?"

"Good point." Tyler scanned the information she'd given him. He looked up at her. "So do we know who authorized these checks or who wrote them? From the email I got, someone knew about them and wanted to point out that there's something fishy going on."

"It's hard to tell because these are electronic checks with the finance officer's electronic signature." She pointed to the address on one of the checks on the screen. "They were mailed to a post office box. Maybe that's the next step. See who's renting the box."

"Good idea. I'll also look into who has check authority. That should be easy to find out."

"You know, I can't help feeling like this was a very amateur operation."

He cocked his head. "How's that?"

"It's as though they wanted to get caught."

"Interesting. Are you sure it's not that they're so bad at covering up, but that you're so good at finding the evidence?"

She laughed and pretended to fluff her hair. "Well, I am pretty good."

She stood close to where he sat. He wrapped his arm around her waist. "Very good work, no matter how easy it was for you." He gave her a squeeze. "Dinner on me tonight."

She grinned down at him. "Didn't you reschedule training for tonight?"

He dropped his arm from around her. "Damn! You're right. Tomorrow night, then?"

"Deal. Besides, I knew you'd be busy so I made plans for dinner with a few of the old friends I ran into at the picnic on Sunday."

"Sounds like fun." He pushed back the chair and stood. "I'm going to go make some phone calls about this before everyone leaves for the day." He leaned in to kiss her and she came into his arms willingly.

She relaxed in his embrace, enjoying the heat of his mouth on hers and the solidness of his body as he held her close. She could easily get used to having him around to do this at will.

"Hey," she said suddenly. "So now that I've figured all this out—at least as far as the financial records go—what am I going to do next?" She slumped in his arms and groaned. "Please don't tell me more physical labor."

He chuckled and held on to her tighter. "Let me work on that. I didn't expect you to figure this out so quickly."

"It's my thing," she said. "I love to know where money goes and why. It's what tells me whether a company is heading for success or failure."

"Well, I'm glad you're so skilled." He gestured to the files on the table. "This was all like a foreign language to me until you explained it." He kissed her nose. "I don't know how late I'll be tonight."

She waited for him to say more.

Instead he kissed her mouth, lingering there while he spoke. "This is where you're supposed to say 'be sure to stop by when you get home.'"

She pulled back a little to look at him and raised her eyebrows. "I am?" She chuckled. "Then be sure to stop by when you get home."

He held her close, ending by grabbing her butt cheeks with both hands and grinding against her.

She moaned as her core heated automatically. She struggled to speak. "You win. You can't get me churned up like this and then not follow through tonight." She tilted her head up and went on tiptoes to kiss him thoroughly.

This time *he* moaned. "Good comeback. I'll make it an early night of training. I'm sure my officers will appreciate it."

So would Callie. Time with Tyler in bed would be an even better reward for finding the financial problem than a dinner date. Who needed food when his magnificent body was available for feasting upon?

He gave her a little wave when he turned to leave. She enjoyed the sight as he disappeared through the doorway and into the hall.

She stood there a moment. If she had to come

back to Whittler's Creek, how lucky was she that it was shortly after Tyler had returned?

She shook her head to come back down from the clouds. She needed to put her work away for the day. There was nothing more for her to do here. The rest was up to Tyler and his investigation. She did wonder how Wendy and her husband played into this. Tyler would have to find out whether Wendy had check-writing approval. Or maybe her husband had someone else producing the checks for him if he was the one cashing them.

Either way, Callie wouldn't be upset when Wendy faced charges if she was somehow involved in what appeared to be embezzlement.

TYLER FOUND HIMSELF whistling as he drove back to his office. Life was good and being with Callie was better than ice cream for dinner.

"You're in a good mood," Donna commented when he stopped at her desk.

He'd already spoken to her about calling local shelters to look for Wendy. "Any luck finding Wendy Pullman?" He'd deliberately ignored her comment.

"One place had someone who matches her description come in with a boy her son's age, but they never spent the night. The director got the feeling the woman was spooked by something and didn't stay. Then I found two other shelters with the same experience."

"Interesting. I wonder what happened."

Donna shrugged. "Don't know, but it's strange that I got the same story three times." She handed him the list of shelters she'd called as well as the notes she'd made about each one.

"I have another job for you," Tyler said. "I need you to find out who has check-writing authority for the town. I also need to know about Wendy Pullman's employment. What she did, when she started, when she left and why."

Donna was furiously writing down what he said. "Anything else?"

"Oh, right. One more thing." He pulled a paper from his pocket and laid it on her desk. "Find out who rented this post office box." Then he headed to his office to figure out his next move.

Callie's community service. That's what he needed to work on. Right now she had nothing to do tomorrow. She was more than halfway through her required hours already. He didn't even want to think about her leaving town once she completed her hours.

He suddenly had an idea. He searched online for a phone number, picked up his desk phone and called a friend who worked at Lewisburg Hospital. Tyler remembered Brian ran the accounting department there. Maybe he had something for Callie to do.

"Hey, Brian, it's Tyler Garrett," he greeted his friend. "How are you?" He and Brian had gone to different schools, Tyler to public and Brian to private, but they'd played on the same youth soccer and baseball teams for years.

"Ty! Great to hear from you. What's up?"

The two men caught up for a few minutes and then Tyler described what he was looking for.

"Hmm. I don't have anything here right now." Brian paused. "But I might know a place she'd be useful."

"Fill me in." Anything was better than sending her to do more dirty, physical labor. Tyler selfishly wanted her to save her energy for him.

"There's a women's shelter on the outskirts of town. Its location is very top secret for obvious reasons. You're sure you can trust this woman?"

"With my life," Tyler told him, recognizing that he hadn't always been as trusting of her. "What kind of work would it be?"

"I know they get a lot of women in who have no idea how to handle money. They've been in abusive relationships with dominant men who control the money, usually giving them an allowance for household items, and that's it. They have no idea how to balance a checkbook or maybe even write a check, let alone how to bank electronically."

"So you're talking about a classroom situation?" Tyler thought Callie would love the opportunity.

"Exactly. Think she can handle it?"

"Absolutely."

Brian gave him the details, including the person to speak to. "Norma Wilson will give you the specifics, including the address. All I know is that it's right outside the town limits."

"Thanks, Brian. I really appreciate this." They disconnected and Tyler immediately called Norma.

"That's a wonderful suggestion," the woman told Tyler after he explained Brian's idea. Norma sounded like someone's grandmother and he pictured a round little woman with white hair wearing an apron. "We've held classes on child care and health issues, but not finances. I think that would be very helpful to many of these women."

They spoke about details for a few minutes and then Norma said she'd meet Tyler and Callie tomorrow morning at a nearby location. She wanted to talk to them about the idea in person and then she'd allow Callie to come to the shelter. Tyler liked that she was so paranoid. That meant she protected the women in her care very well. If he, as Chief of Police, couldn't be given the address, then hopefully none of the abusive men in these women's lives would discover the location, either.

Tyler checked his watch. He had no time left to eat dinner before training with his officers. Maybe he'd make it an extra early evening and get left-overs at Aunt Poppy's.

Most of all, he looked forward to stopping by Callie's room afterward.

THE NEXT MORNING Callie was ready in record time to go with Tyler to meet Norma. Excitement and nervousness didn't even begin to cover how she was feeling. She'd never done anything like this before, but being able to help abused women take their lives back was beyond great.

"Want some coffee?" Tyler asked when she met him in the kitchen.

"I'd love some," she said. "What time are we meeting Norma?"

Tyler laughed. "You're like a child on Christmas morning. Calm down. We've got plenty of time. She said nine o'clock at the Route 40 Diner on the way to Lewisburg. We've still got forty-five minutes."

Callie took the coffee mug he'd poured for her and sat at the kitchen table. "Where are the girls this morning?"

"They went for a walk with Aunt Poppy and they're stopping at the playground."

"They're up and out early." Callie was extremely glad they hadn't gotten up during the night at an inappropriate moment.

He winked at her. "Probably because they slept through the night."

She grinned back. "That's always a good thing."

"Absolutely. That and the locks on our bedroom doors." After forgetting to lock the door one time, they'd been diligent about doing so since, whoever's bedroom they were in.

When they finished their coffee, they left for the diner. Tyler had mentioned his impression of what Norma would look like based on talking to her on the phone, so when they saw a woman matching that description sitting in a booth, they approached her.

"Norma?" Tyler asked.

The older woman dunking a tea bag into her cup of hot water shook her head. "Nope."

"I'm sorry to disturb you, ma'am." Tyler turned to Callie. "Everyone else in here is male or with a man. It's seat yourself, so let's get a table and Norma will find us. She'll know me by my uniform."

"And you're looking pretty darn sexy in it, too," Callie said just loud enough for him to hear.

He chuckled and put a hand on her lower back. Callie pointed to a table where they'd be seen by anyone coming in through the door.

They ordered coffee, which arrived just as a tall woman, probably close to six feet, with dark gray hair and a prominent limp, came directly to their table. "Chief Garrett?" She put her hand out to him. "I'm Norma Wilson." She was nothing like Tyler had guessed.

Tyler rose as they shook hands. "Have a seat." He gestured to Callie. "This is Callie James." Norma shook Callie's hand and sat.

The woman got right down to business. "So tell me what you'd like to teach my girls."

Callie swallowed. "Well, I don't have any experience teaching, but I'm very successful in the financial world. I'm good at what I do."

"Yes, I did a search on you last night. You're very respected in your field."

Callie nodded. "Thank you." She took a breath. "I'll teach whatever the women need. From the basics of a checking account to saving for retirement. Whatever they'd like to learn about."

Norma's head bobbed in agreement. "Good, good. I was hoping you'd be open and not stuck on teaching what you thought they *should* learn. We have women from all different backgrounds at the shelter. From high school dropouts to women with post-graduate degrees."

They spoke for a few more minutes, Norma wanting to know specifics about times.

Tyler piped up. "I would expect that the classes would take prep time that Callie could do either at home or at your shelter." He looked at Callie.

"That time would certainly be counted against your service hours."

"Oh! I nearly forgot." Norma looked at Callie. "That's what I wanted to know. What is it that you did to be given the service hours? I couldn't find anything online about it, and I can't have you coming into contact with these women if you've done something to hurt someone or anything of that nature."

"You have nothing to worry about," Callie told her as calmly as she could. "My ex-boyfriend accused me of breaking an expensive vase of his. I assure you I didn't do it on purpose, and I'm almost certain I didn't accidentally knock it over, either. But I took a plea deal rather than go to trial because he has a so-called witness, and I had no way to prove my innocence."

"I see." Norma paused. "And you have no other incidences of violence? No one who might follow you to the shelter for any reason?"

Callie shook her head. "None."

Norma put out her hand. "Then I'll see you tomorrow morning at ten? The women are assigned chores like laundry but by ten they should be able to attend your class if they choose." She put a finger to her lips and furrowed her brow. "Do you think it would be possible to have an evening class, too?"

Callie looked to Tyler and they both shrugged. "I don't see why not."

"That would be spectacular. Several of the women have day jobs so an evening class would benefit them."

After Norma left the diner, Tyler said, "You didn't mention what you just went through with your dad and stepmother when Norma asked about incidences of violence. Or about Wendy. She's shown up twice now unexpectedly."

"I didn't think they counted. I thought she meant things I'd initiated."

Tyler shrugged one shoulder and changed the subject slightly, filling her in on the search of shelters for her stepsister's whereabouts. "I know you told me you didn't tell your therapist about what happened when you had dinner with your dad." He paused. "But I really do think it would be good to talk it through with him."

"There's really nothing to talk through. It's over. I don't want to relive it."

"I get that. But why don't you tell him about it, anyway, so he can decide if there's more to discuss?"

She sighed. "Maybe. I don't know." She took a sip of her now-cold coffee. "I'm not sure what good it would do to divulge it."

Judging from Tyler's near silence for several

minutes and on the drive back to Poppy's, Callie was pretty sure he wasn't thrilled with her answer.

But she did what had worked for her entire life—kept quiet and avoided an argument.

THINGS WERE PRETTY uncomfortable between Tyler and Callie on their drive to Aunt Poppy's. Unlike most women he knew, she tended to shut down when faced with a conflict. Not that he'd helped the situation by remaining silent himself, but he didn't know what to say. She obviously didn't want to talk to anyone about what had happened with her stepmother. And that included both him and her therapist, who could probably be a huge help to her if she let him.

Tyler drove to the police station after dropping off Callie at his aunt's, anxious to see what information Donna had for him about Wendy. "Whatcha' got for me?" he asked as he stopped in front of her desk.

She smiled at him. "Hopefully all the information you wanted." She pulled a legal tablet from her top desk drawer and began reciting what she'd learned. "Wendy was an employee of the town of Whittler's Creek for just under a year. She resigned abruptly about two weeks ago."

"Resigned? She wasn't fired?"

Donna shook her head. "Not from what I found,

but I didn't speak to her superior. She might have a different story."

Tyler nodded. "Right. Maybe she was given the choice of resigning or being fired. Resigning looks better when you're applying for your next job. What else did you find out? What was her exact job?"

"Turns out that she did *not* have check-writing authority. Her job was an entry-level position. Filing, copying, whatever needed to be done."

"Damn. I was counting on her being the one who wrote the checks that her husband allegedly cashed." Tyler had provided Donna with just enough details so she had a better understanding of what information was important.

"I know. There were two people in her office with check-writing authority. One was Wendy's boss, Michelle Bloom, and the other was James Brack, the town's financial officer. It takes both of them to authorize checks, so I'm not sure how this could have happened unless they're both in on it."

"I doubt it. I don't know anything about Michelle, but Jim Brack is a respected businessman. He's got a thriving insurance office besides being the town's financial officer."

"And I doubt Michelle has anything to do with it, either. We sing in the church choir together and I can't imagine her being involved in embezzlement."

Tyler shrugged. "Sometimes the people who look most innocent are the most guilty."

"That's true, but depressing." The phone on Donna's desk rang and she answered it.

Meanwhile, Tyler went into his office to figure out his next move. He picked up the phone and called Jim Brack first.

"Good morning, Mr. Brack. This is Chief Tyler Garrett. I was hoping to ask you a few questions about some checks that you authorized as Whittler's Creek's financial officer."

"Sure, Chief. Is there a problem?"

Tyler didn't want to divulge too much at this point. "Just checking up on something."

"Okay. What do you need from me?"

"Do you remember authorizing checks to be written to a Pullman Corporation?"

"That's hard to say off the top of my head. I can't remember every check exactly."

"I understand. These checks were issued once a week for about six months. The last one was authorized approximately two weeks ago."

"Pullman Corporation? Like the sleeping cars? It only sounds familiar because of the name. I think I would have remembered it because of that but I don't." Jim Brack paused. "If you pull the authorizations, I can tell you if it's my signature or not."

"I'll do that." The two men disconnected and Tyler gave Donna another job to do.

While she took care of retrieving the authorizations, Tyler debated another problem. After mulling it over for quite a while, he searched his email and came up with the phone number he needed.

"Hello, Dr. Hammond. This is Police Chief Tyler Garrett from Whittler's Creek. You turned Callie James's community service hours over to me."

"Yes, yes, how's it going?"

Tyler filled the therapist in on what Callie had been doing and what was planned for what would probably be her final service hours.

"That's great," Dr. Hammond said. "It sounds like things are going well there."

"Well, yes and no." Tyler took a deep breath and began relating the events of the other night involving Callie and her dad and stepmother.

"I had no idea." Dr. Hammond sounded stunned. "She never mentioned a word."

"That's why I'm calling. She doesn't think telling you is important and I doubt she'll say a word unless you bring it up."

"You do realize that now I'll have to let her know that I'm aware of what happened?"

"I understand. I should also tell you about her reaction when we went back to her dad's house for her car. In her mind, she was back in the house as a child, remembering how she was treated."

"And how was that?"

Tyler hesitated. He'd only meant to tell Dr. Hammond enough so he'd ask Callie questions. "I think that's up to her to tell you."

"I understand. She's told me some of what went on, but I thought there was more." Dr. Hammond cleared his throat. "You seem very concerned about Callie."

"I am. She's been through a lot."

"It sounds like the two of you have developed a personal relationship. I hope it won't interfere in your duty to the court."

"Not at all. Callie and I went to high school together, so we already knew each other." He wouldn't divulge anything more that might hurt Callie's situation.

She was already upset with him and she wouldn't feel any better when she discovered what he'd just told her therapist.

CHAPTER SIXTEEN

"AUNT POPPY! AUNT POPPY!"

She spun around in front of the stove. Madison and Alexis had run into the kitchen. Their faces were flushed and they were dancing around.

"What is it, girls?"

"There's a man at the door with something really special for you." Madison was breathless.

Poppy furrowed her brow. "For me?" She wasn't expecting anything. Maybe she'd ordered something online and didn't recall. She turned down the burner on the stove and wiped her hands on a towel before heading to the front door.

There stood a man with a bouquet of flowers. A *huge* bouquet. "Mrs. Poppy Thompson?" he asked.

"Ye-yes." She'd never seen so many red roses at once.

The delivery man put the flowers in her arms and left before she could even form the words *thank you*.

"They're beautiful, aren't they, Aunt Poppy?" The girls had followed her to the door and were now jumping up to smell the flowers, one on each side of her.

"Yes, they're beautiful." She was in a fog, possibly because of the overpowering fragrance coming from the roses—and from the surprise of their arrival. "We should get these into water." She wasn't even sure she had anything large enough to hold them all. "We might have to divide them into two vases."

By the time she and the girls got the flowers—three dozen by Poppy's count—into vases, the girls were off to their room. Poppy had given them each a single rose and a narrow vase to keep next to their beds.

She was cleaning up the counter when she spied an envelope near the kitchen door. It must have fallen and she hadn't noticed it.

She picked it up, sure it would say the flowers were from Gino. Who else could it be? Though the note would be in someone else's handwriting because he'd probably called in the order.

Instead she recognized Gino's handwriting immediately. His nearly illegible scrawl was difficult to read, but she could tell he'd tried his best.

My Dearest Poppy,
These roses have nothing on your beauty, my love. Please accept this small token as an apology for hurting you. You mean the

world to me and I can't go on without you
in my life.
All my love,
Gino

By the end of the note, Poppy could barely see
through the tears in her eyes.

"I'm glad you got the flowers."

She whirled around to see Gino standing in the
kitchen doorway.

She swallowed her emotions, but her words
came out choppy. "They're beautiful. Thank you."

He nodded and began speaking in a serious
tone. "I know calla lilies are your favorite, but red
roses signify love. And showing you how much
I love you was my goal. That's why there were
three dozen roses. One for our past, one for our
present, one for the wonderful future I anticipate
we'll have together." He cleared his throat. "I was
hoping the flowers would be the beginning of my
apology and that you'd agree to spend the evening with me."

"Gino—"

He held up a hand to stop her. "I know you're
still mad at me. I've had a lot of time to think
about how to make things right between us. I
might have an idea that could work." He paused.
"If you're willing to listen."

She loved this man with all her heart. The past

few days had been torture. She owed it to herself—and to him—to hear him out. "I'm willing to listen."

Gino let out a huge sigh. "Thank you. I wasn't sure what I'd do next if you said no."

"I'm only agreeing to hear you out. This doesn't mean everything is okay between us."

Gino nodded. "I understand." He reached for her hand and she allowed it. "I appreciate the opportunity to make things right."

"So now what?" she asked.

Gino smiled. "Now you finish making that dinner so everyone else can eat. And as soon as Tyler gets home to be with the girls, you and I are going to dinner."

"You're in luck. I'm free tonight." Poppy touched her hair and realized she had no makeup on. "I need time to get ready. I must look a fright."

Gino took a step closer. "You look beautiful." He touched her cheek. "But if you insist, go get ready and I'll finish dinner."

Poppy laughed. "You cook? That's a good one."

"Yes, I know how to cook." He shrugged. "Okay, a little. I'm not great, but I can get by." He looked at what she'd been preparing. "So what do I do with this?"

She chuckled and nudged him aside before explaining how to finish the meal in the oven. "I shouldn't be too long. Just let me know if you need help."

"Go! I can handle this."

Poppy hurried upstairs. She wasn't sure what to wear to dinner. She should have asked Gino. Pretty sure he wouldn't be changing out of his gray slacks, white dress shirt sans tie and black sport coat, she dressed accordingly.

"You are stunning," Gino told her a short time later when she met him at the bottom of the stairs.

Her face heated at his compliment. She'd chosen black pants and a teal blouse that she knew nicely accented her coloring. "Thank you."

Tyler's voice, as well as his daughters' giggles, could be heard in the kitchen. "Sounds like the girls are taken care of."

Gino nodded and offered his bent arm. "Are you ready to go?"

She took his arm and they left the house. All the while she wondered what his solution might be.

"I thought we were going to dinner," Poppy said when Gino pulled into the parking lot behind the Lincoln Hotel. She tensed at the mere sight of the building.

Gino pulled into a parking spot and killed the engine. "We are. Just wait and you'll see what I have planned."

She did as he requested, hoping it was the right

decision. They walked into the hotel through the unlocked front door.

"Don't you keep the building locked?" she asked. "What if someone found out and decided to come in here and cause damage? You know there are people out there who do things like that."

Gino laughed. "I know, I know. Don't worry. I keep the building locked when no one's here." He winked. "But the building isn't empty."

He guided her to the elevator and pressed the up button. Poppy was more confused than ever. Was he going to give her a tour of a construction zone? Should they be wearing hard hats?

She remained silent on the elevator ride while Gino hummed to himself and then smiled at her when the slow-moving elevator finally came to a grinding halt. They had arrived on the fourth level, which was the top floor of the hotel.

Gino exited first, putting his arm out to keep the elevator doors from shutting while Poppy disembarked. They walked down a hallway that looked like a typical hotel corridor until they reached a steel door with a sign that read Stairway on it. Gino opened the door and invited her through.

"I'm afraid there's no elevator to where we're headed," he told Poppy. "But it's just one flight up."

Poppy was hesitant, knowing the building only had four floors. "Are we going to the roof?"

Gino grinned. "You'll see." Again, he offered

her his bent elbow and the two of them ascended one more flight.

What she saw when she stepped onto the roof made her gasp. There were white lights strung from everywhere, barely visible even though the sun had already set behind the large trees on the west side of the building. In the middle of the area was a round table, set for two with fine china and crystal on top of a floor-length, white-linen table-cloth. On either side, two chairs were covered in matching white linen. Soft music played, nearly drowning out the noise of the cars going by on the street below.

"What is all this?" she asked.

"This is all for you," he replied. "Come, have a seat." He stepped quickly to the table and pulled out a chair for her.

She walked hesitantly to where he waited, in awe of the trouble he'd gone to. She sat and he took the seat across from her.

"Champagne?" He lifted a chilled bottle from a standing silver wine cooler beside him.

"Okay." She felt tongue-tied and off balance. As if this was a movie set or maybe she was dreaming.

Gino poured them each a glass of the pale fizzy liquid and he lifted his glass in a toast. "To us."

Poppy froze. "I thought you brought me here to tell me about some compromise." She gestured to their surroundings. "A romantic interlude like this isn't a compromise. I can't drink a toast to us. Not with the way things are right now." She put her glass down on the table and was about to push her chair back to leave.

"Wait, wait!" Gino cried. "Let me explain."

She stayed where she was, waiting for him to do just that.

"I got ahead of myself," he said. "I'll save that toast for later." He seemed jittery, not quite himself. He was usually so calm, so in charge. He held up his glass again and looked her in the eye. "Cheers!"

She smiled slightly. She couldn't help it. She held up her glass and repeated his toast, "Cheers!" They lightly touched their glasses together and each took a sip.

"Would you like to begin with appetizers?" Gino had his phone out. "I only need to send a text and they'll be delivered."

"You've gone to a lot of trouble," she said. "And a little food sounds wonderful." She didn't want the champagne to go straight to her head.

"Good." He sent a text and then put his phone down. He reached for her hand. "Any effort it took to put this all together was worth it. *You're* worth it." He squeezed her hand and she squeezed his back.

"Thank you." She took a sip of her champagne. "Now, can we talk about this compromise?" She wasn't about to let him suck her in with a little wine and ambience.

Gino sighed. "If you insist."

Just then the door opened and two men in black pants and crisp white shirts stepped onto the roof. They carried trays and a folding stand that they placed next to the table.

One server pointed to a platter. "These are coconut shrimp." He pointed to another platter. "These are crab-stuffed mushrooms, and the ones on this plate are bacon-wrapped dates with a chutney and honey dipping sauce." He gave them each a small plate.

"Thank you," Gino told them. "Everything looks delicious."

The men gave a slight bow and left the rooftop.

They served themselves, tasting everything, and Gino spent an inordinate amount of time talking about the appetizers until she finally stopped him. "You're avoiding the real subject," she reminded him.

"You're right," he admitted freely. "I am." He was quiet for several seconds. "I just want to do this right."

She narrowed her eyes. "Do what right?"

As soon as he got up from his seat and reached into his pocket, she knew what he intended. Her blood pressure rose and her pulse pounded in her temples. "Stop right now."

He halted midstride.

She continued to speak. "If you're about to do what I think you are, then don't."

"But, Poppy—" He'd pulled a small black box from his pocket.

She shook her head. "Asking me to marry you isn't the solution to our problem." She pushed her chair back and stood. "I can't believe you'd even think that's the answer."

"I think it can be a good start."

"If that's all you have, then I need you to take me home." She turned to go.

"But, Poppy—"

"Do you have a compromise or not?" When he didn't respond, she repeated her request. "Take me home."

He must have finally realized his mistake because he stopped trying to talk her into staying.

They were both silent all the way back to her house. He pulled to the curb and she unbuckled her seat belt.

"Don't go," Gino said.

She turned to him, giving him one more chance.

"I love you, Poppy." The well of emotion in his voice was nearly her undoing.

She swallowed the lump in her throat. "I love you, too, Gino. But I need you to respect me."

"I *do* respect you. I wouldn't want to marry you if I didn't respect you."

"Then why are you still planning to compete with my business? Why aren't you taking that seriously?"

He stared at her. He obviously had no answer.

Sadly, she opened the car door and went into her house, straight to her bedroom, and flung herself onto her bed for a good long cry.

TYLER COULDN'T IGNORE the fact that Callie was going out of her way to avoid him. She hadn't liked his opinion about telling her therapist everything that had happened the other night. She'd spent the evening in her bedroom with the door closed, even taking her dinner upstairs rather than eating with him and his daughters.

Allowing her time to cool down—even though she had been freezing him out rather than getting angry—he took the girls to visit their new house. They hadn't seen the progress being made for several weeks.

He didn't question why it was so important to him, but he'd also really wanted to invite Callie to see how much work had been done since she'd first been there. He craved her approval.

"This is magical," Madison said as she stepped inside the front door to see the new chandelier, as well as the newly refurbished hardwood floors and intricate stairway with wrought iron balusters and handrails. "Our own castle," she said on a sigh.

Tyler chuckled. The girls and their princess fantasies.

"I love this house, Daddy." That came from Alexis, sounding like she was in awe. "When can we move in?"

He was pleased that they were as excited about moving into the house as he was. "Not long now. I'm thinking we can paint your bedrooms this weekend and move your furniture out of storage."

The girls jumped up and down and then took off to see the rest of the first floor.

Standing alone in the front foyer, the truth of his situation hit him. He was redoing this house for the three of them. This was their fresh start. They'd be a family here.

Not that they weren't now, but this would be their first home where it was just the three of them.

Neither of the girls had even mentioned their mother to him in weeks.

They chattered on about a lot of people, especially Miss Callie. But their mother was no longer one of them.

The girls ran past him and headed up the stairs. He could hear their footsteps on the hardwood floor. He needed to get some area rugs to keep the noise down. They sounded like a herd of wild animals up there.

He smiled and began walking around the house

to check out the work that had been done. After giving Callie the tour, he'd realized how much still needed to be completed and how little free time he had to get it all done. So he'd contacted his contractor and asked him to take on more of the project.

As he inspected the work that had been done in his absence, he was very pleased. The last thing he checked was the powder room, which had been completely gutted when he'd last visited. Everything he'd ordered to finish the space had been in the garage, ready to be installed.

He was amazed when he opened the powder room door. It had come out exactly as he'd pictured it. As with the work his contractor had done everywhere else in the house, he couldn't be happier.

"Daddy, Daddy! Come quick!" the girls called to him from the upstairs hallway.

"I'll be right there." They were probably excited about their rooms and their new bathroom that they'd share.

"Hurry, Daddy," Madison told him. "It's a 'mergency."

He took the steps two at a time. "What is it? What's wrong?"

The girls led him to their bathroom. "Don't go in, just stand right here," Alexis instructed him.

Then Madison chimed in. "We didn't do this, Daddy. We promise."

He stuck his head into the newly finished room and saw that there was water all over the floor. Probably a half inch or so. The flooring outside the bathroom was dry, but only because they'd caught the leak just in time and the threshold held the water back from the hallway. "Did you girls use the toilet or turn on the water?"

Both shook their heads vigorously. "No, Daddy." They spoke in unison.

Alexis explained. "I took a step into the bathroom and my shoe got wet." She lifted her foot to show him. "So I didn't let Madison go in."

"Good thinking. Can you girls go downstairs to the dining room to see if the ceiling is wet down there?"

"Sure, Daddy." They ran off, leaving him to call his contractor. He didn't pick up, so Tyler left a message.

Knowing help was *not* on its way, he took off his shoes to step barefoot into the bathroom to figure out where the leak was coming from. He'd turn off the water in the entire house, only if he couldn't stop the leak by turning off the water to the bathroom.

"Ceiling looks okay, Daddy!" Alexis yelled from the first floor.

"Okay, thanks! You guys stay down there until

I get this figured out." He'd used the job of checking the dining room ceiling as a way to get the girls out of his way. They tended to want to help him whenever possible.

He found the leak under the sink and turned off the water there. After he had stopped the water from rising, he needed a wet vac to get rid of the water on the floor. He wasn't sure there was one in the house.

He had one in his storage unit, which meant he'd need to take the girls with him. He sighed. Was this how it would be when it was just the three of them in the house? He'd been used to having his ex-wife around, and then living with his ailing father, and finally with Aunt Poppy. There had always been another adult to help with the girls.

He blamed Rebecca for putting him in this position. If she hadn't mistreated their daughters, she'd still be around and he wouldn't have to rely on Aunt Poppy's generosity. They'd still be married and his girls would have a mother.

CALLIE HAD KEPT to herself most of the day. She'd been pulling together information she thought essential for not only women but for everyone to know when it came to financial matters.

At a little before nine o'clock, when she came out of her room to take her dinner dishes to the kitchen, she was surprised at how quiet the house was. She and Tyler hadn't spoken since he'd dropped her off after meeting with Norma at the diner. She didn't like that he was pushing her to tell her therapist about what had happened at her dad's. What good could it do to go over the experience again?

Once had been enough, thank you very much.

She hadn't taken notice of anyone else's doors left open or closed, but she assumed Tyler's daughters were in bed by now. Tyler was nowhere to be found, so maybe he was in his room. Poppy had gone out for the evening, so not seeing her anywhere wasn't such a mystery.

The front door suddenly opened, bringing with it several voices. Callie looked to see who was coming in and was surprised to see Tyler and the girls.

"We've been to our new house," Madison told her. "And we had a mess to clean up."

Callie looked at Tyler for more information. "Is everything okay?"

He nodded. "There was a leak under the sink in the girls' bathroom. We had to get my wet vac out of storage and then clean it up."

"You should have called me. I could have helped."

He gave her a look that reminded her they hadn't left things very cordial between them.

"Go get ready for bed, girls. I'll be up in a minute to tuck you in." Tyler waited until they were out of earshot before speaking to Callie. "I wasn't sure you wanted to hear from me."

"I'll admit I didn't like you badgering me the last time we spoke."

"I'm sorry I pushed the issue," Tyler said.

"Apology accepted. And I'm sorry I got so upset." Her mouth turned up in a hint of a smile. "Can I get you a beer? Sounds like you had a crummy night."

His entire body seemed to relax at the suggestion and he smiled back. "That's the best offer I've had all day." He held his arms out. "But first, come here." She gratefully did as he asked, melting into him. He whispered into her hair. "I've missed you. I don't want you to ever leave."

She pulled back to look him in the eye and placed her hands flat on his chest. "You know I'm only here for a few more days. I have a job and a life that's not here. We agreed that this was only temporary."

His arms dropped to his sides. "Sure. Whatever." He stepped back from her.

"Tyler."

He looked at her, not saying a word.

"Do you want to talk about this?" she asked.

"Do you?"

Her heart nearly beat out of her chest. "Yes, I do."

He took a step closer and looked directly into

her eyes. "I know when we originally talked about this—whatever this is between us—we agreed that it would be temporary. Just until you left town." He ran a hand through his hair. "But I like this. Us." He paused. "I don't want you to leave for another decade or so. I want to see where this goes."

Her emotions were choking her. She swallowed. "I didn't realize you felt that way." She hesitated. "I'm not sure how we can make this work."

He put his hands at her waist. "Do you want to figure it out?"

"I do," she whispered.

She wasn't sure who moved, maybe both of them, but she was back in his arms, his mouth on hers, before she could blink.

When she finally had the willpower to pull back, she said, "Do you really think we can make it work?"

"You worry too much." He took her hand in both of his. "I've already got a plan. You know the fourth bedroom at my house?"

She nodded, wondering where he was going with this.

"That's your room."

She cocked her head. "My room?"

"Right. For when you come to visit on the weekends or whenever you can."

"O-kay."

"I can see you're not getting it. Just like we do now, we can each have our own bedroom for propriety sake—aka Madison and Alexis. When you come to visit, then we'll do the same thing we do now." He squeezed the hand he held. "I think you coming to my room after the girls are settled will work best since I'll have a king bed and your room's only big enough for a twin."

"And what if I don't agree?" she teased.

He shrugged. "Okay, we can do it in a single bed if you want."

She hit him playfully on the arm. "That's not what I meant. What if I don't want to make the trip up here every weekend?"

He pursed his lips. "Well, you could find another job and move here permanently."

"I can't do that." Her response was immediate.

"Why not?" His brow furrowed.

"Because I love my job. I can't give it up."

He pulled her close. "But I don't want to give *you* up. I love you."

She stared at him, wide-eyed. "You do?"

He grinned. "I do."

She swallowed. "I love you, too." She really did. Not a false kind of love like she'd thought she felt with Andrew and boyfriends before him. This was the real thing.

She smiled at him. "Maybe it's time for those

beers." She needed a moment to digest their conversation.

"Wait. There's one more thing I need to tell you. It's important."

She froze. That phrase was never a good sign.

"I want you to know that I called your therapist," he said.

She didn't know what to say. "You called him? Why? Have you been checking up on me?"

"No, nothing like that." He hesitated. "I called because you didn't tell him what happened at your dad's. I realized how difficult it would be for you to relive it, but I thought he should know."

"*You* thought?" She couldn't believe he'd gone behind her back like that. "If I'd wanted him to know about it, then I would have told him myself."

"I'm sorry that you don't agree. I just want what's best for you. And your therapy is a big part of that."

"So you think you know better than I do what's best for me? You took control of me, of my life." She'd thought he was different, but it turned out he wasn't.

"That's not true."

She glared at him but kept her tone neutral. "It *is* true. You didn't consult me, you went ahead and did what you thought was best. You're no different than Andrew. He decided I needed to loosen up because I'm supposedly wound too tight."

"Maybe he had a point."

"What?" She wasn't sure how long she could remain calm. Inside she was seething. And all of this right after they'd admitted to being in love with each other.

"Look at you." He pointed at her hands, which were fisting and unfisting. "You're extremely angry right now, but your hands are the only part of you expressing that emotion. Your tone of voice is even. You're not storming around, banging things."

"So? Does that make me crazy or something? You know my history. I've learned quite well how to keep my emotions in check. It doesn't mean I don't have them."

"I know that. But wouldn't you like to just once yell and scream?" He paused. "I get that you don't think I should have called your therapist, but I'd do it again."

"So you're not even sorry?" She was incredulous.

"No, I'm not." He took a step closer but she retreated. "I want you to be whole again, Callie. Not just for you, but for my daughters, as well. I love you, but we can't move forward until you've completely healed. My daughters have been through too much and I won't gamble with their futures."

"And you think I'm some kind of danger to

them?" She refused to think about what kind of mother she would make.

"Can you guarantee that you won't have another break with reality?"

"That's ridiculous. There are no guarantees in life."

"True," he agreed. "But don't you think dealing with your past will give you a brighter future?"

She'd heard enough and spoke deliberately. "My future is not your concern. We will not be *moving forward*. Unless you need to speak to my therapist about my community service, then stay out of things that don't have anything to do with you." She spun on her heel and headed to her bedroom where she allowed her tears to flow freely.

CHAPTER SEVENTEEN

BY THE TIME Callie woke the next morning, after spending most of the night tossing and turning and shedding some quiet tears because of her breakup with Tyler, she was anxious to get to the women's shelter. She wasn't sure what she would have done if she hadn't had something else to occupy her mind.

She drove to the parking lot at the diner to meet Norma as planned. When Norma decided all was safe, Callie would follow her to the shelter.

Everything went well and Callie parked her car behind Norma's on the street. The two women walked together to the front door of a nondescript house in a nondescript neighborhood. "This is it?" Callie asked Norma before they entered.

"This is it," Norma confirmed. "Not what you were expecting?"

"I'm not sure what I expected. It's just another house on the street."

"From the outside, yes. But you'll see when we enter that appearances can be deceiving."

Norma wasn't lying. As the women came to

the living room to meet Callie, she was amazed that there were so many people living in the small house. She had an even harder time believing that there was such an enormous demand for a protective home such as this.

As much as she'd thought she'd been doing good in her own community by donating her clothes and supporting local charities with monetary donations, she'd never been face-to-face with the actual people in need. She didn't count serving food at the community center because she walked by the homeless on a daily basis.

These women were afraid for their lives and for their children's lives. Not because they didn't have enough to eat or warm clothes to wear. They were afraid of the men in their lives.

Much like how Callie had been afraid of her stepmother as a child.

"I think maybe the dining room table would work best." Norma showed her the way. "I've already told everyone why you're here, so anyone interested will join you in there."

Callie smiled at her. "Thank you so much. I really appreciate that you've allowed me to be here."

"Anything that will help these women is okay with me." Norma left Callie alone in the dining room.

She put the bag of supplies she'd brought with her on a chair and began pulling out handouts for the women. When she was ready to begin, five women were sitting around the table.

Another woman walked past the doorway, stopped, then went on.

"I'd like to start by introducing myself. I'm Callie James and I'm a financial analyst at a large firm in Bethesda." She left out that she was in town to complete community service hours. Callie didn't want to spook these women.

The same woman as before walked by the doorway. She stopped as if trying to decide whether to join the group or not.

"We'd love to have you join us," Callie told her.

The woman scrunched her face as if the idea was disgusting. "Not a chance. You come in here as if you know what we need. You haven't had a hard day in your life."

Callie was taken aback by the woman's vitriol. "You'd be surprised by what I've survived. That's why I know the stronger and more knowledgeable you are, the better chance you have of surviving, too."

"That's bullshit!" The woman waved her off and left.

Callie took a few breaths and then continued where she'd left off. "I'd understand if you'd prefer not to tell me your full names, but maybe first names would be okay?"

The others at the table all nodded. They introduced themselves and then Callie questioned them about what they knew so that she knew where she needed to begin.

By the time she left the home a few hours later, she felt more useful than anytime in her life. Even with how successful she'd been in her career, this experience—helping these women take control of their lives—was more rewarding than anything she'd ever done.

AFTER SPEAKING WITH the women at the shelter, as well as Norma, the plan was that Callie would teach her next class the following evening. She'd taken the women's suggestions and devised a lesson plan that she hoped would help the women she'd meet with that evening.

She began the next morning with a run, all the time watching for Wendy. Running during daylight hours seemed less risky than as it got dark. She returned to Poppy's after her run, pleased that it had been incident-free.

By the time she needed to leave for the shelter, Callie had a well thought-out game plan and she'd even had time to work on her paying job.

Even though she'd found time here and there to get some work done since she'd arrived in Whittler's Creek, today she actually felt she'd accomplished something. She knew most people thought numbers were boring, but she was energized by them. Stock prices, interest rates, housing costs. She couldn't contain her excitement.

When she arrived at the shelter, she received a warmer welcome than yesterday when the women were hesitant to befriend her.

"We have two more women who are interested in your class," Norma said as she walked her to the dining room. "There's also a possible third, but she hasn't made up her mind yet."

"That's fine," Callie told her. "She's welcome to join us later if she wants."

Norma nodded and left her alone with her students. "It's nice to see everyone," Callie said. For the sake of her new students, she reintroduced herself and asked them a few questions about what they knew and what they'd like to learn.

"I think online banking would be very useful," one of the new women said. She appeared to be in her early twenties and wore a fast-food uniform. "But I don't own a computer. There's one here to use, but what can I do after I leave?"

"That's a good question," Callie said. "The library's computers are an option. Of course, it's better to use your own because of security reasons, but if you have to use a public computer, then always remember to sign out of your account and close the window and application you were using. That will lessen the chance of the next person using that computer being able to get into your account and access your information."

Callie answered a few more questions concerning electronic banking and was about to move to another subject when Norma came to the doorway. "I have a new student for you." The woman stepped into view and Callie's jaw dropped.

"Wendy."

Callie's stepsister looked as stunned to see Callie as she was to see Wendy.

"Yeah, so what?" She turned to Norma. "I don't need to stay. She won't teach me anything I don't already know."

She knew she should try to urge Wendy to stay, but Callie was busy trying to process the fact that Wendy was residing in a battered women's shelter.

"Of course, that's up to you," Norma told her. "Is there a problem?"

When Wendy didn't speak up, Callie filled Norma in. "Wendy is my stepsister."

Norma looked from one woman to the other. "I take it you're not close?"

"Ha!" Wendy said. "That's exactly right." Before Callie could add anything, Wendy turned and left.

"Can we speak when you're done here?" Norma asked Callie in a tone meant for her alone.

"Of course," Callie said, hoping Norma wasn't

going to tell her that she couldn't come back because she and Wendy didn't get along.

Norma left and Callie continued with her class. Putting Wendy from her mind, she enjoyed the women and their interest in learning. When she reached the end of what she'd planned to teach them that evening, she said she'd like Monday's class to focus on saving. She got a lot of strange looks.

"How can we save money when we don't even have enough to live on?" one woman asked, and several heads bobbed up and down.

"That's what we'll discuss on Monday. I think you'll be surprised when I show you how regularly saving even just a little bit will make a difference when you get to a point when you need it. A car repair or an unexpected medical bill can throw you into debt that you might not be able to recover from. I don't think any of you want to be dependent on someone else if you can help it, correct?"

The women agreed heartily with that statement.

"Then I'll see you Monday night, same time."

Last time she left them they were very reserved. Tonight the women stood around her, asking more questions while she packed up her things. She finally broke away and went to find Norma.

"There you are." Callie popped her head into the kitchen. "You wanted to talk?"

Norma stopped what she was doing and gestured to the back door. They both went outside to a small patio with an old redwood picnic table. Norma's limp seemed more pronounced as she made her way to the table and sat across from Callie.

"I didn't want anyone to overhear us because I want to talk to you about your sister," Norma began.

"Stepsister." It was an automatic correction. "What about her?"

Norma tapped a pointed fingernail with white nail polish on the table. "I can't figure her out."

And Norma was looking to Callie for answers? "I'm afraid I don't know much about Wendy or her life. We've had no contact for years."

Norma nodded. "I was afraid of that. Let me ask you this. Is there anyone else who might be able to fill in the blanks, especially about this husband of hers? She's refused to press charges against him when it was obvious upon her arrival late last week that she had visible bruises that were healing."

Callie recalled first seeing Wendy at the drugstore shortly after arriving in town. She'd appeared to have fading bruises at that time. "I don't know of anyone." She'd never even met Wendy's husband. She only knew that he'd been a few years ahead of her in school. Then she asked, "And you think he was the cause of her bruises?"

Callie couldn't imagine how much worse her

own childhood would have been if she'd had to endure physical abuse on top of everything else.

"Nine times out of ten, it's the husband or boyfriend where these women are concerned." Norma stated it as fact. "If you find out anything else about her situation, please let me know."

"I will." She hesitated. Just as Norma moved to get up, Callie said, "You should know that she's suspected of being involved in a crime. The Whittler's Creek police have been looking for her to question her about an embezzlement case."

Norma's eyebrows rose. "Really? Then I'll need to contact Chief Garrett right away. We don't hide criminals here."

"He'll appreciate that," she told Norma. Callie was relieved that she wouldn't have to speak to Tyler herself, something she'd avoided since their argument.

"I'll call him tomorrow morning and we can arrange a time for him to question Wendy."

"You would allow him to come here?" Callie was surprised after how complicated it had been for her to come to the house.

"No, I think the best option would be for him to go to where she's working. The women here get a little nervous when they see law enforcement. The men in their lives have beaten them down emotionally so they sometimes assume an officer is here to take them back home."

After what she'd endured as a child, Callie could actually imagine how confused and afraid these women probably were.

THE NEXT MORNING Tyler received a call from Norma as soon as he got to his office. He didn't usually go into work this early unless he was called in for something, but today his reasoning was twofold. One, he was avoiding Callie, afraid he'd lower his standards when it came to her mental health. And, two, he needed to clear up the embezzlement case.

"Good morning, Norma," he greeted her. "What can I do for you?"

"Good morning, Chief. It's not what you can do for me, but what I can do for you." She seemed chipper this morning. "Callie tells me you're looking to question Wendy Pullman. She's a resident here and I can give you the address of her new employer so you can speak with her. I trust you won't divulge where she's currently living and that you'll speak with her personally?"

"Absolutely. I have no interest in revealing her whereabouts to anyone who might cause trouble for her or any of your other residents."

"Just as I'd hoped." Norma recited Wendy's employer's name and address and they ended their call.

He checked his email before going to see Wendy

and found a message from his admin. Donna had discovered who was renting that post office box— S. Pullman of the Pullman Corporation. The address associated with it was the same one Tyler had visited the other day when he went to speak to Steve Pullman, Wendy's husband.

"Thanks, Donna," he said aloud to his empty office. "No surprise there."

He headed out to the address Norma had given him for Wendy's employer. It was more than a half hour away. Wendy must have taken the job to be as far away from her husband as possible and still be close enough to her son.

She was employed by a small medical clinic. He wasn't sure exactly where to find her, but he didn't need to ask. She sat at the reception desk behind a glass partition when he came in the door.

Like a deer in headlights, she froze when she saw him.

"I need to ask you a few questions," he told her in a quiet voice when she finally stood to open the partition. He didn't want to alert the other employees to his presence or worry any patients. "Can you take a break?"

Seeming flustered, she looked around to her left and then her right. "Just a minute." She went through a door leading to another room behind her. He hoped she was getting someone to take her place and not running out some back exit.

He gave a sigh of relief when she returned with another woman following behind her.

"Sharon will cover for me during my break. There's a small lounge down the hall where we can talk."

Tyler was surprised at Wendy's attitude, how cordial and accommodating she was being. She was dressed in purple scrubs, the obvious uniform for the employees at the clinic, from what he'd observed. She was also well-groomed, quite different than when he'd seen her at the community center or in the church parking lot.

She came through a door into the waiting room and he followed her to the lounge where there were three tables with plastic chairs at each. The small kitchenette had a refrigerator, a large sink and a single-cup coffeemaker. Currently, he and Wendy were the only occupants.

As soon as they were seated at a table across from each other, Wendy spoke. "So what did you want to ask me? I assume this is an official visit?" She gestured to his uniform.

"Yes, it is. I'd like to know about some checks that were written to the Pullman Corporation."

He watched her face for a sign of guilt when she realized what he was talking about, but all he saw was relief.

"So you figured out what that email meant." She stated a fact, not a question.

He looked at her, his eyes wide. "You sent the email?" He'd thought she'd gotten caught because someone else had figured out what she'd done.

She nodded, her lips twitching. "Yep."

"So who wrote the actual checks?"

She hesitated. "You haven't read me my rights, so you can't use whatever I say against me, right?"

He considered his options. "If you cooperate and give me all the details, I'll see where we stand."

She pursed her lips. "Look. I want my husband in jail. Steve's the guilty one. I'll do whatever it takes to get him there. But I can't get in trouble myself. I have a son to take care of."

"And where is he since you moved out? Is he at the shelter with you?" Steve had thought he was at a friend's, but Tyler didn't consider him a credible source.

"No, he's staying with his friend. I talk to him every night and check in." Her voice caught. "His friend's mother knows why I needed him to stay with them. She's taking good care of him."

This was a very different Wendy than he'd expected. He had no explanation for her change of personality, but he preferred dealing with this Wendy rather than the one who'd threatened Callie.

Tyler took his notebook and pen from his pocket. "I'll need an address for your son since he's a minor. His name is Eric?" He looked up at Wendy and she nodded as she recited the address.

"Let's start at the beginning. Who wrote the checks to the Pullman Corporation?"

"It's kind of complicated," she said. "Steve—my husband—was laid off from his job about seven months ago and we began having money trouble just living on my salary even after his unemployment kicked in. He came up with an idea to have the city pay a dummy corporation—he named it the Pullman Corporation—for services rendered. He wanted me to get the checks written. I tried to tell him that I didn't have access to checks, but he wouldn't listen. I told him we were sure to get caught, but he didn't give me a choice." She twisted her hands and didn't look at Tyler as she spoke.

"What did you do?" From Wendy's nervousness and what he suspected about her marital situation, it wasn't difficult to figure out that Pullman had physically threatened and abused Wendy.

"Since I didn't work in the accounts payable department, I wasn't sure how to get a check cut. But Steve insisted that I figure it out." She paused. "I casually knew someone in the department, so I began getting her to go to lunch with me and spending more time with me."

"Did she agree to write the checks?"

"Oh, no. She has no knowledge of what happened. I began by asking about her job, making her think I wanted to transfer to her department when there was an opening. One day when she got distracted by a call on her cell phone and I was waiting for her to go to lunch, I saw a reimbursement form on her desk. It had been signed by both cosigners. I snatched the form then made a copy of it back in my office after lunch. The next day, I returned it to my friend's desk. She was none the wiser."

"How did making copies of the form help you?"

"The signatures were from black stamps, so my copy looked exactly like the original. Then I just had to white-out the other information and I made copies. So about once a week, I would fill out a reimbursement form from the Pullman Corporation for whatever amount Steve told me. Then I'd sneak it into my friend's pile of reimbursement forms." Wendy was being careful about not revealing the friend's name.

It sounded like the city's payment procedures needed a complete overhaul.

"And who opened up the post office box?"

Her eyes widened. "You know about that, too?"

"It wasn't difficult to find out once the checks came to light."

"I guess not."

"And to be clear, you wrote the email that led to this investigation?"

She nodded vigorously. "When no one figured it out right away, I had no choice. I thought everything I was doing was obvious, but apparently it wasn't. And I thought sending the email would also help the authorities realize I didn't want to be committing a crime."

"You left your job a few weeks ago. Were you fired? Did someone discover what you were doing?"

"I wish I *had* been fired, but no one ever caught on to what I was doing. I never wanted to steal from the city and as long as I was in that job, I had to keep getting money for Steve." She sucked in a breath. "I resigned. I gave no notice, just quit on the spot. Then I told Steve I got fired."

"What happened then?" He prepared himself for the worst.

"He was mad, *very* mad, but not at me. He blamed the people I worked for. I told him I was fired for coming in late several times because of dropping our son off at school."

"He believed you?"

"At the time."

"And then you moved out and into the shelter?"

She shook her head. "Not immediately. It was the next day when he saw a text on my phone from my friend asking why I'd resigned." She folded her hands on her lap and bowed her head. "I thought he was going to kill me. He'd never been that mad before. Sure, he'd hit me numerous times, but never like this. He usually chose body blows that wouldn't show in public. This time, he didn't care. Even when he nearly choked me to death." Her voice became more and more quiet and she was shaking. "So I left as soon as I could after making sure my son could stay at his friend's house where he'd spent that night."

"Did you see a doctor?"

She shook her head. "No. Just bruises, no permanent damage."

Tyler continued to write in his notebook and flipped to a clean page. He looked up. "Is there anything else you'd like to add?"

She seemed to ponder that for several seconds. "Not that I can think of." She hesitated. "I've cooperated and I was the one who reported the crime. I'm not going to get into trouble, am I?"

"Like I said, I'll see what I can do. I'll talk to the assistant state's attorney first thing Monday morning."

She nodded sullenly. "Will you be arresting Steve?"

"I will if you'll go to the police station right after work today and sign an affidavit stating what you just told me. You'll also need to testify against him."

Her eyes widened. "Testify in court? I can't."

She shook her head frantically. "He'll come after me. And next time he'll be sure to kill me."

He'd made a promise when he took his job to protect and serve the citizens of Whittler's Creek. That included Wendy, no matter what she'd done. "I'll see what I can do about protecting you. For now, stay at the shelter until I figure out the next move."

"Okay."

"And one more thing." He needed to take this opportunity to give Wendy a warning. "Stay away from Callie."

She opened her mouth to speak and he held up a hand to stop her.

"No exceptions," he said sternly. "I want you nowhere near her unless it's by her invitation. Is that clear?"

She nodded. "Yes."

"I mean it. If I find out you've hurt her or caused her any more grief, I'll make it my mission to make sure you land in jail. I don't care if you were threatened into embezzling the money or not. Got it?"

"Yes." She was acting uncharacteristically agreeable.

He gave her a questioning look. "You're sure?"

She nodded. "Being here the past week has opened my eyes."

He wasn't sure what her cryptic words meant,

but he'd seen a huge change in her attitude and appearance. "Okay. I'll be in touch. Get to the police station as soon as possible."

When he reached his truck, he radioed one of his officers to give him a heads-up about the arrest. "Once Wendy Pullman signs the affidavit, pick up Steve Pullman and arrest him for embezzlement and attempted murder." He recited Pullman's address and described the mobile home where he could probably be found.

There would be more charges once the ASA took over, but that would be enough to hold Pullman for now and Wendy would be protected from him.

CHAPTER EIGHTEEN

LATER THAT NIGHT Callie was heading upstairs to bed when Tyler stopped her. "I need to ask a favor." Before she could reply, he added, "I wouldn't ask if not for Alexis and Madison."

That got her attention. "What is it?"

"I'm moving things into the house tomorrow and you had told the girls you'd help them set up their bedrooms." He paused. "Is that offer still open? I can make up an excuse if you'd rather not."

She pondered his request for a few seconds. She enjoyed the girls and this might be her last chance to spend time with them. "I'll do it."

His demeanor went from rigid to relaxed. "Thank you."

The next afternoon Callie laughed harder than she had in a long time. The girls were so excited about each of them having their own bedroom and their giggling soon became infectious. After their beds were assembled, she helped them put sheets on them, teaching them how to tuck in the corners properly. They moved on to unloading their books and stuffed animals, so Callie left them on their own while she went downstairs to begin unpacking kitchen boxes.

"Do you have a plan for how you want the kitchen set up?" she asked Tyler, who was attaching the legs to the kitchen table. Until now they'd successfully avoided each other.

He shrugged. "I don't know. You're probably better at figuring out what should go where than I am. The kitchen's not where I shine."

She put her hands on her hips. "That was pretty sexist."

"Whoa, whoa! I didn't mean it that way. I just meant I'm not into cooking. As long as I can find a bowl for cereal and a mug for coffee, then I'm happy. In fact, putting them right next to each other to make it easier for me would suit me just fine."

"I'll do the best I can." She turned her back on him to put plates into a cupboard, hiding her feelings about never coming back here to share breakfast with him.

Callie's phone began ringing. She pulled it from the back pocket of her denim shorts. She didn't recognize the number, thinking it was probably a robo call. She put it back into her pocket.

"Daddy!" Madison called from her bedroom.

Tyler stood to go to his daughter and Callie's phone made a sound to announce a message. She retrieved her phone from her pocket again and after Tyler left the room, she played the message.

"Callie, this is Wendy. I'd really like to talk to you about some things. Mostly about how I've treated you." She paused. "If you're interested in meeting, please call me back at this number."

Callie didn't know what to do. Should she tell Tyler? With the way things were with them, she'd feel awkward. Should she meet Wendy? Was Wendy setting her up?

She finally decided to tell Tyler, just so she'd have some kind of backup in case Wendy was planning something dangerous.

"Damn it! I specifically told her to stay away from you," he said after Callie played Wendy's message for him. "What is she up to now?"

"You saw her?"

"Police business" was all he said.

"I know you wanted to talk to her about the embezzlement, but you can't tell me what she said?"

"Not yet."

She understood, but it didn't help her make a decision about whether or not to meet Wendy. "So what do you think I should do? What if she's planning to hurt me when we meet?"

He seemed to consider it. "She seemed different—civil—when I saw her." He shrugged. "I could go with you."

She pursed her lips. "I don't know. Seeing you

with me might scare her." Would relying on him right now make it more difficult to leave him?

"Maybe she needs to be scared. Remind her that I meant what I said about not harming you."

"That's true." She looked at her phone. "Okay, I'll call her and arrange a time and place." She hit the number on her phone, curious about Wendy's true reason for getting together.

Callie agreed to meet Wendy later that day.

"I can't come with you," Tyler said when he heard what they'd planned. "I assumed you'd pick a day later this week. I don't have anyone to stay with the girls today."

"It's okay. I'll be fine going alone." She hoped. Besides, it was best that she do this on her own. It was too easy to rely on him and soon she'd be leaving him behind. "Just like you said about her yesterday morning, she sounded like a different person. She even asked about my dad." She looked at Tyler with wide eyes. "Can you believe it?"

"I wouldn't if I hadn't talked to her myself." He shrugged. "Maybe it has to do with her relief that this embezzlement thing is out in the open."

"She explained it?" At his nod, she asked, "Will she be charged?"

"Just between us?"

"Of course."

"I'd say probably not. If she's willing to testify

against her husband." Tyler checked his watch. "Turns out he forced her to do it."

"Really? I guess she has no loyalty to him if he forced her to break the law."

He seemed to hesitate as if weighing his next words. "Well, I guess you'll find out soon enough. Her husband has been arrested for both embezzlement *and* attempted murder."

"Murder!" Callie was astonished.

"Attempted murder."

Callie stared at him until he provided more information.

"He's been abusive to Wendy, which you know because she's in the shelter. For how long, I don't know. But the last time before she left him for the shelter, he nearly strangled her to death."

Callie knew Wendy had been having a difficult time but never suspected it was this bad. She checked her watch. "I should go. We're meeting at the same diner where we met Norma."

"Be careful. Don't let her talk you into going anywhere that's not public."

"I won't. She seems changed, but that doesn't make me automatically trust her."

"Good."

Their eyes met and time stopped. More than anything, she wanted to slip into his arms and have him hold her. But that wasn't an option. They had no future, so why make things worse?

By the time Callie arrived at the diner, the sun was low in the sky but the oppressive heat from the day lingered. The moment she stepped into the air-conditioned diner, she saw Wendy seated in a booth and headed in her direction.

"Hi," Wendy said when Callie was settled. "I'm glad you came."

"I was surprised to hear from you," Callie said in greeting.

Wendy nodded. "I know." She was dressed in purple scrubs as if she had come from working at a medical facility. Her clothes were neat, her hair was clean and she even wore a little makeup. Completely different from the other times Callie had run into her.

Callie folded her slightly damp hands on the table and waited for Wendy to speak.

"I ordered a soda," Wendy said instead of explaining why they were meeting. "Would you like something?"

Callie saw a server coming their way with Wendy's drink. "Could I have some water, please?" she asked the young woman when she reached their table.

After the server left, Callie decided she needed to take control since Wendy wasn't offering an explanation or even a single word as to why she'd wanted to meet. "Why are we here, Wendy?" Being forthright was how she'd decided to play it. Wendy had treated her poorly all their lives and Callie was through taking it.

Wendy looked up at the question but didn't meet Callie's eyes. "I've learned something about myself over the past few days." She paused. "You've already seen me at the battered women's shelter."

Callie nodded. She thanked their server when she brought Callie's water. "Go on," Callie said when they were alone.

"There's a woman there who's downright hateful to all of us." Wendy raised her hand. "I know, I know. It's what I deserve, right?"

Callie shrugged. "What does this woman have to do with us meeting?"

"She made me realize how I've treated you all these years. I heard the same things come out of her mouth that I've said to you numerous times."

"And this was the first time you realized how mean you've been to me our entire lives together?" Callie had a difficult time believing that.

"It's true. Let me explain."

"I wish you would." Callie kept her hands on her thighs, opening and closing her fists as she became agitated. "I just have a hard time believing that hearing yourself in one woman's words actually changed you that much."

"I understand your doubt. I don't know if it's just hearing that woman or maybe everything I'm going through right now, but I want to make changes in my life and in my attitude. The other thing that happened was when you were talking to the women about finances. You really cared and wanted to help them. That's when I began to question why I'd always hated you so much."

"I'd love to know what I did to deserve your hatred."

Wendy pushed her hair back from her face and took a sip of her soda. "You were born."

Callie wasn't sure she heard correctly. "Did you say I was born?"

Wendy nodded. "Haven't you ever wondered why my mother treated you so horribly?"

"Every day of my life."

"It's because she always hated that your mother had a child—you—with your father. My mother was in love with your dad from the moment they met in high school. But it was *your* mother he chose."

"But our mothers were best friends," Callie said. "At least, that's what I was always told. Your mother was my mother's maid of honor."

Wendy nodded. "That's right. My mother swallowed her feelings when your parents married. But when your mother died in that carjacking, my mother wasn't about to let your dad get away again. According to what she told me in the last few years, she divorced my dad immediately and it didn't take long for her to get your dad to marry her. He couldn't remain a long-haul trucker with a three-year-old to take care of and no relatives nearby. So my mother filled the bill and she got the husband she'd always wanted."

Callie was stunned. She'd never known that her stepmother resented her mother. "But I still don't quite understand. Why did your mother resent me even after she married my dad? She finally had what she wanted."

"You'd think so, but no. She resented you because you were your father's child and her doctor had told her she'd never be able to have more children after me. I guess I was kind of a miracle baby. But what she'd always wanted was a child with your dad."

Callie was beginning to understand her stepmother's screwed-up ideas. "That explains her resentment of me, but not why you've hated me all these years."

Wendy looked down at her hands on her lap. "You have to understand. All my mother ever did was talk poorly about you. How you were needy and stingy and disagreeable. I wasn't even three when we came to live with you and Bart, so her hatred for you is all I knew."

"So now I should believe that everything's different just because you've run into this horrible woman who treats people as poorly as you do? That you've had some huge revelation?"

Wendy sighed. "Like I've told you, I'm trying to make a new life for myself and my son. Having the opportunity to explain to you why I've acted like I have is just one of the things I'm doing. I know it's too late for us to be sisters, but I need to at least come clean about the past. I've been through a lot recently and being around the other women at the shelter has opened my eyes to how my behavior has affected other people."

"What else is on your list?" Callie still had a difficult time accepting that Wendy had changed for good. "Like admitting to embezzlement?"

"You know about that?" She paused. "Of course you do. You're best buds with the chief of police."

"If you're going to go off about me stealing him from you, then stop right there." Although, truthfully, he wasn't Callie's anymore, either.

Wendy shook her head. "No. I know he was never interested in me. That's just remnants of my mother again. She thought he would make a great husband so she always pushed me to go after him so I wouldn't lose the 'love of my life' like she had. I figured she knew better than I did, so I took her advice. It's almost as if she brainwashed me my entire life."

Wendy used her mother as an excuse for much of her behavior, but then maybe some of what she was saying was the truth.

"I know about the embezzlement because I was the one who uncovered it."

"You did?" Wendy's eyes widened. "Then, thank you."

Callie nodded. "You're welcome. You did a lousy job of covering up your activity."

"I know—that was the idea. I thought someone would figure it out sooner, but no one did. So my next step was to send that email to Tyler. I'm glad he didn't ignore it."

"Me, too." Callie changed the subject. "What are you going to do when you leave the shelter? Will you go back home now that your husband has been arrested?"

"I don't think I can take that chance. He'll be looking for me if he makes bail. Those first few days when I left him I couldn't find a shelter to stay in that he hadn't already contacted to see if I was there."

"What did you do?"

"I spent a couple of nights in my car, but there aren't many places to park overnight in this town. I also did a lot of walking during that time, paranoid that Steve would spot my car and follow me. As I went on job interviews, I saw some business cards in one office that gave a number to call if you were in need of help, with no questions asked. That's how I found Norma."

"I'm sorry you needed the help, but I'm glad you got it."

"You are?" Wendy seemed truly surprised. "After all I've done and said to you? How can you be so nice and understanding?"

"Call me a fool. I'd really like to think that you're trying to change for the better." Callie held up one finger. "But that doesn't mean I'm totally sold on your about-face."

"Fair enough."

"How's your mother? Is she still in the hospital?"

"They're keeping her for a while. She's pretty drugged up right now to keep her calm. She barely recognizes me and when she does, she thinks I'm a little girl and she wants to walk me to school."

"I'm sorry. It must be hard to see her like that." Callie was surprised that she meant it.

Wendy nodded. "It is. But at least she can't hurt anyone while she's there."

Callie couldn't agree more. She and her dad were safe as long as Ellen was hospitalized or under constant supervision. "Have you thought about an assisted living facility? Unless she shows marked improvement, I don't think my dad can continue taking care of her at home."

"I agree. I've been so involved in my own drama that I haven't paid enough attention to their situation until recently. I think I'll be able to find a good living situation for her now that I've taken a job at a medical office. They have a lot of information available for all ages."

They were silent for a few moments before Callie said that she would be doing a final class the following evening. She'd scheduled it for before her appointment with Dr. Hammond. "I hope you can make it if you're interested, Wendy."

"I am. Now that I'm on my own with my son, I need to think about what you mentioned the last time. How to save for those unexpected bills and still provide everyday basics."

They chatted for a little bit longer before Callie left the diner feeling better about a lot of things. She was almost done with her community service hours, she had the possible beginning of a new start with her stepsister, and she finally knew the cause of her stepmother's hatred. Talking with Wendy even made Callie consider coming clean with her therapist about her past.

Only one thing wasn't resolved.

Tyler.

THE NEXT DAY, SINCE Callie was teaching an evening course at the women's shelter, she arranged to visit her dad that afternoon.

Pulling into the driveway, she was more confident than she'd been a few weeks ago when she'd chickened out. Maybe it was knowing her stepmother wasn't there or maybe she had more confidence in herself now to deal with whatever may come. She didn't know, she just enjoyed her new strength.

"Hi, Dad," she said as she came through the unlocked front door. Funny how she was comfortable enough to walk in without knocking now that her dad was the only occupant of her childhood home.

Her dad came from the hallway to greet her. "Callie! How are you?" He hugged her and they took seats in the living room.

"I'm okay. How are you feeling?" Her dad's head bandage was gone, but he still had the wound on his arm covered.

"I saw the doctor Friday and he said I'm doing okay. I don't know about Ellen, though. I haven't been able to drive, so I haven't seen her."

"How did you get to the doctor?"

"My neighbor drove me."

"You should have called me. I would have taken you."

"That's okay. She didn't mind. And Ellen will never know." He leaned over and whispered, "She's a little jealous of other women."

A little? That was an understatement for sure. Visions of Ellen wielding a knife and the hatred she emitted were still fresh in Callie's mind.

She sucked oxygen into her lungs to aid her in

broaching a difficult subject. "Wendy and I met up yesterday."

"That's nice. Two sisters spending time together." He smiled as if everything was normal.

"We got together to talk about things. Bad things. You know we've never gotten along, right?"

"Oh, all sisters have disagreements. At least, that's what Ellen always told me. I never had a sister, so I took her word for it."

Callie decided he'd probably taken her word for a lot of things.

"We had more than disagreements, Dad." Callie kept her tone even, controlling the emotions that wanted her to shout the truth at him. "Wendy has hated me since the first day we met."

Her dad's eyes widened. "She has? Why?"

Callie swallowed. "Because that's what Ellen told her to do. Ellen has always hated me, too."

"That's impossible. She's your stepmother. Of course she doesn't hate you."

She relayed what Wendy told her about Ellen's longtime love for him.

"She never said a word to me." Her dad got quiet. "I had no idea that she resented you or your mother." His eyes filled with tears. "I wish I'd known."

"Me, too." She breathed in and out to calm her quickly beating heart. She needed to know something and couldn't wait any longer. "Dad, did you know how Ellen treated me when you weren't around?"

His brow furrowed. "What do you mean?"

"Did you know that Ellen would lock me in a closet in the basement?"

"Oh, that's impossible. I know she was strict with you, but locking you in a closet? You're making that up."

"No, Dad, I'm not. Sometimes she would leave me there for more than a day at a time. I had no food or water and no bathroom." Her own eyes blurred with tears. "It was cold and dirty and dark. There were bugs that crawled on me and I could hear her laughing when I'd yell for help."

Her dad was shaking his head as if he didn't believe her.

"It's true, Dad. I'm not making this up. She always yelled at me for the littlest things. Sometimes she would make dinner for herself and Wendy, but I wasn't allowed to eat. Not even something I made myself. If I did, then I'd have to go back into the closet."

Her hands were shaking by this time. She had never disclosed this much and she still wasn't sure if her dad believed her.

He was silent for a long time. "I...I don't know what to say." He was also shaken up by her confession. "I know you came to me once about a problem, but I talked to Ellen and she claimed you had exaggerated. She said she was strict with the two of you because I wasn't around much. So she needed to be firm about the rules."

Callie's hands fisted on her lap. "As soon as you left after I talked to you that one time, she locked me up for two days to teach me a lesson."

Her dad slumped, shaking his head. "I'm so sorry. I had no idea. You should have come to me again."

"I couldn't. The thought of being put back into that closet the minute you left for another trip nearly crushed me." She posed another question. "You never had any clue about how she was treating me? Or how she'd brainwashed Wendy into hating me?"

He wiped a tear from his cheek. "No. I thought everything was fine. That's what she always told me."

Callie nodded. From her dad's emotional reaction, she believed him. "The abuse is why I studied so hard to get into Maryland on a full scholarship. It's why I never came back here. At least, part of the reason."

"I can never make up for what you went through and I'm so sorry for that." He pulled himself together before continuing to speak. "I wish…I wish you had been able to trust another adult with what was going on."

"She kept us isolated. Besides, I worried that

if I told a teacher that she'd find out." She hesitated. "I know now that I could have trusted an adult, but as a child I was too scared." She could see the guilt overwhelming him, so she changed the subject. "Why didn't you ever answer my letters after I moved away?"

He cocked his head. "I could ask you the same thing. I was on the road a lot, but I always wrote you a quick note before I left town. Ellen mailed them for me. Oh." He covered his face with his hands. "You never got them, did you?" When she shook her head, he continued. "And you also didn't get the presents she said she sent on your birthdays and Christmas?"

"Nothing. I never heard a word from you. No letters, no gifts." She could feel her emotions bubbling to the surface, but she shoved them down. "And you never got the letters I sent? The invitation to graduation?" She already knew the answer.

Her dad rose, his arms out to her. She met him halfway across the room and they held each other, both allowing their tears to fall freely.

CHAPTER NINETEEN

BY THE TIME Wednesday night rolled around, Tyler couldn't wait to get home from training with his officers. He was exhausted. Aunt Poppy had taken the girls for a sleepover, so he was sure to get a decent night's sleep. Not that he'd had an easy time sleeping since he and Callie had parted ways.

With thoughts of her lingering in his mind, he checked his phone to see a text from her. She wanted to know if she could stop by his house when he got home. He replied.

On my way home now. See you there.

Callie was waiting for him when he arrived. She sat on the top step by the front door. Her arms were crossed over her chest, a serious expression on her face.

"What is it? What's wrong?" He unlocked the door and invited her in.

She remained just inside the entryway. "I came to say goodbye." She spoke calmly. "My bags are packed. I've dealt with all of my family issues, and I'm driving home first thing in the morning. If you think I haven't fulfilled my service hours, then too bad. You're so good at calling people, call my therapist and report me. Or better yet, call the judge and tell him. You have the power. Use it as you wish." She turned to go.

"Callie, wait!"

She was actually leaving. He'd known it was inevitable, but he hadn't prepared himself for the acute pain.

"Can't we work this out?" he asked.

"There's nothing to work out." She stopped but didn't face him. "You've shown me your true self. I can't be with someone who wants to control my life. Talking to my therapist about everything tonight made your deceit fresh again. I can't stay here any longer." She paused as if trying to maintain her composure. "I've already said goodbye to Madison and Alexis." She opened the front door and turned to face him. "This one's for you." She stepped outside and slammed the door hard enough to rattle the windows.

How had things between them gone from near perfect to disastrous in such a short period of time?

CALLIE REACHED HER car and drove about a block before she pulled to the curb and fell apart completely. The anger and hurt came pouring out of her. She banged her fist on her steering wheel several times. Slamming Tyler's front door must have been the catalyst to what was now turning into a maelstrom of released emotions.

Several minutes later she searched her purse for tissues to wipe her tears and blow her nose. When she could finally pull herself together enough to drive, she headed to Poppy's.

Callie found Poppy sitting alone at the kitchen table with a cup of tea, her expression sullen.

"Are you okay?"

Poppy shrugged. "Not really."

"We make quite a pair." Callie hadn't told Poppy why she was going home tomorrow, but she had to know that Tyler and Callie had reached an impasse. "Is it Gino?"

"Isn't it always a man?"

"That's because they think they should be in charge of us."

Poppy's eyes widened. "They do, don't they?" She sipped her tea. "Gino has no idea why I won't marry him. He won't listen, no matter how often I explain it."

"I get it. Tyler went behind my back to speak to my therapist. He thought he knew better than I did what my therapist should know about my life."

Poppy shook her head. "At least he thought he was doing something to benefit you. Gino didn't take me into consideration at all when he bought the Lincoln Hotel."

"You can't come up with a compromise?" Callie asked, glad to focus on someone else's problems instead of her own. "Are you really in direct competition with each other?"

"We both provide meals and lodging."

"But won't they be different and each attract different customers?"

Poppy seemed to mull over the question. "I'm looking for typical bed-and-breakfast clientele."

"And isn't he making the Lincoln Hotel a high-end inn? With a spa and an exercise room? It doesn't even sound like you're in the same price range."

"I never thought about it that way."

"That really surprises me, Poppy. From what I've seen, you're pretty smart about business."

Poppy chewed her lower lip, seeming to think about Callie's observation. "I guess I was too busy being mad about him not hearing me when I talked about making this house into a B and B. That it's been my dream for most of my adult life."

"So what are you going to do now?" Callie asked.

Poppy pushed her chair back and took her cup to the sink. "I need to talk to Gino."

"What are you going to say?"

Poppy's grin started slowly and grew. "That I

think with some ground rules, we might be able to coexist in Whittler's Creek. And I might just accept his marriage proposal."

At least Callie had been able to help Poppy and Gino. Because she and Tyler simply had irreconcilable differences.

POPPY RACED TO her bedroom to freshen up before heading to the Lincoln to see Gino. He had moved his things into his suite there after she'd turned down his marriage proposal.

She drove as quickly as possible, parking in the lot behind the hotel. Because it was after ten at night and all the workers were gone, leaving Gino alone in the hotel, the front doors were locked tight.

Poppy stood outside, wondering what to do. She looked up at the fourth floor where Gino's suite was located. There was a light on, so he was still awake. He'd never hear her if she yelled from the street. So she pulled her cell phone from her purse and texted him.

I came to talk. At the front door of the Lincoln.

He must have taken the steps down because he arrived to unlock the front door faster than the ancient elevator would have gotten him there.

He wore jeans, a threadbare T-shirt and a tentative smile on his face as he welcomed her inside and locked the door again.

"Let's go upstairs," he suggested, leading her to the elevator.

They were silent as they rode the sluggish elevator up to the fourth floor and then walked down the hall to his suite. "Come this way." Gino walked through the living area to a doorway. He stepped aside so she could enter.

She hadn't seen the suite before, but as soon as she walked into the bedroom she couldn't help noticing that the furniture was the same as in her own bedroom. The linens were the same, as were the lamps and other details.

"This looks like my bedroom," she said, taking in every detail.

"I tried my best," he said. "I took pictures and attempted to duplicate the room. I know you redid your bedroom when you expanded into the attic, and I wanted you to be just as comfortable when you're here." He walked over to a framed picture on the nightstand. "I even had this family picture copied. The frame isn't exactly the same, though."

Poppy's eyes blurred with tears. "I can't believe you did all this."

"I was going to show you after dinner on the roof, but we never got that far."

Poppy nodded.

"You said you wanted to talk?" Gino sounded

hopeful, which gave her the incentive to tell him her ideas.

"Yes, I'd like to talk." They returned to the living area and Poppy sat at the end of the couch. Gino chose the chair closest to her.

"Would you like a drink?" he asked.

"No, thank you." She wasn't sure now where to begin. "I talked to Callie tonight and she pointed out that your inn and my B and B will attract different customers."

His eyebrows lifted. "That's true."

She swallowed and continued. "There are some things I think we could work on to make sure we're both operating successful businesses, but we need to come to an agreement first."

"I'll agree to anything," he said. "I've actually been coming up with some ideas of my own, trying to figure out how to resolve this issue between us."

Poppy was glad to hear that. "The biggest issue for me is that you haven't listened to what I want and need. You make decisions based on what you *think* I want or need."

Gino digested her words. "You're absolutely right. And there's actually something I'd like your opinion on right now." He rose and walked to a small desk in the corner of the room. He picked up a folder and brought it over to her. Then he sat next to her on the couch. "Take a look."

She opened the folder and saw a résumé. "What's this?" Below it was another résumé.

"Those are people applying for positions at the hotel like innkeeper and assistant innkeeper."

"Why are you showing me this?"

"Because I'd like to offer you a deal. If you're running a B and B alone, then you'll never be able to take time off. Same goes for me. So I'm suggesting we share an assistant innkeeper."

She considered the idea. "So it would be a full-time position, but we'd each get the person twenty hours a week?"

"Right." He held up a hand. "But if you don't like the idea, it's okay. I can hire someone part-time just for the inn."

"It's not that I don't like it, I had just been thinking that I'm not sure I can afford a second part-time employee."

"A second?"

She grinned. "I was hoping we could hire a chef that would handle the food at both places. Not that I don't want to cook sometimes, but after we're married it would be nice to not have to run back to my house to make breakfast for guests."

"Married?" Gino's jaw dropped and she loved his reaction.

"Unless you've changed your mind?"

"N-not at all," he stammered. "But I never got around to asking you."

Poppy looked at him wide-eyed and waited.

He jumped up from his seat and went to a drawer in the desk. He returned with a small box and gingerly got down on one knee.

"On one condition," Poppy said.

"I haven't asked yet," Gino joked. Then he sobered. "What's the condition?"

"That you listen to me. I know you'll mess up sometimes and I have my faults, too. But I need you to work hard at hearing what I want and not deciding for me."

Gino took her hand. "I promise to do my best." He groaned and shifted positions slightly. "Now can I ask you? My knees aren't made for this."

Poppy laughed. "Now."

"Poppy, you are and always have been the love of my life. Please marry me and make me the happiest man alive."

"Gino, I love you with all my heart and I would be honored to marry you."

He fumbled with the ring box and placed a gorgeous sapphire in a silver setting on her finger. "I love you," he said and then kissed her to seal their promise.

A WEEK AFTER Callie returned home and forced herself back into her usual routine, she arrived at her condo from work to a message on her home phone. She tried not to hope it was Tyler—

she hadn't heard from him since she'd left Whittler's Creek.

The message was from Andrew. Her heart sank in disappointment. What could he possibly want? She could delete it and never think about it again. Her finger hovered over the delete button before moving to the play button.

"Um, hey, Callie. It's Andrew. Andrew Slater." As if she didn't know her scumbag ex-boyfriend by his voice. "I'm calling to tell you that you were right about the vase."

Callie's eyes widened. Not a sentence she'd ever expected to hear from Andrew.

"You didn't break it. I found out last week that Lori was the one who broke it." Lori must be the woman Callie had caught Andrew in bed with. "She accidentally knocked it over right after you left my apartment that day. When she found out its value, she decided to let you take the fall. So, anyway, just thought you should know."

No apology, no nothing. Typical Andrew. She should probably see if she could sue him for false arrest and get her money back, but she'd rather not ever see him again.

She changed out of her work clothes and into running clothes. Connecting her ear buds to her phone and attaching the phone to her upper arm, she headed outside. There was a school a few blocks away where she liked to do laps on the track. She stepped from the air-conditioned hall of her condo building into the unpleasant mugginess outside.

And there, standing on the steps leading to her building, looking as gorgeous as ever, was Tyler.

Her mouth went dry.

"Callie."

The sound of her name coming from him nearly did her in. She reminded herself to be strong. He'd hurt her. He'd disrespected her. She needed to remember that he'd had power over her and he'd used it against her.

"I'm afraid you've come at a bad time." She struggled to keep her tone neutral. "I'm on my way out. Besides, we have nothing more to say to each other."

"I disagree." He stepped closer. "I've thought a lot about what you said. You were absolutely right about me overstepping when I talked to your therapist." He took a breath. "But I'd do it again if I had to."

Callie's eyes widened in astonishment. "Well, now I *know* we're done here."

She tried to go around him, but he caught her arm.

"I'm not explaining this very well. Can we go inside and talk?"

"No, here is fine."

He looked into her eyes. "When I said I'd do it

again, I meant that I love you enough to do something you don't like. I'll do whatever it takes to make you happy. And at the time, pushing you to face your past by revealing something to your therapist was the only way I could see that happening."

"But you *still* don't understand," she said vehemently. "I don't need protection. I've taken care of myself my entire life. I did what I had to do to protect myself against my stepmother and stepsister." She got louder and angrier the more she spoke. "I even accepted a plea deal to protect myself against my ex-boyfriend. I can take care of myself."

"And *you* still don't understand," he said, repeating her words. "You don't have to do everything on your own."

Her eyes widened. "But I don't know how to do it any other way." She was speaking the truth from her heart and it felt unbelievably good to let out her frustration.

"I can't say I understand completely, but you've got to know that I'll try my best to do what you want. I don't necessarily need to protect you, but I want to be there for you when you need it and also when you don't." He ran a hand down her upper arm and his tone softened. "I love you more than I ever thought I could, Callie. Please give me a

second chance to show you we can be equal part-
ners in this relationship."

"First, I need you to be honest with me, Tyler.
Always. Don't go behind my back like you did
with my therapist."

He nodded. "I promise. At the time I thought
it was for the best, but I can see how you would
see it as me using my position to control you." He
paused. "Just like your ex."

Her eyebrows rose. "Exactly."

"I'm sorry." He sounded sincere. "I truly am.
And I promise I'll trust you to know what's best
for you, even if I don't agree."

"Apology accepted." She held up a finger. "By
the way, you were right."

"I was? About what?"

"After my therapist heard everything I went
through, he's been able to help me work through
it."

He smiled. A sad smile, probably because he
understood how difficult living through her childhood again had been for her.

"I joined a boxing gym," she announced, realizing she was changing the subject.

He blinked. "What?"

"After slamming your front door last week and
beating on my steering wheel, I realized how ca-
thartic it was to have a physical outlet for my frustration and anger."

"So you joined a boxing gym?"

"Yes, I'm learning how to punch. It feels really, *really* good."

"Are you planning to punch me?"

She looked at him for several seconds. "I might feel like punching you, but I never would. I'll take my anger out at the gym."

"Does that mean you'll give us another chance?"

She pursed her lips. "Only if I can thank you first."

"Thank me for what?"

"For showing me that running away when life becomes unmanageable isn't the solution. It took me a while to understand why you talked to my therapist. I've never had anyone on my side before and it might take some time for me to get used to it."

"Then, you're welcome, and you can have all the time in the world because I'm not going anywhere."

The fact that he was standing in front of her, even after everything he knew about her, seemed to prove his statement. "I'm glad." She gave him a tentative smile and really meant what she said.

Then he kissed her so passionately that her legs nearly gave out.

EPILOGUE

BY THE TIME Alexis and Madison participated in their school's Holiday Pageant in December, Callie and Tyler had gotten into a routine. Callie looked over at Tyler sitting next to her in the school's cafetorium and smiled. She slipped her hand into his and he squeezed hers.

They'd started off with their original plan for Callie to visit on weekends, but the time went by too quickly. Then one day about a month ago she woke up and had an astounding revelation. Her job meant less to her than Tyler and his girls did. So she went to her superior and asked if she could telecommute. He wasn't thrilled, but the other choice would have been for her to leave and find another job.

Now that she worked from home—she considered Tyler's house her home more than her condo ever was—she was able to get the girls to and from school. She could even get them started on homework before Tyler got home.

She continued to volunteer at the women's shelter since new residents arrived more frequently than she'd ever imagined. Working one-on-one with the women gave her a feeling of satisfaction and pride she hadn't experienced in her successful career.

"Aren't they adorable?" Poppy whispered to Callie and Tyler during the applause. She and Gino were sitting in the row behind them.

Gino leaned close and added, "They've been practicing their songs for weeks. I think *I* know them by heart."

"Shh," Poppy said to him. "They're ready to sing the next one."

Poppy and Gino were each enjoying success in their businesses. Keeping Poppy's a homier bed-and-breakfast and Gino's Lincoln Hotel a high-end establishment had been a wonderful compromise. Sharing the chef and an assistant had also allowed them more time together. Poppy had even accepted Gino's marriage proposal, although they hadn't set a date yet.

The girls had been more than hinting about Tyler and Callie getting married, especially once Poppy and Gino announced their engagement.

Callie was in no hurry to change their current arrangement, at least for now. One thing she'd learned during their time together was that she could be a pretty good mom to Alexis and Madison and any future children she and Tyler might have.

Her dad, sitting on her left, whispered, "I'm sorry I missed so much of your childhood."

Callie looked at him, moved by the emotion she saw in his face. She patted his hand. "I know, Dad. I'm glad we're getting this time together now and that you're getting to know Eric, as well as Alexis and Madison. They need you in their life as much as you need them."

Wendy and her son had moved in with Callie's dad now that her stepmother was in a nursing facility. Ellen's health had declined and she was rarely coherent. Callie thought the arrangement between Wendy and her dad was a good one for both of them. Wendy no longer feared her husband since he'd gone to prison and wouldn't be eligible for parole for several years. Testifying against him hadn't been necessary because he'd been offered a plea deal. They'd revisit Wendy and her son's living situation when and if her husband was paroled.

Callie glanced at Tyler again. He caught her and winked at her. She smiled back, loving this man with her entire being.

His girls might obsess about princesses and think they needed to be "saved" by a prince to be happy. But Callie was proud that she'd saved herself from her unhappy childhood by leaving town and making a successful life for herself. To top it off, she'd been lucky enough to return to find an amazing prince of her own.

For the first time in her life she was surprisingly happy in the town where she'd grown up. Callie had never thought that would be possible, but she was extremely glad she'd returned to Whittler's Creek to find her happily-ever-after.

* * * * *